# VANISHING GIRLS

# VANISHING GIRLS

## LISA REGAN

GC

**GRAND CENTRAL**
PUBLISHING

NEW YORK   BOSTON

Copyright © 2017 by Lisa Regan

Cover design: Ghost. Cover photos: Shutterstock.
Cover copyright © 2020 by Hachette Book Group, Inc.

Grand Central Publishing
Hachette Book Group
1290 Avenue of the Americas, New York, NY 10104
grandcentralpublishing.com
twitter.com/grandcentralpub

Originally published in 2017 as trade paperback and ebook by Bookouture, an imprint of StoryFire Ltd., Carmelite House, 50 Victoria Embankment, London EC4Y 0DZ, www.bookouture.com

First Grand Central Publishing Mass Market Edition: June 2020

Grand Central Publishing is a division of Hachette Book Group, Inc. The Grand Central Publishing name and logo is a trademark of Hachette Book Group, Inc.

The publisher is not responsible for websites (or their content) that are not owned by the publisher.

The Hachette Speakers Bureau provides a wide range of authors for speaking events. To find out more, go to www.hachettespeakersbureau.com or call (866) 376-6591.

ISBNs: 978-1-5387-3411-7 (trade paperback); 978-1-5387-0191-1 (mass market)

Printed in the United States of America

OPM

10  9  8  7  6  5  4  3

For my Aunt Kitty Funk, who always believed

# PROLOGUE

There was a man in the woods, she was sure of it. For as long she could remember, the woods had been her own special kingdom, teeming with plant and wildlife, the perfect setting for all the stories her imagination could conjure. A peaceful oasis away from her mother's hardened gaze and her father's disdain.

She often felt him there: a presence, like a force field, pressing up against her little empire. As she moved through the forest, she heard him. A rustle of leaves. The snap of a branch. She'd seen bears and deer and foxes—even a bobcat once—in these woods, but the sounds he made were deliberate. They matched her own. She was sure it was a person, and judging by the heaviness of the steps, a man. Sometimes, she heard his breath, heavy and labored. But whenever she turned to confront him, her heart pounding like a drumbeat in her chest, he was gone. Twice she had seen eyes peering through the thick foliage.

"Mama," she said one morning at breakfast, when she and her mother were alone.

Her mother gave her a withering look. "What?" she asked.

The words teetered on the tip of her tongue. *There's a man in the woods.*

"There—the—" she stammered, unable to squeeze the words out.

Her mother sighed and looked away. "Eat your eggs."

Her mother would not believe her, anyway. But he was there. She was sure of it.

It became a game. She told herself to stay at least one foot away from the edge of the trees at all times. But it only lured him in further, closer to the clearing behind her house, his body obscured by a tree trunk and branches covering the rest of his face. She couldn't breathe as she ran back to the house, imagining his hands brushing at her dress ties, reaching to yank her back. Only when her feet crossed the threshold of the back door did the air return to her lungs.

For a week, she didn't come out of her room except to eat. After that, she only went outside if her mother, father or sister were out there. For a long time, he disappeared. She stopped sensing him, stopped hearing him. She almost believed that he had gone back to wherever it was he came from. Maybe she had conjured him, after all?

Then one day her sister was hanging clothes on the line while she flitted to the other side of the yard, chasing the yellow monarch butterflies that proliferated on top of the mountain. A white sheet fluttered on the clothesline, blocking her from her sister's view. She got too close to the tree line. A hand shot out and clamped down over her mouth, silencing her screams. An arm wrapped around her waist, lifting her off the ground. Holding her tightly against his chest, he dragged her through the forest that used to be her friend. One thought rose above her panic. *He was real.*

# CHAPTER 1

The Stop and Go gas station had recently installed flat-screen televisions at the gas pumps because people could not possibly take their eyes off a screen long enough to pump gas. Even though it annoyed her, Detective Josie Quinn found herself glued to the screen when the breaking news flashed across it. They'd finally found Isabelle Coleman's cell phone in the woods near her home.

A few miles away, outside the Colemans' two-story white colonial, reporter Trinity Payne, dressed in a puffy blue jacket and yellow scarf, the wind blowing her black hair every which way, struggled through her report while escaped strands snaked all over her face.

"Five days ago, Marla Coleman returned home from work to an empty house. Believing that her seventeen-year-old daughter, Isabelle, had gone out with friends, she thought nothing of it until later that night when Isabelle failed to return home. Police sources tell us that, at that time, they had no reason to believe Isabelle's disappearance was suspicious. Friends and family of Ms. Coleman describe her as a busy young woman with varied interests, likely to have left town on a spontaneous trip. But days later, with calls to her cell phone still going straight to voicemail and her car still parked in the Colemans' driveway, police are now on high alert as the residents here in Denton rally together to form search teams."

The camera panned out to show the Colemans' long, circular driveway with three vehicles parked in it. Trinity continued, "For the last few days, volunteers have combed the area around the Colemans' home, where Isabelle was last seen."

The camera moved further out, swinging from side to side and focusing in on the heavily wooded areas surrounding the Coleman home. Josie knew the house. It was one of the larger homes on the outskirts of Denton, sitting alone along a rural road, its nearest neighbor almost two miles away. She'd once hit a deer with her police cruiser not far from there.

The camera returned to Trinity. "Yesterday, during one of the searches, a cell phone was discovered in one of these wooded areas, which is believed to have belonged to the missing girl. The screen was shattered and police tell us that the battery had been removed. Coleman's parents say that she would never willingly part with her phone. It is now widely believed that Ms. Coleman is the victim of an abduction."

She went on to answer some canned questions from the WYEP anchors and give out the number of the Denton police department helpline with a request for information. The knots in Josie's shoulders that had started forming three weeks earlier tightened. She swiveled her neck and shrugged her shoulders, trying to loosen them. Listening to the latest developments and knowing she could do nothing to help made her want to smash the TV's plasma screen into a million pieces with the gas pump in her hand.

Isabelle had been missing for five days. Why had it taken so long to find evidence that she had been abducted? Why had they waited two days to form search parties around the house? Why had they turned Josie away when she'd offered to join the search? Surely being on paid leave for an alleged use of excessive force didn't render her searching skills useless. It didn't matter that she was showing up as a private citizen; her colleagues, most of whom she outranked, had sent her home. Chief's orders.

She fumed. Every available resource would be devoted to locating the girl. Every resource. Josie knew her colleagues were probably sleeping on cots in the break room at the station, working around the clock just like they'd done during the floods of 2011 when the entire city was under seven feet of water and the only way to get around was by boat. She knew they would have already called in volunteer firefighters, emergency medical services, and every able-bodied person in the city willing to search and run down leads. So why hadn't the chief called her back to work yet?

Denton was roughly twenty-five square miles, many of those miles spanning the untamed mountains of central Pennsylvania with their one-lane winding roads, dense woods and rural residences spread out like carelessly thrown confetti. The population was edging over thirty thousand, just enough to give them about a half dozen murders a year—most of those domestic disputes—and enough rapes, robberies and drunken bar brawls to keep the police department staff of fifty-three moderately busy. Competent as they were, they simply weren't equipped to handle an abduction case. Especially not the kind where the kidnapped girl was blond, vivacious, popular and college-bound. Every photo of Isabelle Coleman that Josie had seen—and the girl's Facebook page boasted thousands of them, all of them set to public—looked like a glamour shot. Even in the photos where she and her friends made funny faces, poking out newly pierced tongues, Isabelle's small pink barbell read "Princess" where it might as well have read "Perfect."

The double doors to the Stop and Go whooshed open and two twenty-somethings made their way toward the gas pumps. Across from Josie sat their tiny yellow Subaru. The woman got in as the man pumped gas. Josie felt their eyes on her but refused to give them the satisfaction of looking back. Not that they'd have the balls to ask her any questions. Most people didn't. They just liked to stare. At least her indiscretion wasn't on the news anymore. In a small city where the standard newsworthy items were car accidents, local charity activities, and who got the biggest buck during hunting season, nobody cared anymore about the crazy lady cop with a temper.

She had hoped that the Coleman case would give her a chance to get off the chief's shit list, that he would make an exception in this case and just let her come back for a week or two, until they had the investigation well in hand. Until they found the girl. But he didn't call. She kept checking her phone to make sure it was working; that the battery hadn't mysteriously drained; that she hadn't accidentally muted it. She hadn't. The phone was fine. It was her chief who was being a hard-ass.

Deciding she wasn't ready to go home just yet, Josie walked back inside the Stop and Go to get a coffee. She killed a good ten minutes fixing it slowly—lots of half-and-half and two sugars—and paying for it. The owner, Dan, a former biker in his late fifties who had never given up leather vests, was an old acquaintance. He made enough small talk with her to let her know he was on her side without actually asking about the case pending against her. He knew her well enough by now not to ask probing questions.

But then there was nothing left to do but go home.

She noticed a small group of customers gathered around another television that hung above the lottery kiosk near the front of the store. She wandered over to them, sipping her coffee and watching as the broadcast she'd seen at the gas pump continued. The words "Students and Faculty React to Coleman Abduction" flashed across the bottom of the screen while a montage they'd been looping since last night played. The first time Josie saw it, WYEP had used the word *disappearance* instead of *abduction*.

"She was, like, a really nice person. I hope they find her. I mean, this is scary to think this could happen in Denton."

"It's just hard to believe, you know? She just vanished. It's a shame. She was really nice."

"We were supposed to go to the mall this weekend. I just can't believe it. I just saw her yesterday. She was my best friend."

"Isabelle is one of the brightest students in my class. All of us are extremely concerned."

A spasm rippled across Josie's shoulder blades. Only Isabelle's history teacher spoke as though she were still alive; everyone else had used the past tense. They had already given up on her being found safe. But why wouldn't they? People didn't vanish into thin air, and beautiful teenage girls who were abducted were rarely returned alive and unharmed. Josie knew that with every second that passed, the odds of Isabelle being found alive grew slimmer and slimmer.

A bead of sweat formed at the nape of her neck and rolled down her spine as she stepped outside, the paper coffee cup burning the skin of her palm as she stared at her Escape for a moment. She really should go home. The owner would need that pump for new customers. But the thought of spending the whole day alone in her house was simply too much to bear. Of course she could always drive around, maybe try to find the crime scene—it would likely be marked and cordoned off now that it had been located—and see if she saw anything that the others had missed.

Josie pulled out her cell phone and punched in a number she had dialed four to six times a day for the last six months. He let most of her calls go right to voicemail, but occasionally he would answer, and today he picked up on the third ring.

"Jo," Sergeant Ray Quinn said, sounding out of breath.

"When did you guys find the scene?" she asked without preamble.

He wasn't too breathless to give her one of his trademark heavy sighs. The kind he always gave her when he thought she was being a pain in the ass. "Jesus Christ," he said. "You're out on leave. Stop calling me. We've got this under control."

"Do you?"

"You think we don't?"

"Why hasn't the chief called in help? He's saying Coleman was abducted. Has he asked for support from the state police or the FBI? We don't have the resources for this."

"You don't know anything about this case, Jo."

"I know enough. If this really is an abduction, you need to call in backup, like, yesterday. You know that missing kids who aren't found in the first forty-eight hours—"

"Stop."

"I'm serious, Ray. This is serious shit. This girl could be anywhere by now. Have you shaken down the registered sex offenders yet? Please tell me you've got someone out there doing that right now. I mean, this isn't rocket science. Pretty blond teenager is abducted? Hiller would be good. You should get him to do it, and I'd have LaMay go with him. Call over to Bowersville and see if they can get a couple of people in their department to hit the register there. That's not that far from here. Tell me you've done this already?"

She could feel his annoyance over the line, but she was used to it. She tried to remember a time when they'd been loving toward one another. Sweet, caring, patient. She had to go all the way back to high school for that memory. They had liked one another once, hadn't they?

Ray sighed, "Here we go again. You think you know everything. You think you're the only one on the force who can do the job. You know what, Jo? You're not. You know nothing. *Nothing*. So shut up and stop fucking calling me. Take up knitting or whatever the fuck women do when they don't work. I'm hanging up now."

She was stung by the force of his words. He used the word *nothing* like a knife. Stabbing her fast and quick, a prison shanking. He was always abrasive—she could be too—but never cruel. Recovering quickly, she blurted, "Sign the divorce papers, Ray, and I'll stop calling."

Silence.

Now it was her turn to stab back. "I'm marrying Luke. He proposed. Yesterday. In bed."

He didn't respond, but she could hear him breathing. They'd been separated for months, but their relationship had been broken for a long time. She knew he hated Luke, hated the thought of another man with his wife. Even if she was his soon-to-be ex-wife.

She was listening so intently to the sound of his breathing, waiting to see what he would say, what tack he was going to take on hearing this news, that it took a moment for her to register the sharp report of gunshots in the distance. It wasn't that unusual in Denton; during hunting season, in the wooded outskirts of the city, shots went off all day long like fireworks. But it wasn't hunting season, or the Fourth of July. It was March, and there was no good reason for anyone to be firing off that many rounds.

Phone still in hand, Josie tossed her coffee cup into a nearby trash can and took a few steps out into the parking lot. The shots were getting closer, shattering the cool stillness of the morning. People at the gas pumps froze in place. All heads craned, searching for the source. Josie met the wide-eyed stares of a few of the patrons, but all they could do was exchange the same puzzled look.

Something was coming, but they didn't know what, or from where.

Instinctively, her free hand reached to her waist for her service weapon, but it wasn't there. Fear was a fist in her chest, squeezing her heart into her throat.

Ray spoke into her silence, "Jo?"

From around the corner, a black, bullet-riddled Escalade barreled toward the Stop and Go, jumped the curb and sailed directly toward Josie. Her feet were like cement blocks. *Move,* she told herself. *Move.* As the Escalade hurtled past her, the driver's side mirror caught the corner of her jacket, spinning her around and sending her flying through the air. She hit the asphalt hard, landing on her left side, her body rolling away from the vehicle until her stomach hit one of the metal pillars that blocked the gas pumps.

The Escalade smashed into the front of the Stop and Go, metal screeching and windows blowing out in a cacophonous boom. Even after the SUV lodged in the wall, the engine continued to rev and squeal. Plumes of dust from the crumbled cinderblock rose around the vehicle. People fled from the building. Josie's lungs screamed for air that wouldn't come.

# CHAPTER 2

Trying to catch her breath, Josie rolled to her other side, causing a sharp pain to shoot through her left leg. A glance at her jeans revealed a large tear going up the side of her calf. Shredded, pink skin peeked out from underneath. She took a deep, full breath at last. Her entire torso felt like a bruise. But she was alive. Nothing appeared to be broken or missing, but her adrenaline pumped too hard to register the relief.

Looking back toward the Escalade, she saw a smattering of people gathered around the back end of it, keeping a careful distance. As she staggered to her feet, Josie noticed a man, bent at the waist, hanging face down from the rear driver's side window of the vehicle. Blood fanned across the back of his white T-shirt. What looked like a TEC-9 had landed in the parking lot about ten feet away from the car. Again, she reached for her service weapon and felt a sense of panic at its absence. She stumbled toward the vehicle, trying to right her posture. Pain prickled across her lower back.

"Get back," she told the crowd.

Two women looked on, faces pale. One covered her mouth with her hands. The other pressed her hands to her chest, which heaved in time with the sound of the car alarm going off inside the Escalade. The twenty-somethings were there too, clinging to one another. Near the pumps an older woman leaned against her car, sobbing.

The driver slumped forward, his forehead on the steering wheel. His window had been shot out. Blood trickled from his ear. His thick black hair was wet with what Josie was sure was more blood. Josie stepped closer to the car and reached gingerly into the driver's side window, pressing two fingers to the side of the driver's neck. No pulse. Her fingers came away red.

The sound of someone retching drew her attention. She raced to the other side of the Escalade. The Stop and Go owner was a few feet away from the rear passenger's side, leaned over and vomiting, a shotgun in one hand.

Josie said, "Give me that."

He didn't protest when she took the gun. Turning back, she saw what had made him sick. Another man hung from the rear passenger's side window, his neck twisted at an awkward angle.

She hefted the shotgun up and fitted the stock into her shoulder, keeping the barrel low but at the ready as she prowled toward the front passenger's seat, cataloging everything she knew so far. Pennsylvania plates. Four occupants, three definitely dead. All three appeared to be of Latino descent, mid to late twenties, and were pretty heavily inked. The two guys in the back had shiny bald heads, and the matching tattoos on the backs of their necks told her they were probably members of a gang. The driver and the man seated behind him had been killed by gunfire, no doubt. The other backseat passenger was more likely killed by the impact of the crash. It looked like a bullet had grazed the side of his head at some point in the gun battle, but she didn't see any obvious gunshot wounds anywhere else.

The sound of the front passenger coughing sent her arms flying upward, the barrel of the gun pointed toward the open window. Cautiously, she approached. Behind her, the owner of the Stop and Go called out, "Detective!" His voice was high-pitched with concern.

Inside the vehicle, the man's body bucked and shook. As she got closer she saw that, unlike the other occupants, he was white and middle-aged with short dark hair and glasses. He had his seat belt on. Where the other men wore T-shirts, this man had on a plaid button-down shirt with a tie. Blood oozed from a bullet hole in his chest. His face was pinched with pain and smeared with blood. Thin, rice-sized pieces of glass sparkled all over his skin, like someone had sprayed him with glitter.

His head swiveled toward her and his hazel eyes took her in. Shock coursed through her. She lowered the shotgun. "Mr. Spencer?" she said.

She drew closer, leaning in toward him. With great effort, he reached a hand through the window. His fingers searched for something to grab onto and found the sleeve of her jacket. Josie locked eyes with him, the look of panic in his face like a sudden splash of cold water down her back. His mouth worked to speak. Blood spilled from his lips. He whispered hoarsely but with a desperation in his tone that went right through her. He said only one word. A name.

"Ramona."

# CHAPTER 3

Josie sat in the back of an ambulance, an unused ice pack in her hand. Too many places on her body hurt. She needed a body pillow filled with ice, not just a pack. Someone had called 911, and they had responded immediately. She counted three Denton cruisers and two state police cars. Evidently, the shootout had started on the interstate and ended when the Escalade had left the highway and crashed at the Stop and Go. The staties had scoured the interstate for miles in each direction, scouting out each exit as they went, but there was no sign of any other bullet-riddled vehicle. No one could say who the men in the Escalade were exchanging gunfire with.

Josie watched her colleagues process the scene. Two of the men she knew, but not well. The third man, Dusty Branson, had been Ray's best friend since elementary school. He had been Josie's friend as well until her marriage collapsed. Now she found it difficult to be in the same space as him. As expected, the Denton officers looked exhausted and bewildered, but moved with purpose and determination: taking witness statements, erecting tarps around the SUV, taking photographs and marking the evidence scattered throughout the scene.

"Don't come over. Don't come over," Josie muttered under her breath as she watched Dusty saunter from the back of the Escalade toward her.

As he came closer, he pulled a notebook from his pocket and flipped it to a blank page. He met her eyes only briefly. She was happy when he looked away. She had never liked his dark, beady eyes, like two pieces of glittering coal. He pushed a hand through his oily brown hair and she felt a small surge of joy to see the premature gray strands at his roots. He wasn't even thirty yet.

"So, you saw this?" he said.

"Yeah," she replied.

His pen poised over the blank page. She concentrated on a small stain on the left side of his uniform shirt, just below his rib cage. It looked like coffee. He scribbled as she spoke, his pen freezing just as she told him about Dirk Spencer's final word before he slipped into unconsciousness.

"You should write that down," she said pointedly. "It's important."

He looked up at her. The smirk he gave her caused a swell in her stomach. "You don't know that it's important," he told her.

"The guy was barely hanging on to life, Dusty. Why would he say the name if it wasn't important? If this Ramona person *wasn't* important?"

He used the tip of the pen to scratch his temple. "So what? It's probably just his wife or daughter's name."

"Maybe," she said, but the whisper of the name kept running loops in her head. She waited for Dusty to write the name down. "Just check it out, okay?"

"You don't get to tell me what to do anymore," he told her, closing his notebook and pocketing it.

She bit back her first response, her hands itching to shove

him. But shoving him would involve actually touching him, and few things repulsed her more than making physical contact with Dusty Branson. Instead, she spat, "Yeah, but that doesn't relieve you of your obligation to do your job, now does it?"

She held his flinty gaze until he looked away. "I gotta work," he said, and meandered away like he had nothing to do at all.

Luckily, no one inside the Stop and Go had been seriously injured. One of the officers had turned the car's engine off but its alarm continued in an angry, rhythmic series of honks that grated on her frayed nerves.

"Jo. Jesus Christ."

It was Ray, in full uniform, except for his hat. He climbed into the ambulance with her and got close enough to pull her to him, but at the last minute decided to keep his distance. They hadn't touched in almost a year. Part of her was relieved to see him and grateful that he had shown up to check on her, but the other part of her shivered at the thought. She never thought she'd feel that way; Ray had been a fixture in her life since middle school. They were friends long before they became high school sweethearts. He had always been good-looking in a sweet, boy-next-door kind of way with his thick, tousled blond hair, blue eyes and athletic body. She'd always been secretly pleased that he was hers. Women were drawn to him. They didn't know he had issues.

"You okay?" he asked, taking a seat on the bench across from her. His gaze raked over her, searching for injuries.

"Yeah," she said. "Just banged up."

He nodded toward her leg. "That looks pretty bad."

"It's just a brush burn."

"Listen, Jo, about earlier. I'm sorry I snapped at you. This Coleman case has us all on edge. I didn't mean—"

A low voice boomed from the outside of the ambulance. "Josie, there you are!"

Luke appeared, also in full uniform. This was going to be awkward.

No matter how many times she saw him in his state police gray, Josie was always struck by how imposing he looked, and she knew Ray would be feeling it too as Luke pulled off his cap and bent to climb into the ambulance.

He was the opposite of Ray in almost every way, which was why she enjoyed him so much, she supposed. As a statie, Luke had to keep his black hair high and tight, shaved close to his head on the sides with a short cap of hair on the top. His face, clean and shaven, was smooth against her cheek when he leaned in to kiss her. He ignored Ray as he folded himself down beside her and slung an arm across her back.

"Are you okay?" he asked.

She smiled. "Yes, I'm fine."

She sensed Ray's scowl before she even looked at him. An hour ago she'd been flaunting their engagement over the phone with Ray, and yet Luke's display of affection in front of him made her uncomfortable. It shouldn't—she hated that it did—but she wasn't able to stop herself. He hated Luke. She knew that he made him feel inferior; he was taller, broader, in better shape. He was even hung better, although she had never told Ray. She was saving that one for a day when he really got under her skin.

She patted Luke's hand and, after assuring him once more that she was fine, said, "Can I have a minute alone with Ray?"

A muscle in Luke's jaw twitched, but he smiled, kissed her softly on the lips and said, "Sure."

He made sure to bump Ray's shoulder on his way out of the ambulance. Ray watched him go, looking both satisfied and wary. "Are you really going to marry that guy?" he asked.

She sighed and pressed the ice pack, now melted, against her left shoulder. "I'm not talking about this again."

"Then why did you want to be alone?"

"Because I want to know why Isabelle Coleman's history teacher was in the passenger seat of that Escalade out there."

# CHAPTER 4

Ray glanced toward the open ambulance doors as though he might be able to see Dirk, but he was already halfway to Geisinger Medical Center in critical condition. He had slipped into unconsciousness after saying that one word to Josie, and neither she nor the paramedics had been able to rouse him. He was the only living witness to the shootout, and he'd be lucky if he survived the next few hours.

"How do you know he was Isabelle Coleman's teacher?"

Josie rolled her eyes. "He was on the news last night and again this morning talking about what a good student Isabelle is. Trinity Payne interviewed him. She interviewed everybody. I thought you were on this case."

"Yeah, well, the chief's got me searching the woods out by the Coleman house. I don't have time to watch the news."

"So, you found the phone?"

His eyes flicked to his lap. "No, a searcher did. It was kind of embarrassing since our guys had already taken a pass in that area right after Coleman went missing. Anyway, this lady found it and called it in. Dusty and I took it into evidence."

"Well, a few minutes before the crash I saw Dirk Spencer on the news talking about what a great girl Isabelle is and how everyone just wants her to come home."

"You think this"—he motioned toward the crash—"has something to do with Isabelle Coleman's disappearance?"

"You mean abduction."

"You know what I mean."

Josie told him about Dirk Spencer whispering the name Ramona before he lapsed into unconsciousness. Three horizontal lines appeared on Ray's forehead. It was the same look he got when she asked him to pick up tampons at the store. Puzzled consternation. "So what?" he replied. "It's probably his girlfriend."

She sighed. "Yeah, I guess. So what's the chief holding back on the Coleman case?"

He stared at her, one eyebrow lifting. "You know I can't tell you that."

Josie's head throbbed. "You think I won't find out eventually?"

Exasperated, Ray said, "Why can't you just follow the rules? Just one time? You're asking me to put my own job in jeopardy, Jo."

She couldn't contain her incredulous "Puh." She laughed. "Your job? You're kidding me, right? You really think the chief would fire you for sharing information with someone in the department? I am your superior," she reminded him.

It was a sore subject. He might have been promoted alongside her if the chief hadn't kept finding empty whiskey bottles in the footwell of his patrol car. Turned out it wasn't that easy to storm out of an ambulance. He stumbled and nearly fell to the asphalt outside. The last thing Josie heard was "Son of a bitch."

Luke slid in beside her with a fresh ice pack, and this time she held it to her temple. Her headache was getting worse by the moment. She needed some ibuprofen. Her adrenaline was fading, leaving her entire body aching.

"What was that about?" he asked.

"Just trying to find out what he knows about the Coleman case."

He put a hand on her knee. "Josie," he began, but he didn't lecture her. She liked that about him.

"What've you got on this mess?" she asked.

Luke sighed and rubbed a hand over his eyes. "Squat, that's what we've got. All we know is that they came from the interstate. But it's like they were shooting at an invisible car. We know there was another vehicle involved because of all the rounds shot into the Escalade, but all we've got are spent bullets."

"What kind?"

"Nine millimeter, 30.06 and some 7.62 by 39s," Luke said.

Josie moved the ice pack to her left shoulder. "A handgun and a hunting rifle? Well, that narrows it down. Practically every male in the state has those. The 7.62s are a little less common around here."

"AK-47s take 7.62 by 39 rounds. Lots of inner-city gangs use those."

"So you think this was a gang thing?"

"Vehicle is registered to one Carlos Garza of Philadelphia—the driver. He's a known member of The 23, a Latino gang out of Philadelphia."

"That's the number the other two had tattooed on the backs of their necks. Whatever this was may have started on the interstate, but Philadelphia is two hours away."

"You know as well as I do the drug trade doesn't respect borders," Luke pointed out.

"So this could all be over drugs?"

"Sure looks that way."

"Then what was Denton East High's twelfth-grade history teacher doing in the passenger's seat, and who's Ramona?"

Luke shrugged. "Who knows? Hopefully Spencer will make it through and be able to tell us himself."

# CHAPTER 5

Josie hated not being on the job. She wanted to be out there working. If not on the Coleman case, then on the shooting. That made two extremely unusual crimes in Denton in the past week, and she didn't get to be a part of solving either of them. She lingered around the Stop and Go for as long as she could but when Trinity Payne pulled up in her WYEP news van, Josie knew it was time to go.

At home, she locked the door, stripped off her torn clothes and headed straight for the bathroom. She turned the faucet on to fill the tub and inspected herself in the full-length mirror; her entire left side was starting to turn a nasty plum color. She was lucky to have narrowly escaped the Escalade, inches away from being the fourth fatality. Goosebumps prickled her skin. She wished Luke was there. For once, she wished he had the kind of job where he could just call off and spend the rest of the day with her, quieting her anxiety.

But she was alone for the rest of the day, and it was only noon. She sat on the edge of the tub and eased her lower left leg into it, hissing through gritted teeth as the open skin met the hot water like dipping it in hot lava. The wound wasn't deep, but it was big. She cleaned it with anti-bacterial soap, patted it dry and, limping, she made her way into the bedroom and sprawled out on her bed. Tucking a pillow beneath her calf to elevate it, she found two ibuprofens in her nightstand and swallowed them dry.

Flinging her arms wide, she stared at the ceiling and concentrated on breathing through the pain until it subsided. She listened to cars passing outside and the noises of her house—the hum of the fridge, the roar of the forced-air heating system as it kicked on, and then the deafening silence when it kicked off. She still wasn't used to the house, having only moved in three months earlier. It was a proud moment for her, finally owning her own house. She hadn't been able to stay in the home she and Ray had shared. Sure, it was painful—how could the end of a marriage not be painful?—but mostly, living there made her irrationally angry. He had had the good sense to move out, living on Dusty's couch for months while she looked for a new place to live. He had offered to give her the house. He had cheated, he reasoned, so he should have to leave. It was the most intelligent thing he had said in the last decade.

Josie tried it. She tried to move on while living in the home they'd bought together as a young married couple. The home where they'd celebrated their promotions. The home where they'd entertained mutual friends—almost all of whom were on Denton's police force—on holidays and on nights when their jobs had been particularly difficult. The home they'd furnished and decorated together, arguing over their choices in perfect matrimony.

She couldn't do it; she didn't want to stay there. The thought of using her own money that she had earned to buy her own house was so appealing to her, it made her giddy. She'd found the three-bedroom bungalow-style home on two acres of land after only a month of searching. It was her house;

she knew it the moment she saw the front of it. She didn't even need to go inside, but the realtor had insisted. A college professor had owned it. He'd been abruptly transferred and wanted a quick sale. It was a match made in heaven.

She let Ray keep all of their furniture. She didn't want any remnants from their life together. The downside of that decision was that since she had sunk all her money into the new house, she had had very little left to spend on new furniture. It was a work in progress. With her work hours she was rarely home anyway, and she didn't entertain, except for Luke, and they spent ninety-five percent of their time in her bedroom.

Her one extravagance had been the enormous bed she lay on now. A small compensation for her shitty childhood; a king-sized bed in a huge master bedroom with high ceilings and a wall of windows was about as far as you could get from the two-foot-by-four-foot closet where she began.

Usually Josie reveled in sprawling out in the luxurious bed with its fifteen different-sized pillows, but she couldn't stop thinking about Dirk Spencer: shot and bleeding out, eyes panic-stricken, struggling to utter just one word. Why that word? Why that name? Who was Ramona? Why was Spencer in an SUV with a bunch of gangbangers from Philadelphia? Had he been in Philadelphia? Did they take him under duress? Who was shooting at them?

There were too many unanswered questions. Too many for Josie to possibly stay home in bed.

# CHAPTER 6

It only took a few minutes for Josie to google an address for Dirk Spencer. His house was on top of a mountain in a development called Briar Lane. The small collection of modular homes could only be reached by one of the long, narrow rural roads that snaked from Denton proper out into the thick forests surrounding it. Josie actually passed the Coleman driveway on her way out there; the two lay along the same road. A large yellow mailbox with hand-painted cardinals on it stood alone on the shoulder of the road where the mouth of the small one-lane driveway that snaked its way through the woods to the Colemans' home started. She expected to see crime scene tape, a cruiser, or another WYEP news van parked at the turn-off, but it was deserted.

Like most of the new developments in Denton, all the houses in Briar Lane looked the same. They came in three colors: tan, gray, and white. Some of the residents had added a little character with landscaping and lawn ornaments. Dirk Spencer's house was gray and nondescript. He hadn't bothered to add any distinguishing touches. If Josie didn't know any better, she would think the house was unoccupied.

She parked out front even though the driveway was empty.

She had no idea who else lived there, if he had a wife who might arrive at any moment. She didn't want to be blocked in. She knocked on the door a few times and then rang the doorbell, but no one came to the door. No sounds came from the house at all. No barking dogs or cats in the windows. She peeked in through the gauzy curtains and she saw furniture, but nothing inside moved.

"Oh, honey, he's not home." A woman's voice came from behind her. Josie turned to see a white-haired woman at the end of the driveway. She wore a camouflage-green raincoat even though it wasn't raining, and held a cane in one hand. She smiled at Josie. "You missed him. Someone picked him up this morning in a big car."

So, Spencer had gone willingly with the men in the Escalade.

"You saw him leave?" she asked the woman.

"Well, yeah. That big old truck was parked out here, same place you parked. They beeped twice. That's what made me come to the window. Dirk came running out a few minutes later, hopped right in."

He'd been expecting them. He must have left his own car in the garage.

"It's probably best you missed him with all that fighting between you two. Did you forget where he keeps the spare key?"

It was only then that Josie realized the woman was mistaking her for someone else. Someone who knew Dirk Spencer quite well. Before she could answer, the woman hobbled up the driveway, picked up a round, palm-sized stone from beside the porch steps and shook it until a small flap opened up along its surface and a shiny key fell out. Quickly, Josie stooped and snatched the key from the ground. "Thanks," she said.

Another smile. Up close, the woman's face was lined with

wrinkles and she had the kind of look that people get when they can't really hear what someone is saying but are too embarrassed to admit it, so they simply smile and nod along.

"You colored your hair," the woman said.

Josie returned her smile but said nothing. Later, if her unsanctioned visit to Dirk Spencer's house became an issue, she could say truthfully that she had not encouraged the woman.

"The darker color looks good on you," the woman added. When Josie didn't respond, the woman said, "It's a shame it didn't work out with you two. He really loves you."

The corners of Josie's mouth tightened. "Oh well, that's nice of you to say."

"You still work at that restaurant in town?"

"Uh, no," Josie replied.

The woman stared at her for a long moment, eyes narrowing, like she was trying to puzzle something out. Josie waited, a cold sweat gathering on her top lip; the woman had realized her mistake, surely. But then she smiled again, her eyes going blank once more. She turned and began shuffling back down the driveway to the street. "I'll leave you to it," she said over her shoulder.

She wanted to stop her and ask if she knew where she might find someone named Ramona, but she stopped herself. What if Spencer's ex *was* Ramona? Josie waved and watched the old lady move slowly down the block before she turned and tried the key in the lock.

The living room had two mismatched couches with blankets thrown over their backs. Bookcases dominated one wall, and the tomes that didn't fit there were stacked on end tables. A blue sweatshirt was thrown carelessly over one of the couch arms. The local newspaper—an edition from three days earlier—lay spread out across the coffee table, open at one of the first features they had done on the disappearance of Isabelle Coleman. Beside that was a coffee mug, its dregs congealing in the bottom in a thick brown goo.

In the kitchen was a sink filled with unwashed dishes. Crumbs dotted the countertops. A butter knife lay next to the chrome-colored toaster, sheathed in a coating of dried-up butter. A cell phone charger was plugged into the wall next to the toaster, its cord dangling over the side of the countertop. Josie made a mental note to try to find out what, if anything, was found on Spencer's cell phone. On the fridge were photographs affixed with magnets from various places Spencer had obviously been: New York City, Baltimore's Inner Harbor, the Rock and Roll Hall of Fame in Cleveland, Hersheypark, and San Francisco. In most of the photos Spencer smiled happily into the camera, alongside a woman with long brown hair and blue eyes. Other than having long hair, she didn't really resemble Josie. She was probably a few years older, early thirties maybe. This, Josie assumed, was the ex-girlfriend. In one photo she wore a green apron and stood in front of a bar in a restaurant that Josie vaguely recognized.

Mixed in with the photos of the ex-girlfriend were photos of Dirk with a different woman and a teenage girl. This woman was older, maybe mid-forties, thicker around the middle with brittle, sandy-colored hair and dark eyes. The teenager looked like a combination of the two of them, only her skin was more olive-colored. Her hair was dark, like Dirk's.

She assumed this was Spencer's family. Perhaps he was divorced. She wondered where this woman and teenage girl were now. Someone would have to notify his next of kin if he didn't make it; someone had probably already been in touch as it seemed likely he wouldn't make it another day. She used her cell phone to snap a few pictures of the photos on Spencer's fridge and checked the upstairs. The queen-size bed in the master bedroom was unmade. Down the hall from that, the other bedroom had a neatly made twin bed in it with a dust-covered nightstand and dresser, but the room had no adornments. It didn't look lived in at all. Nothing of interest. Josie made her way back toward the front door, careful not to disturb anything. On the porch, she closed the door and turned the key to lock it.

"What the hell are you doing here?"

Josie froze at the sound of Trinity's voice. Her right hand was still turning the key, her stomach somewhere around her ankles. This was not good. She sucked in a deep breath, shored herself up and turned, trying to look put out and annoyed. "What are *you* doing here?" she countered.

Trinity still wore the same puffy blue coat she'd had on that morning; a black, knee-length A-line skirt peeked from beneath it, followed by long, toned legs in thin stockings and finished with four-inch heels. At least Josie didn't have to worry about Trinity chasing her down, not in those shoes.

Josie's gaze drifted back to Trinity's face. As always, she was struck by the similarities. The two women weren't related—Trinity had grown up a few towns away in relative wealth, raised in a two-parent home, while Josie had been raised by a single mother who never quite found her way out of abject poverty—but they both had long, jet-black hair, porcelain skin, and striking blue eyes with long lashes. Josie's fingers reached up and pulled her hair forward, making sure it covered the long, jagged scar that ran down the side of her right cheek. It was the most striking difference between them. Josie had always been grateful the scar was close to her ear so that if she wore her hair down with some concealer, it was barely noticeable.

Trinity pointed to her own chest. "Me? I'm working a

story. A story that just got a whole lot more interesting now that I've found a suspended cop breaking into a shooting victim's house."

Josie looked beyond her to the street but the WYEP van was not in sight. She knew from experience that sometimes Trinity purposely had the cameraman park the van around the corner so that the people she wanted to talk to wouldn't get spooked by it and scatter. Trinity was as sneaky as she was desperate. Two years earlier she had been on the fast track to a major morning news show when a bad source gave her a false story. She went on air with it. Later, when it came out that the entire story was a lie, she had taken the fall. The scandal made national headlines. Disgraced, she had returned to central Pennsylvania and landed a job as a roving reporter for the small news station that covered the central part of the state. Josie suspected Trinity was looking for the story that would put her back in the good graces of the major markets and the viewing public. She wasn't going to find it here, Josie thought.

"I wasn't breaking in," Josie said, pulling the key out of the lock and waving it in Trinity's face.

"You know Dirk Spencer?"

"Sort of," Josie answered. She moved to walk past Trinity, but she moved with her.

"Either you know him, or you don't. So, which is it? I know you're not here on official police business."

"Get out of my way," Josie said. "I don't have to talk to you."

A cell phone appeared, as if by magic, in Trinity's hand. Her eyes narrowed. "Do you want to wait here while I call your chief and ask him why I found the detective he suspended coming out of Dirk Spencer's house hours after he was nearly killed in a gang-related shootout on the interstate?"

Josie stared into her smug, overly made-up face with ice in

her eyes. She could have slapped her, but that was exactly the sort of thing that had gotten her in trouble in the first place. She wondered how much force she could use to push Trinity out of her way before it became assault. Trinity's cameraman was probably hidden somewhere behind the rhododendron across the street, taping this entire exchange. There was no shoving her way out of this, so she got right to the point. "What do you want?"

Slowly, Trinity lowered her cell phone. "I want a comment about the woman you assaulted. Tell me your side of the story."

Josie sighed. "You know I can't talk about that, not while the investigation is pending."

Trinity rolled her eyes. "That's public relations bullshit. Don't you want your side of the story told?"

Josie didn't. She had no desire to hash the whole thing out in any type of public forum. What she really wanted was to move on with her life. Get back to work and find Isabelle Coleman, or find out why Dirk Spencer had been shot. She said, "It doesn't matter what I want. I can't discuss it."

Trinity placed a well-manicured hand on her hip. "What about this morning? You were a witness. Surely you can talk about that?"

"If I talk to you about this morning, will you back off?"

Trinity bit her lower lip briefly. "Until the investigation into your excessive force charge is complete. I can't promise you anything once that happens. Our viewers will want to know what happened."

"I'm not going on camera."

"Then I'm not backing off."

"Giving you an on-camera interview isn't necessarily a decision I can make on my own. I have superiors to answer to, you know that."

Trinity said, "I have superiors too. They're going to want an interview. So, what's it going to be? Am I calling your chief right now or are we going to have a conversation about this morning?"

Josie was furious with herself for getting caught at Dirk Spencer's house. There was no explanation that would satisfy her chief, so she lied. "Fine. I'll give you an exclusive on the excessive force thing once the investigation is over. But I do not go on camera today. I'll talk to you about this morning, but you never saw me here."

Josie thought she saw the tiniest flicker of satisfaction pass over Trinity's face. "You have a deal."

# CHAPTER 7

Josie kept it brief, discussing only the basic facts of what she had seen that morning and nothing else. She figured she couldn't possibly get herself in trouble by merely describing what a half dozen other Stop and Go patrons had also seen. She left Trinity pouting and drove down the mountain, still cursing herself for having gotten snagged in Trinity's web. She was going to be furious when she realized that Josie had no intention of giving her an exclusive interview about the investigation involving the allegation against her, or anything else for that matter.

She slowed the car as she came to the turn-off to the Colemans' home and made the left into the driveway. Halfway to the house she found a Denton police cruiser. In it, his head lolling, eyes closed, sat patrol officer Noah Fraley. Josie pulled up behind him and got out, her lower back protesting and her leg throbbing as she put weight on it again. As she approached, she could hear Noah snoring.

Leaning into the car window, the flutter of yellow crime scene tape in the tree line caught her eye. So, he was there to guard the scene. Gently, Josie nudged his shoulder and he jolted awake, confusion blanketing his face momentarily. As she registered her presence, a crimson flush stained his cheeks. "Jos—Detective Quinn," he stammered. "What're you doing here?"

Flustered by having been caught sleeping on the job, he spoke too fast, words piling on top of one another. When she smiled at him, the color in his cheeks deepened. He had always had a crush on her. Noah wasn't bad-looking, but it was impossible to see him that way. He had no swagger. You had to have some degree of confidence to be a cop. Even if it was fake. Noah's decided lack of self-assurance was exactly the reason he kept getting assignments like this—sitting in a car all day making sure no one went into the woods.

"Is that the crime scene?" she asked him.

He glanced over at the crime scene tape tied across the trees on the shoulder of the road and then back at her. She could see the hesitation in his face. "Uh, yeah, it's through the woods there."

The trees were thick and the woodland dense; there was no path that Josie could see. "Through the woods? How far from the road?"

Noah shrugged. "I don't know. You have to go back a ways."

She rested her forearms on the window's edge and leaned closer. "Do you mind if I take a look?"

"I—uh, I can't, you know, I'm not supposed to, I really shouldn't—"

"Noah," she said, her tone conspiratorial. "I'm an experienced investigator. You know I won't disturb the scene."

"But the chief said no one except—"

"It's already been processed, hasn't it?"

"Well, yeah, but I still have to keep a log of everyone who comes in and out," he said.

"You don't even have to put me on the log. It will be like I was never here."

"But the point of the log is so we know who was on the scene and when."

She tried another tack. "Officer Fraley, am I or am I not your superior?"

He shifted uncomfortably, looking away from her. "But you're not, you're—you're on suspension."

"You don't think the chief will call me back soon? I know you guys are running on empty. He's got everyone on around the clock, doesn't he?"

Noah nodded. He let out a long breath. "It's been awful," he admitted.

"And now with this shooting…" she added.

He met her eyes again. "I, uh, heard you were there. Glad you're okay, by the way."

"Me too," she said. She was close enough to smell the stale scent of old sweat. He probably hadn't been home to shower or change for a good three days. "Noah," she tried again. "The chief is going to call me back any minute now. Ray told me so. When he does I'm going to need to be up to speed. You don't have to tell anyone I was here, and I don't have to tell anyone that you fell asleep at your post."

He closed his eyes, resignation and shame warring for dominance on his face. "Please, just be quick, okay?"

She patted his shoulder and half-ran, half-hobbled off toward the woods before he could change his mind.

"Don't leave your car here!" he shouted after her.

He was right. If someone from the department came while she was in the woods, there was no way he could explain away her vehicle. Of course, there weren't many places she could leave her car without giving away the fact that she was nosing around the Coleman scene. She couldn't park up near the house, so the best she could do was park along the shoulder of the main road about a half mile back. Anyone coming from town to the Coleman home would not pass her vehicle. If someone showed up while she was at the abduction scene, she could always find her way back to her car through the woods and take off with no one the wiser. She just had to hope no one on the force decided to pass the Coleman home and head toward Dirk Spencer's development while she was at the scene.

By the time she got to the Colemans' mailbox she was sweating pretty heavily, and the left side of her body had gone from a dull ache to an angry throb. She took off her jacket and tied it around her waist. As she passed the mailbox, she saw something bright and pink in the grass a few feet from it. A closer inspection revealed an acrylic nail: hot pink with yellow stripes. She snapped a few pictures of it with her phone before picking it up with a tissue and putting it in her pocket.

She knew the woods around the Colemans' home had been searched extensively. They would have come to the edge of the road. They probably had even gone a few miles into the woods on the other side of the road, across from the mailbox. She was sure this nail would have been seen by someone already. It should have been taken into evidence, at least until they could determine whether or not it belonged to Isabelle. Unless it was from one of the searchers, which was entirely possible. Or perhaps Mrs. Coleman had stopped for the mail and lost it. Josie sighed as she trudged up the long driveway. This was the sort of thing that drove her crazy. There was no way to know whether or not it was important. If she hadn't had to give up her badge, she would go right to Mrs. Coleman with it and ask if she recognized it. But she wasn't a cop right now.

She nodded at Noah as she stepped gingerly behind the crime scene tape. More yellow tape tied from tree to tree formed a narrow path that led to the clearing. The ground was covered with mud, decomposing leaves, and snapped-off tree branches. She estimated the scene was about forty feet from the side of the driveway. It was just a small clearing with a large stone to one side. There was nothing to it, really. All the evidence had been processed and removed.

Josie spun in a slow circle, taking in the scene.

"What the hell was she doing out here?" she muttered to herself.

There was nothing remarkable about the clearing at all. It was like a thousand other clearings in the Pennsylvania woods surrounding Denton and its neighboring towns. It wasn't even necessarily a clearing so much as a slightly larger gap between trees. What had Isabelle been doing this deep in the woods? As Josie picked her way back toward the road, she wondered if the girl had been on the driveway and had run into the woods when she realized she was being pursued. Or perhaps there had been a struggle and she had escaped into the trees.

Josie didn't have enough information. All she knew was what she could glean from Trinity Payne's news reports. As far as anyone knew, Isabelle had been home alone when she disappeared. Nothing in her home was disturbed, and her cell phone had been missing.

At the driveway Josie waved a thank you at Noah, who looked considerably relieved to see her go. On the way back to her car, she fingered the wad of tissue holding the acrylic nail and wondered when the chief was going to call her to come back to work.

# CHAPTER 8

It took two slow circles through downtown Denton for Josie to find the restaurant she was looking for. Sandman's Bar and Grill. She and Luke had eaten there once; it was one of the first places they had gone publicly. The inside was just as she remembered it—and just as it had appeared in the photo on Dirk Spencer's fridge. It was dimly lit, with a long bar, its wood lacquered and shiny, taking up one wall. Across from it were two dozen tables for two, some of which had been pushed together for parties of four or more. The walls were red brick adorned with signs for beer that had long since been discontinued. Falstaff, Meister Brau, Rheingold.

It was after lunch but before happy hour, and the place only had a few patrons. Josie limped up to the bar, her leg pulsating steadily with pain in time with the ache in her back. She needed more ibuprofen. The bartender was young, probably just twenty-one, and his attention was riveted to one of the large televisions hanging on the wall behind the bar. It showed Trinity Payne—Josie couldn't escape the woman—this time in front of the Stop and Go. There was no sound, but the bartender watched with intense concentration. Josie wondered if he was more interested in the shooting or Trinity.

The sound of her dragging her stool closer to the bar drew his attention. He gave her a fake, practiced smile and asked what he could get her. She was going to say nothing, but the pain in her body was getting so bad a shot of something sounded perfect right about then. "Two shots of Wild Turkey," she said.

He looked behind her and then toward the door.

She smiled tightly. "They're both for me. It's been a long day."

His smile faltered for a moment but he recovered quickly. "No problem."

She waited until he had returned with the shot glasses and liquor before she asked, "Do you guys have anyone working here named Ramona? A waitress?"

There was no recognition. His pasted-on smile gave way to genuine confusion. "No one by that name," he said. "What's she look like?"

Josie pulled out her cell phone, located the photo she'd taken of Dirk Spencer and his ex-girlfriend, zoomed in on the woman and showed him.

"Oh, that's Solange," he said easily. "She's on tonight. Should be here in about a half hour if you want to wait. I can—" He stopped speaking abruptly, as if just realizing that maybe he shouldn't be giving out so much information without knowing who Josie was or what she wanted.

"Don't worry. I'm a police officer," Josie offered. "But that's not really why I'm here. I'm off duty. She's not in any trouble, I just need to talk to her about something."

He looked doubtful, and she prayed he wouldn't ask for her credentials. After a moment he shrugged and said, "Okay. Can I get you anything else?"

She smiled. "Just a soda."

As promised, Solange arrived about twenty minutes later,

following the bartender from the back and looking concerned. When she saw Josie, she smiled awkwardly. Her hands fidgeted with her green apron as she tied it around her waist. She came around the bar and offered her hand. "Hey, aren't you the lady cop that was on the news—"

"Detective Josie Quinn, yes. I'm not working right now."

"You're suspended."

"Yes."

Solange's face had closed off, her lips pressed into a straight line. "What is this about?"

"Do you know anyone named Ramona?"

No flicker of recognition at all. Solange's expression didn't change. "No."

Josie sighed. "This morning there was a shooting on the interstate that ended when an Escalade crashed into the Stop and Go."

Solange crossed her arms over her chest. "I saw it on the news. What's it got to do with me?"

"No one from the police department has been by to speak with you yet?" Josie asked.

"No, why?"

"Dirk Spencer was a passenger in the Escalade," Josie said.

Solange's hand flew to her mouth, her eyes wide with shock. Stumbling backward, she found a stool and half-sat, half-leaned on it. "Oh my God," she said. "Is he—is he . . . ?"

"As far as I know he's still alive," Josie said. "He was life-flighted to Geisinger Medical Center. From what I understand, his injuries are very serious. I don't know what your relationship is, or was, but you may want to go see him."

The woman gathered her composure, her face closing back down. She smoothed the apron down over her waist and legs. "We haven't been together for almost two years. We broke up."

"There was no answer at Mr. Spencer's house," Josie said

carefully. "Does he have any other family or anyone we should notify?"

"I thought you were on suspension," Solange said pointedly.

"I am," Josie admitted. "I'm not here because I'm a police officer. I mean, I am, but I'm not. I'm here because I was there this morning. I was almost killed when that Escalade crashed." Josie lifted her shirt slightly and turned so Solange could see the bruising already darkening the left side of her body. "Before Mr. Spencer lost consciousness, he said the name Ramona. Does that mean anything to you?"

Solange shook her head. "No. I don't know anyone by that name. Neither does he. At least, not that I'm aware of. Maybe he met someone since we broke up."

The thought didn't seem to sit well with Solange.

Josie said, "I'm sure you're aware that with the Isabelle Coleman abduction, the department is stretched. I recognized Mr. Spencer from the local high school, and since I was there, and the last person he spoke to before he passed out, I thought maybe I'd talk to his next of kin personally."

It wasn't warm in the restaurant, but Solange started fanning herself with one hand. Her eyes looked everywhere but at Josie. "Oh well, he has no next of kin here. He has a sister in Philadelphia, Lara, but they don't talk much. She's . . . she's always in a lot of trouble, you know, like with the law. He has a niece, June. She was living with him, but she ran away over a year ago and no one's seen her since."

"How old is June?" Josie asked.

Solange shrugged. "I'm not sure. By now she's sixteen or seventeen. You'll never find her though."

"Why do you say that?"

Another shrug. "Because Dirk looked. Believe me, he looked. That girl doesn't want to be found."

# CHAPTER 9

According to Solange, June Spencer was a troubled girl. With her dad out of the picture, she had lived in Philadelphia with her mother, and by the time she was fifteen she had been expelled from four high schools, arrested a half dozen times, overdosed twice and tried to slit her wrists.

"Her mother isn't much better," Solange said, spreading her hands in a what-do-you-expect gesture. "That woman has been in and out of rehab more times than I can count, and don't get me started on her criminal record. She might as well have a bench named after her down there in the Criminal Justice Center. It's no wonder that June is such a hot mess."

Josie bristled. She knew a thing or two about moms like that. If Solange was to be believed, she also knew that June had most likely been a helpless victim in all of the chaos: a child with no resources and no one to turn to, a captive audience to her own mother's destructive lifestyle. Sometimes even an unwilling participant. Josie pushed those thoughts aside and focused on Solange. "How did June end up here?"

Solange started to roll her eyes and then stopped when she saw the seriousness in Josie's face. "She was Dirk's personal crusade. He didn't want her turning out like his sister. They were both raised by a single mom who died of a heart attack when they were in their twenties so, besides him, June really has no family at all. It took some convincing, but he got his sister to let her come live with him on a trial basis. He wanted to adopt her."

"His sister wouldn't allow it?"

Solange shook her head. "No. That bitch is nothing if not spiteful. The only reason she even let June come up here was because she had to serve six months for probation violations, and child services told her if she didn't sign over temporary guardianship to Dirk, June was going into foster care."

"How long ago was this?" Josie asked.

"About two years ago. She had just turned fifteen."

"Isn't that how long you two have been broken up?"

Solange's shoulders slumped. The bartender slid a coke across the bar to her, and she gave him a weak smile in return. With a pained look she said, "Yeah. Look, I appreciated that Dirk wanted to save his niece, I really did. But I'm, like, ten years younger than him. I wanted us to settle down, start our own family. That was our plan. Taking on a damaged, rebellious teenage girl was not something we had ever discussed."

"So you left?"

"I tried to stick it out. I figured she would turn eighteen in a few years, and then maybe Dirk and I could start our life together, but I didn't last that long. Dirk and I kept in touch even after I left; our break was supposed to be temporary, but at some point it became pretty clear that we were moving in different directions. Dirk asked me to keep coming around and be a 'positive female role model' for June, so I tried doing things with her now and then. I did my best to try to relate to June, for Dirk's sake, but she was a closed book."

Josie could find out from Ray or Noah if June had ever been arrested in Denton, but she didn't personally recall any incidents involving the girl. "Did she have trouble when she came here?"

Solange put her glass back on the bar and swirled the straw around in the brown liquid, making the ice cubes clink. "She wasn't as bad as we expected. She got in trouble for cutting school, and Dirk caught her smoking weed a few times. She smoked cigarettes. He didn't like that very much. But mostly she was just very depressed and withdrawn. He had her seeing a therapist twice a week. We never could tell if it helped, or if she even talked to the woman. He was at the high school with her so he kept a close watch on her there, but she never made friends."

"How were her grades?" Josie asked.

"So-so. Passing. Dirk wanted her to join some clubs at school, but she thought they were all lame." She coughed a laugh. "Actually, what I think she said was, 'I ain't joining no dumbass school shit.' Mostly she was just so depressed. Did you grow up here?"

"Born and raised," Josie replied.

"So, you know then. Unless you're super popular at school or find some niche there, there is absolutely nothing for a teenager to do around here."

It was true. Josie had gotten into some trouble when she was a teen, but it was mostly her mother's doing. Still, even after her mother left, she remembered being in that strange no man's land that was pre-adulthood. You weren't old enough to do anything that was truly interesting to you. It seemed like everyone just wanted to get drunk or high, or both, and see what the hell happened. Push the limits. If you didn't fall into a group at school, you found yourself on the fringe, restless to explore life but unable to actually do anything. There wasn't much left to do other than get into trouble—especially in a place as small as Denton. Even though it was a city, it still had many of the features and pitfalls of a small town.

As a teenager, Josie had had few friends. The only person who had ever really understood her was Ray, and when her other friends had mocked her sudden decision to get the hell out of Denton and go to college, he had been the only one to defend her.

Coming from a city the size of Philadelphia, Josie could see how Denton must have seemed like the most depressing place on earth for a girl like June.

"Did she keep in touch with her friends in Philly?" Josie asked.

"At first, yeah, but then Dirk wouldn't let her go back for visits on the weekends, and one by one they dropped off. After a year, she really had no one. I think she was pretty lonely. Dirk did his best, and like I said, I tried to have some sort of relationship with her because he begged me to, but she was miserable. I wasn't surprised when she ran away."

"Did she go back to Philly?"

"That's what Dirk thought, yeah, but no one who knew her ever saw her there. Then Dirk and his sister convinced themselves that someone took her."

Josie felt her skin prickle. "Why is that?"

"Just because they couldn't find her, I guess. He went to the police here, and then him and his sister went to the police in Philadelphia, but they never found anything."

Josie frowned. "This was a year ago?"

Solange nodded. "Yeah. She didn't take her phone, but some of her personal things were missing. She had this old, ratty brown messenger bag she dragged around everywhere. We never did find it."

Josie would definitely have to get Noah to look her up. "She disappeared from home?"

"Yeah. Dirk took his car to get serviced one Saturday morning, and when he came home she was gone."

"No sign that anyone had been in the house?" Josie asked.

"Nope. She was just gone. We talked to all the neighbors—there's this one really nosy older lady who is always in everyone's business—but no one saw anything. We thought—well, I thought—maybe she had gone off into the woods, and you know, killed herself or something."

Josie knew from experience that this was more common in central Pennsylvania than anyone would care to admit.

"You searched the woods?"

"Dirk got a bunch of other teachers from school to help. It took weeks, but yeah, we searched the woods in every direction. No sign of her at all. No one saw anything. He tried to get it on the news, but they said runaways weren't news. He put up some flyers around town, but nothing ever came of it."

At this, Josie felt a stab of recognition. "When she disappeared, June had dark hair," she said, "and lots of piercings. Eyebrow and nose, right?"

"Yeah. That's right. Dirk hated those things, but her mom let her do whatever she wanted."

A memory floated to the surface of Josie's mind. The mention of the flyers brought it back. She *had* seen June's face before: older and with more face jewelry than in the photos on Dirk's fridge, but definitely the same girl. Josie had asked her chief why they weren't aiding in the search, and he had told her they'd already expended as many resources as they could to look for the girl, but that in his estimation the most likely scenario was that she'd simply gone back to Philadelphia and taken up with people there. Philadelphia was out of their jurisdiction. Josie hadn't questioned it at the time. She had no reason to question it and no reason to seek out more details about the case. They did get runaways in Denton: troubled kids, kids with terrible home lives, kids who were addicted to drugs. Most of the time, the families' efforts to bring their troubled souls back into the fold were half-hearted at best. By the time those kids ran away, it came as a relief. It was sad, but Josie had seen it again and again on the job.

But something about June Spencer's disappearance didn't sit well with her now that she knew the details. The only reason that June had been deemed a runaway was her tortured history. Josie had just been out to Dirk Spencer's house—in the boonies, as they liked to say in Denton—and there was no way that June had just walked off. She would have been miles from anything. She had to have gone somewhere, with someone. Perhaps she had intended to run away, had been walking along the lonely mountain road and been picked up by someone, but there was no way she had run away from Dirk's house alone, on foot. She may have gotten a lift, but whether she made it to her destination was another story. Josie could see why Dirk had insisted on searching.

"Does Dirk go to Philadelphia often?" Josie asked.

"Hardly ever. He hates it there."

"Does he keep in touch with anyone from there?"

"Other than his sister? No."

"No old friends who might be members of a gang?"

Solange's eyes widened. She pointed to the television. "Oh, right. They're saying on TV that the men in the car were in a gang, right? What kind of gang?"

"The 23," Josie told her. "Latino."

Solange looked even more nonplussed than she had earlier. "I never knew Dirk to have any friends from Philadelphia, much less friends who were in a gang. You've, um, seen him, right?"

She nodded; she knew what she meant.

"He's kind of like, a nerd, you know? I mean, he's not like, a tough guy or anything. He's into books and theater and art history."

Josie thought about the bookshelves lining Dirk's living room walls. "Yeah, I got that."

"I don't think he ever even shot a gun."

He hadn't had a gun that morning when Josie had seen him. In fact, he'd been the only person in the vehicle dutifully wearing his seat belt. He didn't fit. They'd come to pick him up at his home. He'd gotten into the SUV willingly. But he didn't fit.

Nothing that Josie had heard so far that day fit.

# CHAPTER 10

The girl woke to total darkness. She lay very still, panic rising in her chest as she blinked several times to make sure her eyes were really open. They were. Around her there was only blackness. Could it have all been a dream? The man in the woods. His hand over her mouth. Him dragging her deeper and deeper into the forest. Then she remembered her very real fear as his hand squeezed more tightly over her mouth and her nose, cutting off her air until her lungs burned and her vision grayed.

Now this. A blackness so complete that she couldn't even see her own body. This was no nightmare. She had been taken.

Beneath her was what felt like a bed of dirt, rocks, and twigs. The soil slid through her fingers as she felt for something—*anything*—familiar. The air was moist and fetid. She wondered if she'd been buried alive. No, she told herself as she stood on wobbly legs. The space she was in was too large; she could move around it, and she should. Her hands reached desperately for the walls and a way out, but found nothing except cold, wet stone. The sound of her own sobbing bounced back at her every which way she turned. She used the hem of her shirt to wipe her nose and kept moving, frantically chasing the sides of the chamber, her hands running up and down the brickwork until she was certain there was no way out. "Hello?" she screamed into the thick, muting darkness. Not even an echo returned.

She forced herself to slow down, taking long slow breaths to calm her racing heart as she moved her hands methodically around her, feeling every inch of her cell until, at last, her fingers found something wooden. A door. She pushed against it with all her might but it was thick and immovable. She swept along the edges of it, digging her fingers into the seams, searching for light. There was not one crack, no handle, no lock. Her small fists pounded against the wood until her bones filled with fire and all she could do was scream and scream until her throat was raw and the sound broken.

No one came.

She collapsed, curling into a tiny ball as the chamber grew colder and colder around her. She folded her legs up and inside her skirt to cover them completely, tucked her arms inside her shirt and held her trembling body close.

"Please," she whispered, rocking back and forth. "I want to go home."

# CHAPTER 11

Josie resisted the urge to have more shots before she left Sandman's. All the talk about June's horrific childhood had agitated some of Josie's own demons—black, amorphous ghosts that lay dormant until disturbed and then threatened to suffocate her. Too much had happened that day, too much had been said. They'd been summoned, and now she felt them swirling around her, pulling her under like a rip current, carrying her off to a dark, fathomless sea. Her limbs dragged as she walked back to her vehicle.

Luke would be working into the night on the interstate shootout, which meant she would be alone. Alone with the stirred-up memories of her past. Luke didn't know about any of it. She didn't want him to. She preferred him to see her as she was now—capable, confident, fearless, and whole. Only Ray knew about her past, and he was her past now too. Josie didn't have many friends who weren't on the force, which meant everyone was working. There was her grandmother, Lisette—probably her best friend, above all—but she lived in an assisted living facility on the outskirts of town. There really was no one she could call.

Everything had been fine when she was on the job; she

worked more than she didn't, and she loved it. When she wasn't working, she was with Luke. Tonight she had only her ghosts, her suspicions, a head full of questions and nothing to distract her. She doubled back as she drove past the liquor store; maybe Jim Beam would be a good friend to her tonight.

She was browsing the aisles slowly when she saw a woman from the corner of her eye. At first, Josie nearly didn't recognize her. She was standing in front of the boxed wine, wearing more clothes than she had probably ever worn in her life. Her long blond hair was pulled back into a ponytail and she wore no makeup or body glitter, just a pair of jeans and a thin blue T-shirt under a brown denim jacket. The transformation was quite amazing, actually. Looking at her in regular clothes, browsing the shelves, Josie would never peg her for the scantily clad, notoriously promiscuous dancer at the local strip club.

Misty must have felt Josie's heated gaze bearing down on her because she looked up, her eyes widening, cartoon-like, as she saw Josie at the other end of the aisle. Josie noticed she was carrying both a wallet and a cell phone in her hands. No pockets, Josie guessed, as she bit back a joke about there being plenty of room in her panties.

Misty said, "Leave me alone."

Josie laughed. She couldn't help it. The sound made Misty jump. She was only a few years younger than Josie. In fact, she had probably been a freshman at Denton East when Ray and Josie were seniors. Josie didn't remember her. Didn't know what had driven her to work at Denton's one and only strip club, Foxy Tails. Still, she had a childlike quality about her and Josie hated that. She always looked like she was genuinely surprised by other people's animosity, which Josie found strange. Surely she wasn't the only wife to catch her husband in bed with Misty. She was certain that Misty had been confronted by angry wives many times. Josie took a step toward her.

"I mean it," Misty said. "I'll call Ray."

"Go ahead," Josie said.

A flush crept upward from Misty's throat to the roots of her hair. She held up her cell phone. "I mean it. Leave me alone."

Josie put a hand on her hip and narrowed her eyes. "What do you think I'm going to do to you, Misty?"

Her doe eyes went blank. "I . . . I don't have to talk to you."

Josie laughed again, causing Misty to shrink backward. "Oh, I have no interest in talking to you, but people go to jail for doing the things I'd like to do to you."

The flush deepened. "Is . . . is that a threat?"

Josie lowered her voice. "Are you afraid?"

Misty's voice went up an octave. Her fingers scrabbled across the phone's screen. "I'm calling Ray."

Josie didn't take her eyes off Misty. She could hear the thin sound of Ray's phone ringing and ringing and then his voicemail clicking on. *"You have reached Ray Quinn . . ."*

"He's not going to answer. He's busy," she told Misty.

Misty lowered the cell phone from her ear. She backed up two steps. "Get away from me," she said without conviction.

Josie advanced on her. "Why? Why should I? You have no respect for other people. Why should I respect you?"

Misty's face twisted, and Josie knew she was about to see her real side. "Oh, please. Maybe if you could keep your husband happy he wouldn't have come looking for me."

The words stung. Wasn't that at the root of Josie's grief over her failed marriage? That she wasn't enough for him? That maybe if she had been able to forgive him for what had happened he wouldn't have gone looking elsewhere? She had always told herself that it wasn't her fault. They'd been together since high school. On her weaker days, she could see that maybe he had grown bored—she had felt that way sometimes as well. But Ray sleeping with Misty wasn't what truly wounded her. It was that he had fallen in love with her.

Who fell in love with a woman named Misty? A stripper, no less. It was such a cliché. It made her physically ill.

"I wouldn't be proud of being a homewrecker," Josie told her.

A thin, cruel smile spread across Misty's face like a snake. "Ray said you don't satisfy him anymore," she said, quietly.

Maybe it was the alcohol, or the day she had just had, or the suspension, or the months of rage over the dissolution of her marriage and then Ray's refusal to sign the divorce papers. Maybe it was all of those things. But it happened, lightning fast. Before she even had time to realize what she was doing, Josie stepped forward and drove her shoulder into Misty's chest, knocking her back so she stumbled, her arms flailing as she tried to keep her balance, her feet flying out from beneath her as she crashed into a wall of bottles behind her. Bottles of red wine shattered onto the floor, splashing crimson liquid everywhere. The sound was deafening.

Before Misty or anyone else in the store could react, Josie fled, squeezing through the automatic exit door before it had a chance to fully open. The cool evening air felt good on her face as she walked quickly toward her car, her whole body trembling.

She leaned against her car door, sucking in the fresh air and willing her body to calm down. Looking down at her hands, she saw that they were clenched into fists. She opened them only to discover that her fingers too, were shaking.

"You bitch!" Misty's voice was a screech. She stood twenty feet away, outside of the liquor store, covered in red wine and shards of glass. Josie stared at her for a long moment. Misty's chest heaved, tears streaming down her cheeks as she shrieked at Josie once more, "You stupid bitch!"

Josie couldn't speak. She could barely breathe. She had thought the sight of Misty, visibly shaken and humiliated, would make her feel better. But she felt worse. She felt empty and hollow and ashamed.

She couldn't get home fast enough.

# CHAPTER 12

Josie woke to an incessant dinging, her head foggy and thick, like someone had stuffed gauze into her eye sockets and cotton into her mouth. Dry-heaving over the side of the bed, she spied the digital clock. She'd slept past noon. The last time that had happened she was in college. The sound came rapid-fire now, the headache behind her eyes pulsing in time with it. She rolled over and tried to sit up on the edge of the bed. Huge mistake. She tried to think back to a time in her life when her body hurt this badly, and she couldn't think of one. A dull ache spread across her lower back and the throbbing in her leg was a like a drumbeat. Items flew from her nightstand drawer as she searched desperately for the ibuprofen. She tried taking them dry like she always did, but the pills turned to a bitter paste in her mouth.

*Dingdingdingdingdingding.*

A quick scan of the room didn't turn up her cell phone. Next to her pillow lay a bottle of tequila, a finger of amber liquid still in the bottom. She used it to wash the painkillers down and stood gingerly.

*Dingdingdingdingdingding.*

Then a familiar voice. It was muffled, but she could just make out the words. "Goddamn it, Jo! I know you're in there."

Only Ray ever called her Jo. She let him machine-gun her doorbell and holler until his throat was raw as she took her time getting down the stairs. The door swung open and blinding sunlight flooded her foyer. Ray was just a blurred, headless blob in her light-stung vision. She put a hand to her head. Her hair was matted on one side. She must look like hell.

"Is Luke here?" he asked.

She blinked, trying to bring him into focus. "What do you think?"

"I think you look like shit. Are you sick?" He sniffed the air and recoiled. "Tequila? Really, Jo?"

She sighed. She wasn't sure how much longer she could remain standing, the pain in her body was so intense, but she didn't want to invite him in. She didn't want him in her sanctuary. "I'm not the one with the drinking problem, Ray," she muttered, knowing it would sting. "What do you want?"

As her eyes adjusted she saw that he held his hat in both hands, squeezing. He always looked like this now—hat in both hands, like some kind of supplicant. Like he was going to beg her for something. He said, "Misty told me what happened last night."

She squinted at him. "So?"

"You can't treat her like that, Jo."

"Fuck you."

"You're lucky she isn't pressing charges," he said.

"Oh, please."

"I'm serious. Just leave her alone. I'm the one who cheated."

"Yeah, I guess you're right. She's just a garden-variety whore."

A muscle in his jaw quivered. "Jo," he cautioned.

Josie rolled her eyes. "Ray, I didn't do anything to her. I was just walking down the aisle."

He gave her a skeptical look. He was coming into focus

now, and she could see how terrible he really looked. A patchy beard had grown in on his face. His eyes were glassy, with large bags beneath them. His blue Denton PD uniform hung off him. "She said you pushed her."

"I might have bumped into her."

"Jo, really."

"Oh, come on, Ray. How can a woman who can take so much pounding be so sensitive about me bumping into her? She's not made of glass, for Chrissake."

He closed his eyes, white-knuckling the hat in his hands. She could see him silently counting to ten.

"We can keep arguing about this," she added, "but you're never going to be right. Why are you really here?"

His eyes popped open. He sighed loudly. "You know how you said to shake down all the registered sex offenders in the area?"

A spiral of excitement shot up through Josie. "You found Isabelle Coleman?"

"No. Not Coleman. A different girl. We didn't—we didn't realize she was missing. She was marked as a runaway."

She knew what he was going to say before he even said it, but she let him speak anyway.

"Her name is June Spencer."

# CHAPTER 13

"Wait, you said her name *is* June Spencer. So, she's alive?"

"Yeah."

Josie's relief quickly turned to unease. June had been missing for a year; that was a long time to be in captivity. She couldn't even imagine what the girl had been through. The nausea she had fought earlier came back with a vengeance. Her body folded in half, and she puked up what was left of the tequila on her front stoop.

"Jesus," Ray said, putting a comforting hand on her lower back. She wriggled away from him.

"Don't touch me," she snapped.

"Are you okay?"

She stood upright, fighting a wave of dizziness, and swiped at her mouth with the back of her hand. "I'm fine. How is June?"

"She's catatonic."

"What do you mean?"

Ray continued to look at her like he was face to face with a wild animal. He reached out as if to touch her and then shrunk back when she glared at him. "I mean, she's catatonic," he said. "The lights are on but no one's home. She won't talk, won't react or respond. When you look into her eyes, it's like she's looking right through you. But the doctor said she's neurologically intact."

Josie reached up with both hands and attempted to smooth down her hair as she tried to comprehend. She really needed a hot shower and some coffee. "Where is she now?"

"Denton Memorial. She's in good shape, they said. Physically. Strong, actually. This pervert must have fed her pretty well. But they had to check her out. Do a rape kit and all," Ray said.

She dropped her hands, leaned against the doorjamb. She needed water. She wanted to sit down, brush her teeth, change her clothes, and take some Alka-Seltzer, but she didn't want to invite Ray in. "Who was he?"

"Donald Drummond. He lived in a house across town, on 7th Street. Used to be his mother's house. After he got out of prison, he lived with her there till she passed."

Josie knew the name, and the street. She kept a mental list of all the registered sex offenders in Denton, and her own list of suspicious men. "The big guy?"

"Yeah, huge. Almost seven feet tall, and not lean muscle, that's for sure."

"Did he go willingly?"

She was trying to imagine how many Denton police officers it must have taken to cuff Donald Drummond when Ray said, "No, he didn't. Chief shot him in the chest. Took three rounds to take him down."

She didn't feel bad for him; she only wished she had been there to see it, that she had been first through the door. The department must be in dire straits if the chief had been on the scene. She'd been on the Denton PD for five years and had never seen him outside the station house except for the holiday party, and the couple of times he'd gone to get his ATV so he could lend it to the department.

"Holy shit," was all she could muster.

Ray gave her something between a smile and a grimace. "Yeah, it was intense."

"Where was she? Where was he keeping her?"

"Second-floor bedroom. He had it outfitted like a cell. Reinforced. She never had a chance. Chief's got a bunch of people tearing the place apart looking for others."

She shifted her weight, trying to relieve her injured leg which throbbed no matter how she stood. She was going to need something stronger than ibuprofen soon. Maybe more tequila. "Others?"

"Yeah, like in the yard and shit. They're waiting on cadaver dogs now. We have to dig the whole yard up, make sure there are no bodies buried back there. Chief's worried maybe he took Isabelle Coleman too."

"Was there anything fresh in the backyard? Like he was digging back there recently?"

"No, I don't think so."

Of course there wasn't. It didn't make sense. This guy had kept June for a year. Isabelle had been missing for six days. Why would he dispose of her so soon if he was a collector? No, Isabelle had been abducted by someone else. Which only increased the nausea roiling in Josie's stomach. Ray looked like he might try to touch her again. "You know, you can invite me in. I don't have to be back for two more hours."

Josie raised a hand as if to ward him off. "No," she told him. "I don't want you in here." The hurt on his face stirred up some guilt for her until she remembered exactly why she didn't want him in her house in the first place. "If you've got two hours, why aren't you spending it with your girlfriend? The only way I'm letting you into this house is to sign the divorce papers."

He looked at the ground. "It's just, I needed to talk to you about me and Misty, especially after what you did last night."

Rage shot through her. "That's all you care about, isn't it? Never mind everything that's going on in this town. All you care about is your girlfriend and making sure I leave her alone. Yet, you won't sign the papers. I don't get you, Ray. Why are you doing this? I did nothing wrong. Nothing! Why are you doing this to me?"

Her voice had become unusually high-pitched and loud. Unbidden tears stung her eyes, spilling onto her cheeks and making her humiliation complete. She reached out and used both hands to shove his chest as hard as she could. "I hate you!" she screamed.

He didn't fall, he didn't turn or walk away. He absorbed the force of her hands and let it push him back a couple of steps, and then he stepped forward again, offering his chest. He kept his hands at his sides, not bothering to block her blows. She shoved him a few more times and he took it. He kept his eyes cast downward, a gesture of humility. She needed to push and he let her. That he still knew what she needed, and gave it to her willingly, only made her feel worse. Her hands fell to her sides. She felt deflated, sick, and more exhausted than she could ever remember feeling. Bile and tequila burned the back of her throat.

"Go away, Ray."

They were halfway down her driveway. He picked up his hat and walked toward the street where his car was parked. "Maybe another time," he muttered.

He got to the end of the driveway, his hand on his door handle, before turning back to her. "Wait a minute," he said. "You already knew who June Spencer was, didn't you?"

She said nothing.

His hand dropped away. "How did you know?"

She refused to answer.

"Jo," he said. "Tell me you haven't been running your own investigation."

"I found an acrylic nail near the Coleman's mailbox," she said.

He shook his head. "Jo. Jesus."

"It's pink—hot pink—with yellow stripes. I'll send you a picture later."

"Don't," he said. He pointed a finger at her. "Don't do anything else. The chief will have your ass if he finds out. I told you about June Spencer as a courtesy, because I knew you'd see it on the news later and call me, and because Dirk Spencer was in the car that almost killed you yesterday. But I'm telling you right now to stop."

She went on as if he hadn't spoken. "You should find out whose it is—Isabelle's, her mother's, a searcher's? Isabelle wore acrylic nails—I saw photos of her and her friends on her Facebook page. Apparently, she and her friends got their nails done regularly. Anyway, it could be important."

"I mean it, Jo. You need to stop this. For your own good. Go inside and get some rest. Then call Luke. Take a trip. Get a Netflix subscription. Something. But for God's sake, leave the Coleman thing alone."

# CHAPTER 14

The state police barracks that Luke was assigned to lay twenty-three miles outside of Denton on a stretch of two-lane road where the speed limit was fifty-five miles an hour. It was a squat, flat-roofed building flanked by forest on three sides. The next closest building of any kind was two miles away. Josie had been there many times and was always struck by the isolation of the place and its utilitarian feel. Every Christmas and Fourth of July, some of the guys would try to punch the place up a bit with decorations bought at the closest Walmart. Usually the multicolored lights and gaudy gold tinsel hung outside the entrance until sometime in June, the tinsel sagging and threadbare by that time, when it was replaced by patriotic fringe garland and big red, white and blue bows. Those would remain until Halloween, and from mid-October through Thanksgiving, a lone pumpkin atop a small, decorative bale of hay would guard the stoop. It was better than nothing, she supposed, but it didn't make the place look any less depressing.

She didn't know how Luke could stand it. She loved the old, historic three-story building that housed the Denton police department; it used to be the town hall but had been converted to the police station sixty years ago. It was huge and gray, with ornate molding over its many double-casement arched windows and an old bell tower at one corner. It looked almost like a castle. With each season and holiday, someone from the historical society would come around and dress the place up. It had character. Josie missed it.

She was thinking about her desk on the second floor as she pulled into the barracks parking lot. Two cruisers sat in the lot along with a handful of personal vehicles, including Luke's white Ford F-150. She knew he would be there. The day before, while she was outside melting down in front of Ray, he'd left her four text messages and three voicemails, each one more frantic than the last. By the time she located her cell phone and called him back, he was ready to send a SWAT team to check on her. He hadn't been able to get away from work, but he was clearly very worried about her. He asked if she'd gone to the hospital to have her leg checked out and sounded annoyed when she told him she hadn't. It took everything in her not to snap at him.

"I really need to get some rest," she'd said instead, hoping her tone came across less irritable than she felt.

She'd taken a hot shower, turned on her coffeemaker and then slept for twelve straight hours. When she finally awoke to even more missed messages, she had promised to meet him at the barracks for lunch the next day.

She felt a frisson of excitement as he slipped through the double doors to meet her. He was in full uniform and she knew what waited for her beneath. The thought of him naked woke her up more than the pot of coffee she had consumed before she'd left the house.

With a smile, he leaned into her open window. "Ma'am," he said with mock formality. "Do you know why I pulled you over?"

She grinned at him. "I don't know, officer, but I'm hoping for a full cavity search."

He leaned down to kiss her as she got out of the car, wrapping her in his long arms and gathering her into him. It was long, slow and tender, as always. Her body responded to him, a thunderous need rising inside her. She wanted his mouth on her body, his hands. She wanted him to blot out the frustration of the last two days. She kissed him harder, biting his lower lip lightly.

"Whoa," he said, pushing her away gently.

Releasing her completely, he gave her a quizzical smile and studied her face. "What was that about? You okay?"

She hoped her smile didn't look as awkward as it felt. "Fine," she said. "I missed you."

He reached up and tucked a strand of hair behind her ear. "I'm sorry I wasn't there for you."

"I'm fine, but I could really have used some company the last two days."

One of his hands found hers, his fingers stroking her palm and sliding over the band of the engagement ring she'd remembered to wear. "I'll make it up to you," he promised.

She raised a brow. "When?"

He laughed. "Starting now. I wanted to take you to lunch."

But she didn't want to go to lunch. She didn't need food. She didn't need to talk about her feelings. She needed him. Lacing her fingers through his, she tugged him away from her car and the parking lot, toward the thickest copse of woods she could find surrounding the barracks. Reluctantly, he let her lead him. "Josie," he said. "What's going on? Where are we going?"

"You'll see," she said over her shoulder.

They picked their way over branches and rocks. Every few feet, she glanced over her shoulder, ignoring the look of

confusion and concern blanketing Luke's face, to check if
any part of the barracks was still visible. When the building
finally disappeared from view, she stopped walking and
turned to Luke.

"What are we doing out here?" he asked.

Her jacket dropped to the forest floor, followed by her faded
Rascal Flatts T-shirt and bra. Luke didn't speak, but he smiled
nervously as she kicked off her boots and unzipped her pants.
His hands were on his hips. "You're bat-shit crazy, you know
that?" he said, but his eyes roved greedily over her body as
she stripped off the rest of her clothes.

"I don't see you running away," she challenged.

His voice was husky. "Never." His gaze moved from her
breasts to her leg, which she had had the good sense to wrap
with an ACE bandage that morning. "How's your leg?"

"It's fine."

He nodded, continuing to stare. "You're pretty bruised up.
You feeling okay?"

"I'm fine," she replied, a tinge of impatience creeping into
her voice.

He glanced around briefly. "We're in the middle of the
woods."

"I know."

She knew these woods, she trusted them. She and Ray had
been exploring them since they were nine years old. They'd
even named a few places where there were distinctive cliffs,
valleys, or rock formations. There were few places in the
county she hadn't scoured. This was a more private place than
either one of their vehicles.

Luke started to unsnap his holster belt. It was secured to his
pants belt by four belt keepers and held his SIG P227, baton,
mace, handcuffs, and portable radio. "You have any idea how
long it takes to get this damn thing on and off?"

Her eyes narrowed and she licked her lips.

He stopped unfastening his belt, looking suddenly confused, as though he didn't recognize the woman before him. "What's going on with you?"

She strode toward him. "Shut up," she said, yanking at the keepers and divesting him of his belts. She dropped them onto the ground beside them. He was still looking at her like she was a stranger. Before he could speak, she rocked up onto her toes and captured his mouth, kissing him hungrily. Her hands tore at his zipper.

Luke gripped her upper arms, breaking the kiss but keeping her close to his body. "Josie," he rasped, searching her face.

"Make it up to me, Luke," she said, her tone a challenge. "Right here, right now."

For a long, pregnant moment, her command hung in the air above their heads. She wondered if he was going to shut her down. She plunged her hand into his pants and took hold of him. Regardless of what his brain was telling him, his body was ready for her. "Do it," she said. The next thing she knew his pants were around his ankles and her back was against a tree. He lifted and held her there as if she weighed nothing, pushing inside her with a gentle firmness that quickly turned urgent. The bark of the tree scraped into her back, hard and rhythmic, smarting against her earlier injuries.

"Harder," she breathed into his ear as the pain went from sharp to exquisite and exhilarating, blotting out every other feeling in her mind and her body. As her own body tightened around him, she let out a long cry of pleasure. This, she could always count on. As they walked back to her car, disheveled, sweaty and satisfied, Josie felt more clear-headed than she had in days.

# CHAPTER 15

They ate at a diner a few miles from the barracks but in the opposite direction from Denton. It was a relief to be somewhere else for a while. Josie ordered a half-pound cheeseburger with fries and a side of mozzarella sticks. Sex always made her ravenous, made her buzz with energy. She felt like she could do anything. Ray always said that's what cocaine was like. They'd taken a break from one another in college—she had tried other men and he had tried drugs. Sex with Luke had always been good but never near what it had been like with Ray. Until today. She felt high, like she was on top of the world with no chance of falling off.

Across from her, Luke picked at his own burger and used the longest French fry on his plate to marshal the smaller fries into formation.

"Something on your mind?" she asked.

He didn't look up. "Ray sign those papers?"

"Not yet. You know he's busy with the Coleman case, and now with this Spencer thing..."

At the mention of June Spencer, he looked up at her. "I heard about that. Crazy shit. Did you hear her uncle is still holding on?"

She hadn't. "Has he said anything?"

Luke shook his head. "No. Still in a coma. They didn't find anything useful on his phone either. A few texts between him and the driver arranging the pick-up, but that doesn't tell us anything we don't already know. Word from your department is that they can't even locate his next of kin."

"He has a sister in Philadelphia."

"Yeah, she's AWOL. No one can find her."

"So, June Spencer has no one." It was a statement, not a question. June would be released from the hospital eventually and Josie wondered where she would go. Dirk's house was her home, but if she was as out of it as Ray had said, she would need someone to care for her. She wondered if Solange would take the girl in, and then decided no. Solange didn't have that kind of grit.

Luke shrugged. "Unless her uncle recovers or her mom turns up, I guess. Don't know."

"Anything new on the shootout?"

He took a bite of his cheeseburger and then placed it back on the plate and wiped his hands on a napkin. "Not much. We had some of our guys in Philly notify next of kin and do some interviews but no one is talking. Big surprise there. We have no idea who was shooting at them, but we do know that they were traveling west. They'd gotten on at the Bowersville exit."

Josie frowned. "That's the closest exit to Dirk Spencer's house," she said. "So they picked him up and got onto the interstate there. But where were they headed? The next exit is Denton—where they got off at the Stop and Go. They were traveling away from Philadelphia and the next decent-sized town is almost two hundred miles away."

"Don't know," Luke said. "We may never know. Unless Dirk wakes up and can tell us. I'm sure they only got off the interstate at the Denton exit because they were getting shot at."

"Makes sense," Josie said. "Not many places to hide on the interstate. Any idea where the shooting started?"

"Looks like about halfway between the exits. We found rounds about three miles from the Bowersville entrance ramp."

So they got on Route 80 and drove for three miles before the shooting started. It was two more miles to the exit where they'd gotten off, already badly wounded and in trouble. "I wonder if they were being pursued before they even got on the interstate. Maybe that's *why* they got on the interstate, so they could get away fast without drawing much attention."

"We thought of that. Someone's pulling surveillance of various businesses in Bowersville to see if we can see the Escalade passing through at any point, see if anyone was tailing them."

"No connection between Spencer and the guys in the car?" Josie asked.

"None that we can turn up. Just that they came from Philly, and he used to live there. Everyone who was interviewed in Philly said they never heard of him."

"It's just strange, don't you think?"

"Lots of strange things going on lately," Luke muttered, his eyes back on his plate.

Josie paused in her eating, a mozzarella stick poised halfway to her mouth. "What does that mean?"

He met her eyes. "What was that about today? Out in the woods?"

She resisted the urge to roll her eyes. Most men would be grateful. Being with Luke was a double-edged sword: she could count on him utterly to never put her in the position that Ray had put her in, but at the same time his level of care and concern grated on her. "Why do you ask?"

"I'm worried about you. With everything going on...the

suspension, what happened at the Stop and Go. Plus, I know you want to work. I know this is killing you. Isabelle Coleman is still missing and you have to sit it out. I just want to make sure you're, you know, okay."

Josie forced a smile. She wasn't okay. For every reason he had just listed, and then some, but the last thing she wanted to do was talk about it. Luke had already done everything he could do for her back in the woods. She reached across the table and patted his hand. "Don't worry," she said. "I'm fine."

# CHAPTER 16

Lisette Matson's gnarled hands shuffled the deck of playing cards like a magician. Josie was always fascinated by her grandmother's dexterity when it came to playing solitaire. Or, when Josie was there, kings in the corner. The two of them sat at a table in the cafeteria of Rockview Ridge, the only nursing home in Denton. It was after dinner and most residents lingered in their wheelchairs or at tables—reading books, doing crossword puzzles, or chatting quietly. One man used his feet to pull his wheelchair along, going from nurse to nurse to complain that "Sherri took my larynx," his fingers pressing an artificial device to the hole in his throat to say those very words. Throat cancer. Although Josie couldn't remember his name, she remembered her grandmother telling her about him. Her grandmother knew everyone's diagnosis. The doctors had had to cut a stoma into his throat to give him a permanent airway which was why he needed an artificial larynx to speak. A nurse in blue scrubs acknowledged him as she pushed her medication cart past the cafeteria doors. "Now, Alton, why would Sherri do a thing like that?"

He pressed the thing to his throat again, his voice robotic. "Because she's a bitch," he said and laughed, silently.

Several women in the room, including Lisette, called, "Shut up, Alton!"

The nurse frowned at him before continuing on her way. She tutted. "Alton, that profanity is not necessary."

Lisette muttered, "He just lives to get under people's skins, that one. You should hear the disgusting things he says to us when the nurses aren't around, and he accuses poor Sherri of taking his stupid larynx at least once a week. Yet he's never without the damn thing. Someone ought to take it and shove it up his—"

"Gram!" Josie hissed, holding back her laughter.

Lisette batted her eyelashes in a look that said, "What did I say?" and looked back at her cards.

Across the room, Alton waved a dismissive hand in the nurse's direction and turned his wheelchair back to the television in the corner of the room, which was playing the local news.

Following his gaze, Josie watched as an old Facebook photo of June Spencer flashed across the screen, the words FOUND ALIVE huge and bold and capitalized beneath her sullen visage. Josie wondered if that was the best Facebook photo Trinity Payne could find of the girl. Or maybe she never smiled. It would certainly fit with what Solange had told her. The screen cut to Trinity Payne, standing outside Denton's police headquarters in the same puffy coat she'd been wearing two days ago.

Lisette eyed Josie's left hand as she dealt the final card. "Nice ring."

Josie smiled tightly. "Luke proposed," she said.

Lisette's left eyebrow rose. "You should have led with that."

Josie picked up her hand as Lisette placed the draw pile squarely between them. "I'm sorry. I should have called."

"I suppose you said yes, or you wouldn't be wearing the ring."

Josie drew her first card. "Yes," she said. "I said yes."

"I haven't even met this boy," Lisette said. "And, you're not divorced yet. You know, cheating isn't the worst thing a husband can do."

"Don't," Josie said.

"I'm just saying," Lisette went on, "couples recover from infidelity all the time. I'm pretty sure marriage counselors make their living on helping people do just that. No papers have been signed. You two could move into that big old house you just bought and rent out your old one—maybe all you need is a fresh start."

Josie closed her eyes and took a deep breath. It was true. Infidelity was not the worst thing a husband could do. She knew that because what Ray had done to her had been far worse. She could have lived with the cheating, possibly. She might have tried, but this ran deeper than that. She couldn't bear to relive it and she just didn't have the words to tell her gram. Lisette loved Ray deeply. He was as much a part of her life as he was Josie's, and he had been for over a decade. When Lisette was in her early seventies, and still living independently in her own home, Ray was the one who cut her grass in the summer and shoveled her walk in the winter. He kept her house in good repair and picked up her prescriptions. Between him and Josie, Lisette never wanted for anything.

"You might even convince Ray to go to AA," Lisette added.

"Gram, stop."

After her third fall at home, Lisette had moved in with Ray and Josie and lived with them for nearly a year. Her mind was sharp, but her body was failing. "I'm not sick," she always said. "Just old." The osteoarthritis in her knees and hips made it more and more difficult for her to get around. She started with a cane and then a walker, refusing to get the knee and hip replacements she so obviously needed, saying she was too old to put her body through all that trauma. She managed the pain well enough, but just after she turned seventy-two, it became clear that she needed more care than they could give her.

It broke Ray's heart just as much as Josie's, but they began the exhaustive search for a nursing home. Rockview Ridge wasn't the cheapest or even the highest rated, but it was the closest, and Josie needed her grandmother close. She knew that Ray still secretly visited Lisette. Josie had told her grandmother that he had cheated, but she hadn't given her any details. She also knew that Lisette had given Ray a stern talking-to, but that she loved him too much not to forgive him.

"Does Ray know about the proposal?" Lisette asked.

Josie nodded as she watched Lisette pull a king of spades from her hand and place it diagonal from the draw pile. She quickly laid down a queen of hearts and a jack of clubs as Josie drew from the pile again. "Yes, I told him two days ago. No, we haven't had a chance to discuss it—not that we need to because we're not getting back together." She motioned toward the television. "Besides, he's been a little busy."

The deeply etched lines in Lisette's pale, thin face tightened into a grim frown. "It's truly terrible," she said. "I hope they find the Coleman girl alive too. Her poor mother. To lose a child—"

Her voice cracked, and she pulled a crumpled tissue from the cuff of her sweater and wiped her eyes. Josie placed her cards face down on the table and reached across to stroke her grandmother's hand. Lisette always thought of the mothers— when a young boy fell through the ice of a rural pond and drowned; when a teenage girl was struck and killed by a drunk driver; when a grown person overdosed on heroin—Lisette would always think of their mothers. Ever since Josie was six years old and her father had walked off into the woods behind their trailer and shot himself. No note, no explanation, no signs beforehand that he had even been depressed. Lisette had lost her only child that day, and the pain was always close at hand.

Josie had been so young, the actual grief of losing her father hadn't hit her as hard. There were good memories, but they were few and hard to bring into focus. What hurt the most was that he had left Josie alone with her mother, a monster who would hold Josie's palm over an open flame of the stove just to hear her beg. And when she grew tired of seeing her, then came the closet—sometimes for days at a time.

At the tender age of nine, when she and Ray had first become friends, he had handed her a small navy blue backpack containing a flashlight, extra batteries, a dog-eared copy of the first Harry Potter book, his beloved Stretch Armstrong doll and a couple of granola bars. "Hide this in the closet," he said, "then when she puts you in there, it will be there waiting for you, and you don't have to be scared anymore." It was the next best thing to having him there with her during those dark, desolate hours.

Lisette had fought for custody from the day Josie's father died, and lost each time they went to court. It wasn't until Josie was fourteen and her mother left in the middle of the night, never to be heard from again, that she was finally able to escape and live with Lisette full time. Life got better after that; Josie was fed, had routine, a bedroom of her own. She even went to the movies and on vacations. Ray never left her side. Little by little, her home life started to mirror those of her classmates and she took the memories of those dark years and packed them away deep in her mind.

Lisette sniffed, drawing Josie's attention back to the present. "I'm sorry," she said, tucking her balled-up tissue back into her sweater sleeve. She picked up a new card from the draw pile and immediately set it down opposite the first corner she had started: a king of hearts. Josie laid a queen of clubs on top of it.

The sound of a raised female voice cut through the quiet of the dining room. Josie and Lisette turned toward the doorway. From the nurses' station they caught the words, "...can't keep her here. We can't take her."

A blast of cold air shot across the floor of the room, tickling at Josie's jean-clad legs. The double doors to the lobby whooshed open and let in the sound of metal clanging and rubber wheels squeaking. A new resident was arriving. An unwanted resident. The next thing she heard was Ray's voice. "We've got nowhere else to take her."

Josie jumped up and made her way to the hall where she spotted Ray standing at the nurses' station, one hand on the high counter and one hand motioning to the gurney. Two paramedics flanked the patient. The girl's face wasn't gaunt or drawn as Josie would have expected, but it was pale to the point of being translucent. All of the eyebrow and nose rings Josie remembered from her missing persons flyer were gone. Her eyes stared sightlessly and unblinking at the ceiling. Her dark hair was long and matted. If Josie didn't know better, she might have mistaken her for a corpse.

But she wasn't a corpse. Josie knew this because June Spencer had been found alive.

# CHAPTER 17

"Jo." Ray looked shocked. "What are you doing here?"

Josie put a hand on her hip. She wondered fleetingly if he had been drinking. "That may be the dumbest thing you've ever asked me."

He shook his head quickly. He looked even more exhausted than he had two days earlier, his cheeks sunken, with hefty bags beneath his eyes. He was tired, she realized, not drunk. She wondered when he had last slept. "Sorry. How's Lisette?"

"She's fine. You can go in and say hello before you leave. What's going on?"

He spoke to Josie but was looking at the nurse behind the counter, a woman not much older than Josie, dressed in maroon-colored scrubs, her dark hair swept up off her neck in a loose bun and bright red lipstick smothering her lips. "As you know, Miss Spencer's next of kin is her mother, who we cannot locate. That leaves her uncle Dirk Spencer, who is in intensive care at Geisinger for multiple gunshot wounds in a medically induced coma. She was just rescued from a year in captivity, and she is in a catatonic state. We can't just leave her alone at Mr. Spencer's house. She needs to be looked after."

"Then the hospital should keep her," the nurse said.

"There's a norovirus outbreak at the college. Half the damn student body is at the hospital right now. Believe me, they don't have the beds." Ray gave the nurse a pleading look. "Come on. She has nowhere to go. It would only be for a day or two until we can make other arrangements. She needs to be monitored, and we need to know where to find her if she comes around and can start telling us what happened to her."

"This is a nursing home."

"It's also a rehab facility," Josie interjected.

"Do you mind?" the nurse said, shooting her a dirty look.

Josie was sure she was the only one who saw the smile fighting to stay hidden on Ray's lips. "Actually, Detective Quinn is my superior," he told the nurse. "And she's right. This is also a rehab facility."

The nurse's shoulders slumped. She rolled her eyes. "Yeah, for people who have knee replacements and hip fractures. Not...this."

Josie advanced on the woman and, in spite of the high counter between them, the nurse backed up a few steps. Josie leveled her index finger at the woman like the barrel of a gun. "This girl was abducted by a known sexual predator and held prisoner in a single room for a year. A year. What she needs right now—what she deserves right now—is our empathy and compassion. Anything short of that is inhumane and, quite frankly, a disgrace. You've got a private room three doors down from Mrs. Matson. It hasn't been filled since Mr. Wallis died. This isn't forever. This is for a few days until more suitable arrangements can be made. It's quiet here, and you've got trained medical personnel on staff. This place is much more comfortable than the hospital. So, you've got two choices. You can admit this young lady and do everything you can to care for her while she is here, or you can call your administrator—use her cell because she bowls on

Saturdays—and make her come in and talk to me about this situation. What's it gonna be?"

While Josie spoke, the woman's haughty posture slowly deflated. She looked over the counter at June and sighed, "Fine, she can stay."

# CHAPTER 18

June Spencer's eyes were open. She lay on her back in the center of the bed, her long hair fanned out on the pillow, arms at her sides, and eyes fixed upward and unmoving. Like a corpse on display at a funeral. Almost the moment Ray left, and expressly against his instructions, Josie snuck into June's room to speak to her. She still wore a hospital gown, and Josie resolved to bring some clothes for the girl from home the next day. She was annoyed that no one had thought of this; hospital gowns were flimsy and undignified, and the last thing a sexual assault victim would want is the risk of further exposure. But of course, no one on Denton PD had thought of this. They were all men. All men, except Josie. The chief had hired two female patrol officers the year before, but one was out on maternity leave and the other had quit to go to law school.

Josie stood at June's bedside, her hand floating over the girl's forearm. She wouldn't touch her, not until she had the girl's consent, but it was difficult to know how to get her attention. Was it even possible? Instead, she talked in a low tone, so as not to be overhead from the hallway, where nurses, nursing aides, and other residents flitted past, craning their necks to see the catatonic girl inside the room.

"June, my name is Detective Josie Quinn," she said. "I am so glad you're with us. I know you've been through a lot. I'm not sure how much they told you, but the man who hurt you is dead. You're safe now. Soon we'll find your mom, and she'll come and be with you. As soon as your uncle Dirk is able, he'll come too. I don't know if you can hear me or not, but I'll be close by if you need anything. My grandmother lives here. Tomorrow I'll bring you some regular clothes to wear. That might make you more comfortable."

June blinked.

Josie stood frozen for a long moment, waiting to see if she would blink again. She said, "Can you hear me, June?"

Blink.

Josie was leaning in closer, looking for answers, when a scratchy voice from the doorway said, "Don't get too excited, hon. Even zombies blink sometimes. It's a purely physical thing."

Josie looked up to see Sherri Gosnell, a chunky nurse in her sixties—the alleged larynx thief—pushing a medicine cart through the door. The computer screen atop it glowed, and Josie could see that June's electronic chart was open. There was no information in it other than her name and date of birth. Lisette had once told Josie that Sherri had worked at Rockview since she was a teenager—as a nurse assistant while she finished nursing school and eventually securing a spot on the staff as an RN. Josie was hard-pressed to remember a time she'd visited her grandmother and not seen Sherri there. She wondered if Sherri ever took any days off.

"Gotta do her admission," she said as she drew closer to the bed. Looking June over, the woman shook her head. "Don't know what we'll do with this one."

An alarm blared from down the hall. By this time, Josie recognized the various alarms that the staff affixed to the chairs, beds, and sometimes even the clothing of residents considered fall risks to alert the staff to when they were getting up without assistance. "That sounds like Mrs. Sole," she said to Sherri.

The nurse rolled her eyes. "All day long she's trying to get out of that chair." With a glance back at June she added, "I'll have the girls sit this one up in the chair and get her a dinner tray. I can do the admission after I deal with Mrs. Sole."

With that, she was gone. Josie glanced down at June. The girl's eyes blinked rapidly for several seconds. Then they stopped, and she floated back off to wherever it was she had found to hide inside her head.

# CHAPTER 19

Josie found excuses to walk past June Spencer's room two more times after that—retrieving a blanket for Lisette's lap from her room and then going back again for the butterscotch candies she kept in her nightstand. Each time she passed, she slowed and peered inside. The nursing aides had, as instructed, moved June from her bed to the guest chair next to it. She sat unmoving with her hands on the armrests. Her pale legs—hairy from a year of not having shaved them—peeked out from beneath the hospital gown. Someone had put those awful brown non-skid socks on her feet. Pushed up in front of her was the rolling tray table and dinner: turkey breast with gravy, applesauce, Jell-O, a tiny can of ginger ale and a hot tea. All of it was untouched, the silverware perfectly lined up beside her plate, which meant no one had tried to feed her. Josie wondered if she would eat. Perhaps, if she was hungry enough? She remembered Ray saying she was healthy. Perhaps the act of eating was an automatic thing for her.

"Come now," Lisette called from the cafeteria, and Josie tore herself from June's doorway to return to the dining room with the candy.

"There's nothing more you can do for her right now. Leave

her," she said, as Josie dealt a new hand of kings in the corner. They played in silence, finishing two games before Lisette suggested rummy. "Since you obviously have no plans to go home." She winked at Josie and started shuffling the cards again as they heard Sherri push her cart past the dining room entrance, heading back in the direction of June's room. "I've got to do this admission," she called to someone at the nurses' station.

Lisette dealt as Josie tried to remember how to play, her ears straining for the click of the door down the hall, hoping that Sherri had the good sense to give the poor girl some privacy.

"You don't remember how to play, do you?" Lisette broke in.

Josie gave her a sheepish smile as Lisette offered her another butterscotch candy and took her through the basics of the game. Slowly it came back to her as they played a few practice hands, before Lisette took the deck and began shuffling it again. "Now we'll play to win," she said.

"Don't we need a notepad to keep track of the score?"

Lisette raised a brow. "I don't suppose you want to take a walk back to my room to get one?"

"I don't," Josie said pointedly.

"You don't have some fancy snap on that phone of yours we can use?"

"You mean app, Grandma."

She waved one hand in the air. "Whatever. Or is it whatevs? I heard Mrs. Sole's great-granddaughter in here the other day and she said, 'whatevs.' Is that the new thing? Young people are too lazy to even finish saying words?"

Josie was laughing so hard it took a moment to register the commotion coming from down the hallway. Then a bloodcurdling scream sliced the air, followed by another and another, from more than one person, until it sounded like a pack of hysterical, panicked wolves howling. Josie raced into the hallway and saw a gaggle of nursing aides standing outside June's room. Their mouths were stretched wide in horror, their faces ashen. One woman stopped screaming just long enough to be sick. Another fell to her knees and covered her eyes as more staff rushed to the door.

Josie ran for the room, the world revolving in slow motion around her. She was moving toward something terrible, she knew it, a large stone of dread pressing down hard on her center of gravity. Sherri's cart stood untouched and unattended outside the room, June's electronic chart aglow on its screen.

Pushing through the crowd, she made it to the threshold at last. Sherri lay on the floor near the foot of the bed, face up. Her hands lay limp on her chest. She was gone. A pool of blood spread quickly beneath her, her throat in shreds, a tiny geyser of blood still gushing from the torn flesh. Her eyes were huge and glassy, frozen. Not so much in horror or even panic. She simply looked surprised, like someone had jumped out of the closet and startled her. *Your face will freeze like that.* Josie's mother's voice rang in her ears.

She dragged her gaze to the far side of the room, where June squatted beneath the window, her naked rounded spine facing the door. The non-skid socks on her feet were thick with blood and the hem of the hospital gown swished back and forth in the crimson puddle. From where she stood, Josie could see she clutched a fork in one bloody hand, a small shard of flesh dangling from its tongs. She was doing something with the other hand. Josie couldn't see what, but her shoulder and elbow worked at a frenzied pace, up and down, back and forth.

"Call 911," Josie said quietly to the sobbing women at her back. "And do not come into this room."

She took a halting step inside. Then another. Whatever June was doing, it was to the wall beneath the windows, her movement smooth and steady, her crouched body blocking Josie's view.

A few feet from Sherri's head lay a white foam cup at rest on its side. The lid had been removed and was still on the tray table. The water for the hot tea. She must have flung it in Sherri's face, then gone for the jugular.

Josie sidestepped the pool of blood edging along the tile floor. Now she was close enough to see that June had written a word on the wall in Sherri's bright, warm red blood in large streaks using her fingertips. Not a word, actually. A name.

RAMONA.

# CHAPTER 20

Josie felt hollow staring down at June as she traced the R in *Ramona* again and again with a steady, blood-soaked hand. After everything she had been exposed to in her childhood, Josie didn't think there was much that could shock her, but this—this was difficult to take in.

Carefully avoiding the widening swath of blood, she circled around Sherri's body and knelt about four feet away from the girl. June didn't look at her as she moved on to the first A in *Ramona,* her palm rubbing the letter into the drywall. Her chin jutted forward—in concentration or determination, Josie couldn't tell. Maybe both.

Josie said, "June, it's me, Detective Quinn."

No acknowledgment. It was as if she were the only person there—not just in the room, Josie realized, but in the entire world. Her hand reached back and scooped a fresh gob of Sherri's blood with which she began stroking the long, straight lines of the letter M.

Josie inched forward. "June, I'm only here to talk to you. Do you think you could put down the fork?"

The fork flew across the room, clattering against the wall opposite Josie and falling to the floor. The girl had reacted with such speed and nimble assurance, Josie hardly believed her eyes. She wondered how deeply hidden *was* the real June?

Josie swallowed. Her face felt unusually hot. "Thank you," she said as June swept more blood into the oval shape of the letter O in a rhythmic motion.

Josie looked at the door. The nursing staff had left the doorway, likely rounding up all the residents and sheltering them in the common area. She didn't have much time. She scooted forward a bit more and swallowed again. "June, I need to ask you something. Who is Ramona?"

Nothing. Round and round the O she went. "June," Josie tried again. "Who is Ramona? I want to help you, but I can't do that if you don't tell me what's happening. Do you know Ramona? Is she in trouble? June, if this Ramona is in trouble, then I need to find her as soon as possible. I can help her. Let me help her. Who is she? Where can I find her?"

Up and down, up and down her hand went, now working on the letter N.

"I saw your uncle the other day," Josie tried. "Your uncle Dirk. Right after his accident. I was there. He said her name. He whispered it to me. He said, 'Ramona.' If you could just tell me who—"

The rest of the sentence lodged in Josie's throat so hard and fast she started coughing. June's head snapped in her direction and her amber eyes zeroed in on Josie like a predatory bird. They flashed with intelligence and awareness. For that split second, June was there. Really and truly there, in the room with Josie. Then she was gone. She turned back to the wall, and continued.

Josie recovered herself. "June, please. You can trust me. Please tell me what's going on. Who is Ramona?"

The sound of sirens, muffled but getting closer, invaded the room. Disappointment mixed with desperation rounded

Josie's shoulders. The cavalry was arriving. June would be taken into custody, and with her any chance Josie had of discovering who the hell Ramona was and where Josie could find her.

She glanced at the empty doorway, and when she looked back at June the girl was staring at her again, the lucidity in her light-brown eyes so stark and startling that Josie's breath caught. Panic welled inside her.

The girl leaned forward and Josie instinctively flinched, throwing a hand up—but no attack came. Craning her neck, June brought her face within inches of Josie's, opened her mouth, and stuck her tongue out as far as she could. In the center of it was a small pink ball with a word written on it. Lizard-like, June retracted her tongue before Josie's brain could properly process the word. Tiny, white letters. Barely readable. *Princess.*

"Where did you—where did you get that, June?" Josie asked.

But the moment was over. The girl retreated back into herself, her eyes as blank and empty as polished stones, her scarlet palm massaging Sherri Gosnell's blood into the final letter.

# CHAPTER 21

Josie sat in a chair next to Noah Fraley's desk, staring down at her sneakers and waiting to talk with the chief while Noah made awkward attempts at conversation. "Did you know Mrs. Gosnell's father-in-law is a patient at Rockview?"

She had tried like hell to stay away from Sherri's blood, but there it was—a browning crust around her soles. There was no avoiding it. Not in that room. Not after the way June had killed her. "They're called residents," she told Noah, absently.

"What?"

She was trying to focus on Noah, but kept seeing June's tongue extended toward her. *Princess.* What was Isabelle Coleman's tongue barbell doing in June Spencer's mouth? Noah stared at her expectantly. She said, "In nursing homes, they're not called patients. They're called residents. They live there."

Noah's face flushed. "Oh."

She hadn't meant to embarrass him. Quickly, she said, "I knew that Sherri's father-in-law is a resident there. I see him there sometimes when I visit my grandmother. Saw him today, actually. He's the one with the artificial larynx, always accusing Sherri of stealing it. Must be a family joke. Sherri's husband is—was—the plumber, right?"

Josie couldn't remember his first name, but knew he was a Gosnell. She knew this because over a year ago, when their hot water heater burst, Ray had categorically refused to call the man—or any plumber—insisting on installing the new one himself, even though he had no plumbing experience whatsoever. The fight that ensued between Josie and Ray had been a big one. It was almost as though letting another man fix something in his house was a violation. As if letting a plumber install a hot water heater was the equivalent of letting a stranger have a go at your wife. The irony was not lost on Josie.

"Nick," Noah supplied. "Nick Gosnell. They told him about an hour ago. He was out on an emergency call. Dusty tracked him down. Poor guy. Can you imagine? I heard they were high school sweethearts."

Josie frowned. "That's not all it's cracked up to be."

She expected more blushing from Noah, perhaps a muttered apology or a palm to his forehead in a gesture of embarrassment. But all he said was, "I guess not."

She followed his gaze to where Ray stood, just outside the chief's door, talking with another officer. Slowly he walked toward her, and she had the strange sensation of being one of those military wives who saw the soldiers in their shiny dress uniforms coming up the driveway, knowing it only meant bad news. When he got closer, she stood up and wiped her sweaty palms on her jeans.

The phone rang on Noah's desk and he answered it with a brisk, "Fraley."

Ray said, "You okay?"

*No.* She felt shaken by what had happened with June. She'd given a brief statement to Ray when he arrived at the nursing home with a small group of other officers, but she hadn't told him about the tongue piercing.

"Jo?"

She said, "Yeah, I'm fine. Where's June?"

"Downstairs in holding."

Josie kept picturing June being led away from the home by two Denton PD officers, her pale wrists locked in handcuffs behind her back, her eyes looking straight ahead but not seeing anything. She hadn't put up a fight. It broke Josie's heart to watch the girl chained up after having spent a year in captivity. She felt sad and horrified by Sherri's barbaric murder, and her heart went out to the nurse's family. But she couldn't get June's face out of her head.

"Are you listening to me?" Ray waved a hand in front of her face.

She focused on him. A five o'clock shadow stubbled his jaw line. They were now standing outside the chief's office. They'd crossed the room without her even realizing it. "Sorry," she mumbled.

"I said I checked out the acrylic nail. It belongs to one of the searchers."

"Thanks," she said.

"The chief wants to see you. Don't wind him up, okay?"

# CHAPTER 22

From across his desk, Chief Wayland Harris eyed Josie like he'd caught her shoplifting. In fact, the look he gave her over the top of his reading glasses was worse than the one he had given her when he asked her to turn in her gun and badge and put her on paid suspension. Then he had looked at her with disappointment, but today it was almost as if she were someone else—a stranger dragged into his office for questioning. She didn't get it. Back then, she'd done something wrong. She knew that. She'd never say it out loud because she loved her job too much to jeopardize it, but she knew it was true. This time, she had merely been a bystander. She'd even disarmed June Spencer. Sort of.

"Quinn," he said. The fact that he didn't call her by her rank bothered her, but she kept her composure. "Why is it that every time there is a catastrophe in this town, you're right in the middle of it? Did I not make myself clear when I told you to stay home? Do you not understand the meaning of a suspension?"

"Sir," Josie said. "I was just visiting my grandmother."

"And you were just getting gas when that SUV crashed into the Stop and Go, is that right?"

"It is. Wrong place, wrong time—or the right place at the right time, depending on how you look at it."

He hunched forward, leaning his elbows on his desk. He was a large man. Some of the officers had nicknamed him Grizzly, or Grizz for short, because of his large, barrel-shaped frame. That, and the hair protruding from his bulbous nose. "The way I look at it is that I suspended you three weeks ago and yet you've shown up at every major crime in this city since then. Are you *trying* to get fired?"

Her face flushed. Not from embarrassment, but from frustration. "Sir, I promise you, none of this was on purpose."

His ice-blue eyes flicked toward the door quickly, then back to her. "Why did you go into that room tonight?"

"What?"

"Why did you go into the room with June Spencer tonight? That girl could have killed you. You weren't armed. You're not a cop right now. What she did to Sherri Gosnell . . ." He shook his head. "Let me ask you this: are you trying to get killed?"

"No, I just—"

"I told you to keep your head down, Quinn. You're like a damn feral cat. Into every damn thing."

"Chief," she said, "I think June Spencer was with Isabelle Coleman."

"What?"

Her words tumbled over one another as she told him about the strange encounter with June. "I saw a Facebook photo of Isabelle Coleman with that same tongue barbell. It was taken a few months before she was abducted."

As she spoke, he stared at her, his expression carefully blank. It was his specialty. Good or bad, his face was unreadable. When she finished, he let out a lengthy sigh. "Quinn, I hate to break it to you, but nowadays all these teenage girls have piercings. Hell, my oldest got one last year. I wanted to kill her."

"But sir, June Spencer would not have a barbell that said 'Princess'," Josie said. "Hers would say 'Bitch' or it would have a skull on it, or something. Listen to me, I don't think that June was with Drummond for the last year. I think she was being held by the same person who took Isabelle Coleman. I think she saw Coleman sometime in the last week, and they swapped. It's a message, don't you see?"

The wiry hairs of the chief's left eyebrow lifted skeptically. "Quinn, do you hear yourself? Sending messages with tongue piercings?"

"It's too big a coincidence. Please, look at Coleman's Facebook page. You'll see." Josie kept going. "What if Isabelle Coleman and June Spencer saw one another? Did you finish the search of Drummond's property?"

"There's nothing there. We took the whole place apart and dug up his entire yard—four feet down. You could drop a pool in there now. There's nothing. No sign of Coleman."

"So, she wasn't with Drummond. They were both being held somewhere else and then they got separated. What if June saw Coleman after she was abducted, but before she ended up with Drummond? Have you checked Drummond's known associates?"

"Drummond didn't have any known associates. He doesn't even have any friends. I tried calling his only known relative, an uncle in Colorado. The guy told me Drummond doesn't deserve a funeral. City's paying for it."

"What about from prison?"

The chief pointed a finger at her. "Quinn. I mean it, now. Stop. I appreciate your telling me what happened with that girl, but you need to go home. We will follow up every lead. You know that. But you're out. Leave the police work to us."

Josie sensed this might be her only chance to plead her

case for getting back on the force. When would she next be in front of him? When he called her back, whenever the hell that would be. She wasn't about to hold her breath. "I'm sorry, but listen to me. Things are moving quickly. You're short-staffed. You're working a high-profile abduction where there might be more than one person involved, a shootout, a kidnapping—again, where multiple possible suspects are involved—and now a murder."

"You think I don't know what we're dealing with right now, Quinn?"

"That's not what I said. You need help. Let me come back. Two weeks. You can put me back out on suspension after things settle down."

"That's not how it works, and you know it. As always, I appreciate your enthusiasm, but you're on thin ice here. The DA is all over my ass to conduct a proper investigation. You have a better chance of winning the lottery than that woman deciding not to press charges. I'm trying to figure out a way to get you out of the mess you made before all this shit started. You being in the middle of every other damn mess isn't helping."

"She won't press charges," Josie said.

His voice rose to a near shout. "Quinn, you knocked out two of her teeth! How in the hell do you know she won't press charges?"

*Because what she did was far worse than me elbowing her in the face,* Josie thought. She kept her mouth shut this time; the last time they'd had this conversation it had sounded like a justification. Instead, she tried, "I'm sorry. I'll try to . . . fly under the radar from now on. But please, just think about it. We can do it quietly. Put me on the tip line or let me guard June Spencer while she's in holding. I'll keep my head down, I promise."

He sighed. "I said no, Quinn. I brought you in here to put you on notice. Stay out of the shit, will you?"

She wanted to scream. Instead, she asked, as calmly as possible, "What about the Ramona thing?"

Slowly, his eyelids dropped. He raised his head to the ceiling and inhaled deeply, his way of counting to ten. She'd pushed him too far. His blue eyes locked on her again. "Did you not hear a *goddamn* thing I said?"

"I did. I was just wondering. Now more than ever, we need to find her, don't you think? What if she's connected to Isabelle Coleman somehow? What if she knows where Coleman is?"

The chief rubbed a hand over his eyes. "There's no Ramona. I got the report after the shootout, and we checked *every* possibility. There are six Ramonas in the NAMUS database listed as missing, and none of them are from Pennsylvania. Not even close. We checked out Spencer's house. Talked to coworkers, friends, his ex-girlfriend. No one knows anyone with that name. We don't even have anyone named Ramona in the city—accounted for or unaccounted for. It's a dead end, Quinn."

"But don't you think it's weird that both Spencers brought the name up? It must mean something. Whoever Ramona is, she must be important."

"What's weird is you pushing all this when you're suspended. I don't appreciate you second-guessing the quality of work that this department is putting out. Now unless you want to be on unpaid suspension, you better get out of my office right now."

"Chief."

"Now," he hollered.

His words hit her like a physical slap. She gripped the armrests of her chair and pushed herself to standing. It wasn't that he had yelled at her. The chief was well known for his big, booming voice. It was the way he looked at her. For the second time in the last five minutes, she felt like a stranger in her own world.

She kept her eyes on him and backed out of the room.

# CHAPTER 23

She had no idea how long she'd been sleeping, but she was startled awake when the door swung open, pushing against her prone form. As she opened her eyes, daylight slashed into the room, blinding her. The pain in her head was instant and excruciating. The girl clenched her eyes closed as tightly as she could, threw her forearm over her face and scrambled backward until her body slammed hard into the stone wall. Before she could catch her breath, a rough hand dragged her up from the ground.

"Stand up," a man's voice commanded.

She followed the pain in her scalp more than his command. Her legs wobbled and shook as she stood upright. She tried opening her eyes again but the light was too harsh.

"Please," she croaked. "I want to go home."

He laughed, his breath hot in her ear. "You can't go home, girlie," he said. "You're mine now."

# CHAPTER 24

It was nearing ten o'clock and Josie was three shots of Wild Turkey deep by the time Luke arrived at her house. She met him at the door, flinging her arms around his neck and kissing him deeply. She felt the stir of her lust for him, intensified by booze. Before he could catch his breath, she was undoing his belt.

Laughing softly, he grasped her hands and held them between his large palms, like he was warming them on a cold day. "Not so fast," he murmured. "I heard about what happened at Rockview. Is your grandmother okay?"

"She's fine," Josie replied. The last thing she wanted to do was talk about what happened at Rockview. She could still see her grandmother standing in the doorway of June's empty room, open-mouthed and white with shock like the rest of them. Josie had felt terrible leaving her there, and felt even worse now, remembering.

Pulling her hands from his grip, Josie pushed Luke until his back was against her foyer wall. Her hands returned frantically to his belt.

"Josie," he said, and she felt a stab of annoyance at the tone of his voice. Was that pity?

"Shut up," she said as she finally released his belt and snaked a hand up, behind his head, grabbing a fistful of his hair and pulling him down to her hungry mouth. He didn't fight her.

He broke the kiss and looked at the steps. "Should we go upstairs?"

She pulled her shirt off. "No," she said. "I want you now."

He brushed her cheek gently with the back of his hand. "We can slow down, you know."

But she didn't want to slow down. She didn't want tenderness, or a slow burn. She needed a raging inferno that would burn up every anxiety twisting and turning inside her head. She needed the heat, that fire they'd achieved in the woods.

She dropped to her knees before him. "No," she said. "We can't."

❧ ✿ ❧

Josie picked up the clothes she had strewn all over the floor and put them back on. The numbing effect of the Wild Turkey had burned away, leaving her feeling as though she had downed a pot of coffee. Her mind felt clear, her anxiety eased for the moment. Luke sat bare-chested at her kitchen table. He had, at least, pulled on his boxer shorts and watched as she went back to work on the late dinner she'd been attempting to make for him before he arrived.

"I brought you something," he said, eventually.

She smiled at him. "Oh yeah?"

"It's in my truck."

"Are you going to bring it inside?"

"Yeah, it's a door. You know, for your bedroom closet."

Josie froze, the knife in her hand poised over a piece of grilled chicken breast. The buzzed feeling she'd had since she took him in the foyer drained out of her. "My, uh, my bedroom closet?"

"Yeah. There's no door." He laughed. "You didn't notice?"

She laughed along with him, hoping he didn't hear the high note of nervousness in her voice. "I, uh, kind of like it without a door," she said. "It's more open, airy."

It was a lie, but it was the best she could do in that moment. What could she say? Nothing that wouldn't lead to questions she didn't want to answer.

When she and Ray first moved in together after college they'd lived in a tiny apartment with a huge bedroom closet. Big enough for her to walk in and out of, but not quite a walk-in closet. She'd been moving things around inside of it when Ray had closed the door without thinking, not realizing Josie was still in there. The click of the latch, the sudden darkness, broke something in her and caused an unexpected, furious panic attack. Paralyzed, she had started hyperventilating. It had felt like the walls were reaching for her, the dark space getting smaller by the second. She had nearly passed out.

Ray had felt terrible. Once he calmed her down, he'd taken the door off the hinges and thrown it out for trash. It had come out of their security deposit when they moved but Ray said it didn't matter. In each one of the string of crappy apartments they'd rented, and then, finally, in the house they'd bought together, he routinely removed all closet doors. It became their normal.

It was only natural to then do the same in her own place. It helped her sleep at night. But she couldn't tell Luke that. She couldn't tell him the truth. He couldn't know that Josie.

"Airy?" Luke said. "But it looks terrible. I mean, all your stuff is just there. Josie, closets are where you shove all your unused stuff. They're meant to have doors."

The knife clanged onto the counter, startling him. "Not all of them," she replied, through gritted teeth, then took a deep breath and reminded herself that he was trying to do something nice for her.

Luke was a fixer. That was one of the things that had initially attracted her to him. If he saw something in disrepair, he quietly fixed it. He'd been mending things around her house for as long as they'd been together: touching up the paint, replacing the leaky faucet in her bathroom sink, patching a hole in the drywall in her kitchen left by the previous owner. She had always appreciated it—until now. This time it felt like he was trying to fix *her,* but she didn't need to be fixed. She wasn't broken. She was fine.

But he means well, she told herself. He wasn't attempting to control her. He didn't understand what putting that door up would mean. She forced a smile onto her face. "I'm sorry," she said. "I meant to say that I want to paint my bedroom. It was really wonderful of you to go out and buy a door for me, but let's just put it in the garage until I paint the room, okay?"

"Oh, I can paint it for—"

"No, no," she said quickly. "I kind of wanted to do it myself."

He looked half-disappointed and half-confused. She had to change the subject, and fast. She hated to do it, but it was the first thing that came to mind. "How did you know about Rockview?" she asked, picking the knife back up as casually as she could.

"Oh, I called to see if anyone had claimed any of the bodies from the shootout—no one has yet—and Noah told me. Hard to believe."

Josie turned to get something from her fridge and knocked a mess of cooking utensils onto the floor. Luke jumped up to help her retrieve them.

"Just throw them into the sink," Josie said with a heavy sigh. "I'll wash them later."

"What is that, exactly?" he asked, pointing to the mess on her counter: chicken, pasta and some creamy concoction. She had lost track of what she'd put into that particular bowl.

"Creamy chicken lasagna," she told him. She scrolled through her phone until she found the recipe and handed it to him.

His brow furrowed as he looked back and forth from the recipe to Josie's countertop. Before Luke had arrived, she'd had the bright idea that cooking would take her mind off the work that she wasn't able to do and all the questions firing around in her head. Cooking hadn't helped at all. The truth was she hated cooking. It was boring and frustrating. She had been living on bagels, microwave dinners and salads since she left Ray.

"Do you mind?" Luke asked, pointing to the cooked chicken breast piled on a plate on the counter.

Her heart just wasn't in it, especially now. "Sure," she said. "Have at it."

First, he rearranged all the plates and bowls on her counter. Then he searched her cabinets for more supplies: measuring cups, basil, salt and a large knife and cutting board. He started dicing the chicken. Josie pulled a chair up to her kitchen table and sat down, tucking her feet beneath her. "You think you can save it?" she asked. There he was again, fixing things.

"Guess we'll find out," he said as his hands worked quickly and deftly, chopping the chicken in half the time it would have taken her. "Tell me about today."

Relieved to be off the subject of the closet door, she took him through the whole episode at Rockview, from June's arrival to finding Sherri murdered on the floor of her room. She told him about everything but the Princess tongue barbell. She already regretted telling the chief; maybe he was right, maybe she did sound crazy. Maybe she shouldn't be taking it so seriously or trying so hard to connect June to Coleman. Luke listened intently as he moved on to the creamy concoction, tasting it with a spoon then adding ingredients, stirring, tasting, adding, stirring some more.

"No missing persons named Ramona?" he asked.

"The chief said there aren't any. There aren't any Ramonas at all in Denton."

"But obviously the Spencers know someone named Ramona."

"Except Dirk Spencer's ex-girlfriend says they *didn't*."

He waved a wooden spoon in the air. "Wait, why were you talking to Dirk Spencer's ex-girlfriend?"

"That's not important," Josie said.

Luke's grin told her he wasn't going to make an issue of this, and for that she loved him. He filled a large pot with water and put it on the stove to boil, adding in a few dashes of salt and a capful of olive oil. "Maybe Ramona isn't a person," he said. "Maybe it's a place."

"No, I think it's a person," Josie said. "Maybe not a missing person. Just a person."

The scene with June played out in Josie's mind again from beginning to end but brought her no closer to figuring out the mystery of Ramona.

And what about Drummond? Where did he fit in? The chief had said they'd found no trace of Coleman or any other girl at his property. Where was Coleman, and how had she and June come into contact with one another?

Josie retrieved her phone from the countertop and pulled up a search screen. She wouldn't have access to the police databases now that she was suspended, but she would have access to the Megan's Law list in Pennsylvania which would tell her what Drummond had been in prison for.

A few minutes of searching was all it took to find him.

He'd been convicted ten years earlier of forcible rape and unlawful restraint. He'd served seven years. His photo showed a wide-faced man with features that seemed better suited to a giant. He looked easily ten years older than his stated age of thirty-three and stared at the camera with a flat affect—almost the same expression June had had when they brought her into Rockview. Physically there, but not mentally.

Drummond was in his early twenties when he committed the crime that landed him on the registry, likely to have been his first. It looked as though he'd been on his best behavior once he got out, under the watchful eye of his mother.

Josie searched for her and found her obituary. She had died a few months before June went missing. In theory, with his mother gone, Drummond could have held June for a year and no one would have been the wiser. It was possible that June had packed up her messenger bag and walked away from her uncle's house, then been picked up by Drummond.

Josie wondered if June's messenger bag had been recovered at Drummond's house. She fired off a quick text to Ray, asking him. She could sense his eye roll across the city of Denton. His response came back within minutes: *No. No bag. Now stay out of it before the chief fires you.*

She typed back: *Have you checked out Drummond's prison friends?*

*Chief already asked me to look into it. DON'T TEXT ME AGAIN.*

She typed in a cutting reply, but then deleted it and simply wrote thank you instead. She might need Ray in the future.

"Are you online?" Luke asked.

She looked up to see him feeding stiff, uncooked lasagna noodles into the boiling pot of water.

"Uh, yeah," she said.

Coleman had not been found at Drummond's house, and

neither had June's messenger bag, which meant there was another location and someone else involved. Yet she couldn't see Drummond being involved in trafficking. It made no sense. He was a collector. He had prepared a room—what had Ray said? He had outfitted it like a cell. Drummond had likely been planning to take someone. He'd wanted June for his own gratification, not to make money from her. Traffickers made money from the women and children they bought and sold.

Round and round it all went in her mind. Going nowhere.

"Josie?"

She looked up from her phone. Luke was standing beside her, an uncertain smile on his face. He laid a hand on her shoulder. "I said the lasagna will be ready in a half hour. Did you want to open a bottle of wine?"

She flashed him a smile. "I'd love to."

*Not as much as I'd love to do some digging in the police database,* she added silently.

# CHAPTER 25

The lasagna turned out rich and exquisite. Even following the recipe, Josie doubted she could reproduce the flavor that Luke had. After dinner, they finally made it to the bedroom where Luke carefully inventoried and kissed all of her injuries from the Stop and Go, before he fell asleep, exhausted and snoring, in Josie's bed. Her alarm clock read 12:58 as she slid out of bed, slipped into some sweats and a faded Denton PD T-shirt, and took her laptop into the kitchen.

She logged into her Facebook first, finding June Spencer's page and running through her posts and profile pictures. There weren't many. Going by what Solange had told her, Josie could imagine that the girl simply had very little to post about.

Next, she brought up Google and entered June Spencer's name into the search bar to see if Trinity Payne had come up with anything new on the case, or if the story had been picked up by the national news outlets. There was a smattering of headlines proclaiming: "Denton Girl Missing for One Year Found Alive" and "Teen Runaway Kept as Sex Slave for a Year." Josie checked the sources. They were all local, mostly WYEP and the few local newspapers in the area. A few listings below the stories about June, an older headline caught Josie's eye: "Missing PA Housewife Found Alive in Denton." Josie clicked on the story from *USA Today* and quickly scanned it. Then she opened a new browser window and entered the housewife's name into the search bar. It turned up hundreds of news reports, the headlines all screaming the same thing:

> MISSING PENNSYLVANIA WOMAN FOUND
> ALIVE AFTER EXHAUSTIVE SEARCH
> MISSING PA MOTHER FOUND ALIVE
> MISSING ALCOTT COUNTY WOMAN FOUND
> ALIVE AFTER 3 WEEKS

One by one, Josie clicked through and read each piece. Six years ago, Ginger Blackwell, a thirty-two-year-old mother of three from Bowersville, the next town over, west of Denton, disappeared on her way home from the grocery store. Her vehicle and all of her personal belongings—purse, phone, keys—were found on the side of a rural road between the grocery store and her home. Her groceries were still in the back of her car and her driver's side front tire was flat. She had vanished without a trace.

The Bowersville police, the state police and the FBI searched day and night. A command center was established near the grocery store where she was last seen. Even a tip line was set up. All the major networks picked up the story. Blackwell's husband was an early suspect even though he had an alibi. Once he passed a polygraph the police focused their investigation elsewhere, but with absolutely no leads the investigation ground to a halt. Josie vaguely remembered the case. Back then she hadn't yet joined the police force; she was fresh out of college, living with her grandmother and still partying more than anything else. She was sure she was aware of it since it had happened so close by, but it hadn't stayed vividly in her mind.

After three weeks, Ginger was found on the shoulder of Interstate 80 between the two Denton exits, bound and naked. She claimed that a woman had stopped to help her with her flat tire, and the next thing she knew she was being held prisoner, but she could not describe where she had been held or the person, or persons, who had held her. "It was just complete darkness," she was quoted as saying. "Like being kept in a cupboard. The darkness was absolute. Like a black box."

Josie sucked in a sharp breath as invisible fingers crawled up her spine. Like a cupboard. Like a closet. She didn't have to imagine; she knew Blackwell's terror. Was it too much of a coincidence? Blackwell had vanished without a trace along a lonely rural stretch of road, just like Spencer and Coleman. All three women had disappeared within a six-year period. That was a lot in a short amount of time for an area as small as Denton. Had the same person who had taken Isabelle Coleman, and possibly June Spencer, also taken Ginger Blackwell? Josie pulled up the Megan's Law site in a new window and checked Donald Drummond's page again. He had been in prison when Ginger Blackwell was abducted.

She flipped back to the tab with the Blackwell story on it and read on. Blackwell remembered next to nothing. She had no idea whether the woman who stopped to help her had been involved in her abduction or not. A Bowersville woman, the owner of a local hair salon, came forward later to say that she had stopped when she saw Blackwell's vehicle broken down on the side of the road but that Blackwell was nowhere to be found. Ginger couldn't remember if the salon owner was the same woman she spoke with. She didn't remember being dumped on the interstate. Her injuries were minor. The news reports didn't address whether or not she had been sexually assaulted.

Because she was found on the interstate, the state police had jurisdiction, but because she was found in Denton, Chief Harris fought to keep her case. Ultimately, the Alcott County district attorney appointed a special investigator to conduct an independent investigation. It was an unusual move, but Josie understood the amount of pressure all of law enforcement and the DA's office would have been under to solve the case given the amount of national press coverage.

Ginger's case was quickly labeled a hoax. Josie scrolled through at least twenty articles outlining why police believed that her abduction had been faked. In each one Ginger's husband was quoted, perhaps to cast doubt on the hoax theory. He said, "My wife did not stage her own kidnapping. This was no hoax. She went through hell. Tell me, if she did all this herself, then how did she tie herself up and dump herself on the side of the highway?"

How indeed.

Studying the photos of Ginger, it was hard to believe the woman had been thirty-two. She looked like a teenager. She was thin with long, lustrous auburn hair and eyes the blue of tropical waters. Her pale skin glowed in every picture. In some, she held squirming toddlers in her lap; in others, she stood in front of a monument or landmark. All taken before her abduction. All showing her radiant and impossibly happy. Josie wondered if she had gotten that smile back in the years after her recovery.

A hand brushing through the back of her hair made her jump. "Jesus," Luke said. "What are you doing? Did you sleep at all last night?"

Her heart thudded against her sternum as she looked around the kitchen and noticed the muted gray daylight flooding in through the windows. She had been awake the entire night. "I—I couldn't sleep," she said.

He yawned. "You must be exhausted."

But she wasn't. She felt more keenly awake than ever before. Luke sat beside her at the table, still bare-chested, wearing only the low-slung sweatpants that he kept in the top left-hand drawer of her dresser. "What are you doing?" he asked, squinting at her computer screen, which displayed her search for Ginger Blackwell. "You really need to give Google a break," he added, jokingly.

Josie clicked on one of the news stories, and a photo of Ginger Blackwell with her wide, infectious smile filled the screen. Below that, a video of the ninety-second news piece began to play. "Do you remember this case?" she asked. "She was kidnapped and then dumped on I-80 three weeks later. Ginger Blackwell?"

Luke pushed a hand through his hair and studied Blackwell's photo. In the video, Trinity Payne appeared next to a large-screen television showing a slideshow of photos of Blackwell and began reciting the scant facts of the woman's disappearance. The sight of Trinity sent a jolt through Josie. Trinity had been a correspondent for one of the major networks at the time of Blackwell's abduction. Perhaps she had gotten the story because of her ties to the area.

"I remember the case," Luke said. "But only because it was on the news. I was stationed near Greensburg back then. I thought the whole thing was a hoax."

Sighing, Josie snapped her laptop shut. "That seems to be the consensus," she replied, but she wasn't so sure. She wished she could see the Blackwell file and decide for herself. It wasn't that far out of the realm of possibility; hoaxes had been known to happen before, but usually the culprit was then charged, or at least fined, for the unnecessary use of police resources. It cost money to put on a search as large as the one mounted for Ginger Blackwell. Money a county like Alcott just didn't have. Josie knew for a fact that Denton had probably blown its annual budget within three days of Isabelle Coleman's disappearance. If Blackwell had staged her abduction, why hadn't she been punished for it? Something was missing; something was in the Blackwell file that hadn't made it onto the news. She knew it.

Josie watched Luke as he stood and made his way to her counter, scooped coffee grounds into the coffeemaker, poured water into it and turned it on. She wondered if she could trust him. Really trust him. She had learned at the tender age of eleven that not all men were trustworthy, possibly before that when, at six, her father had chosen a bullet over her.

The only man she had ever really trusted was Ray, but he was a boy when she met him. And look how that turned out. He had grown into a man and destroyed the most sacred period of their life together—their marriage—proving to her, once and for all, definitively, that men could not be trusted.

Yet she wore Luke's engagement ring on her finger. She had said yes. Without hesitation. Which implied some trust on her part, didn't it? Could she talk to him about the Princess barbell? About her theory that Blackwell, Coleman and June Spencer were all connected? Would he dismiss her as easily as the chief had? Would he think she was crazy?

She thought of the incident that had landed her in the unholy mess she was in now, suspended and at loose ends. After it happened, Ray had called her exactly that. Crazy. Then he had said, "You can't do shit like that. You can't just hit people." Of course she couldn't. She knew that. But nearly every officer on the Denton PD shared Ray's opinion: she had gone crazy. She may have lost control but she knew she wasn't crazy.

Quite honestly, she had expected more support from her colleagues. Like none of them had ever lost his temper in the heat of the moment, been driven to do something regrettable, something stupid or maybe, yes, a little crazy. Sometimes it happened. What they dealt with day after day was the worst humanity had to offer. If it didn't get to you now and then, you weren't human. Only Noah had given any indication that he understood. He had quietly said to her, as she left the station house in disgrace, gunless and badgeless, "She had it coming."

Josie took the steaming cup of coffee Luke offered her, fixed just the way she liked it—two sugars and lots of half-and-half. "Luke," she said, as he sat down next to her. "Remember the incident with that woman, you know, the one I got suspended for?"

He laughed. "Hard to forget it."

"Do you think I did the right thing? Hitting her like that? Or do you think I was…I don't know…crazy?"

His face turned serious. "No," he said, not a hint of laughter in his tone. "I don't think you were crazy at all. I would have shot her."

# CHAPTER 26

They went out to breakfast, and in a hushed tone she told him what June had shown her after Sherri Gosnell's murder, following up with her theory that the Princess tongue barbell in June's mouth actually belonged to Isabelle Coleman. He didn't tell her she was crazy. He didn't question her competence. He didn't tell her she had too much time on her hands, or that she should give it a rest. Instead, he raised an eyebrow, chewed his toast thoughtfully, swallowed and asked, "Did you check June Spencer's Facebook page to see if there are any photos of her with this tongue piercing?"

Her fork paused, floating over her plate. "I did. There wasn't anything useful. Wait—you think I'm right?"

Luke shrugged. "Don't know. I can see what the chief is saying. It's not a definitive piece of evidence that points to Coleman, but given everything you've told me, I can also see where you're coming from."

"You think there is something bigger at work here? Like Drummond was involved with someone else? Maybe more than one person?"

He finished off his toast. "I don't know. Anything's possible."

"You think it's some kind of trafficking ring?"

His brow furrowed as he took a sip of coffee, then he said, "Traffickers spend a lot of time grooming their girls. They don't usually take by force. I'm not saying they never kidnap women, I'm just saying the usual MO is for them to find a girl with low self-esteem—family issues, desperate for attention, that sort of thing—and then they pull the bait and switch. It's usually one guy making the girl feel like she's the most special person in the whole world, that he loves her like crazy, giving her all kinds of gifts, lavishing her with attention and then when she is so gaga for him that she'll do anything, he introduces the sex-for-money thing. It's all about manipulation. It's a game, and these guys are good at it. We do a lot of busts at truck stops. I see a lot of these girls. Unfortunately, there's no shortage of them. So a trafficking ring that abducts teenage girls and then either gives them or sells them to known sex offenders to keep? It's possible, but I'm really not sold on that."

"But you think it's possible that the same person or people who took Ginger Blackwell also took Coleman, and possibly June Spencer?"

Another shrug. "Could be. Worth checking out. You should tell your chief to request a copy of the Blackwell file and check for any connections to the Coleman case—assuming that the Blackwell case really wasn't a hoax. If there is anything useful, I'm sure he'll find it. Who has the file?"

"The state police would have a file. They were the first responders, and they had the case until the chief raised holy hell and got an investigator from the DA's office involved. The state police lab processed the evidence."

"You got all that from Google?"

"Trinity Payne did a pretty detailed story on the whole thing."

Luke said nothing and they ate in silence for a few

moments. Then Josie asked him the question she'd been working up to the entire time, "Can you get me a copy of the Ginger Blackwell file?"

He stared at her. "Josie."

"I know. I'm asking a lot. Especially because I'm not on the job right now."

The truth was that even if she was on the job, asking for a copy of the file was putting Luke in an awkward position. It was a closed case and she was with another law enforcement agency. "Please," she added.

He put his fork down and put both his hands on the table on either side of his plate. "Why?"

"Because I don't believe that her case was a hoax, but I won't know for sure unless I know what the police held back from the press. And what if there really are connections between her case and Isabelle Coleman's? What if Coleman is being held in the same place Blackwell was taken? I could find her."

He looked away from her for a moment, at a point over her shoulder. A small vertical crease appeared above the bridge of his nose. He looked uncomfortable, like the time she'd had to tell him that she was still, technically, married to Ray. She could tell he was considering his words carefully. Whatever he was about to say, he didn't want to offend her or patronize her. Finally, he forged ahead. "Josie, Denton PD is perfectly capable of following up on these leads. Googling missing girls in this area and trying to connect their cases is one thing; accessing a police file illegally for no other reason than..." He drifted off, unwilling or unable to finish the sentence. "I know it's hard for you, being suspended, especially with everything that's going on right now, and I know you want to be a hero and find Coleman on your own, redeem yourself or whatever, but maybe you would... I don't know, get more sleep at night if you found something else to, you know, take up your time."

"What, like knitting?"

His cheeks colored. "No, yes...no. I mean..."

She stabbed her fork in the air in his direction. "This isn't a hobby, Luke. I'm not doing this because I'm bored—"

He leaned his elbows on the table, folding his hands together over the top of his plate. "Then why? Why are you doing it?"

From the look in his eyes, she knew it was a genuine question. The flat white of her napkin was suddenly wildly distracting. Staring down at it, she ran her fingertips over the stippled edge of it. *Because it's who I am.*

"I'm just saying that most people would be perfectly happy with a few weeks off from work. Most people have other things to do. Me? If I had time off from work, I'd be fishing from sunup to sundown. Sure, I'd miss the work, but I'd be happy for the break."

She looked back up at him. "If I get a hobby, will you at least think about getting me the file?"

He shook his head, letting out a heavy sigh, but as he returned to eating she could see a half smile on his face, and she knew he would do what he could.

After they finished eating, Luke went to work and Josie went home. She had planned to get a few hours' sleep—what else did she have to do? But she lay in her bed wide awake, sunlight slipping around the sides of her mini-blinds. She wasn't sure why the Ginger Blackwell case bothered her so much, or even why she had asked Luke for the file. Why did it matter? What connection could it possibly have to June or Isabelle Coleman's case?

Then it came to her. Ginger Blackwell's disappearance had gained national attention. Within the first week, her face was the centerpiece of every news program in the country. Josie had even found stories about her abduction on the evening celebrity magazine shows: *Access Hollywood, TMZ* and the like. It was like the entire world had been wallpapered with Ginger Blackwell. Two weeks later she was dumped on the side of the highway.

"Why?" Josie muttered to herself. Had the news coverage had something to do with her abductor letting her go? Had Blackwell's abductor made a mistake? The woman could easily have been mistaken for a college-aged kid. Had her abductor, or abductors, taken her because they assumed she was young? Had they intended to keep her or even kill her, but felt compelled to release her under the relentless pressure of the media attention?

In spite of the sheer volume of news coverage about Ginger's disappearance, there were few details about what the woman had experienced and seen during the three weeks she was missing.

Josie had to talk to Ginger Blackwell.

# CHAPTER 27

Josie scoured the internet for Blackwell's address for an hour before her eyes started to burn and her head grew heavy and clouded by sleep deprivation. There was an address for a rural route outside of Bowersville, but Josie knew the Blackwells no longer lived there because the entire area had been developed into a miniature golf course. She searched using Blackwell's husband's name but nothing came up. Where the hell had they gone? Even if they had moved, it would have been impossible to keep their new address off the internet in this day and age, surely? She tried using a private address search database that the department subscribed to using Ray's login. This database she could log into without him knowing she was using his credentials, and he used the same password for everything: JoRay0803, their names followed by the date they'd gotten back together after college. But the database turned up nothing beyond the Blackwells' old Bowersville address.

A high-pitched buzzing started inside her head, her body begging her for sleep. She was suddenly aware of the dull ache along the left side of her body from the accident at the Stop and Go. She hadn't changed the dressing on her leg in two days. That needed to be done, but fatigue hit her so hard she felt like she could just slide down onto the floor and sleep for days under her kitchen table. She had barely hit her mattress before the blackness engulfed her.

A loud, steady knocking woke her a few hours later, and much too soon. The sun had fallen to the other side of the sky but its rays clung on, sneaking around the blinds with much less vigor. She looked at her clock, rolled over, and tried to go back to sleep. The knocking went on. Josie pulled one of her pillows over her head, but she still heard it. Finally, after fifteen minutes of constant knocking, she stood up, stomped down her stairs, and flung her door open.

Trinity Payne stood on her stoop in her signature coat, a tight little black skirt, and tall, taupe-colored heels. Strands of her black hair lifted gently in the wind. Josie squinted. Her hair was so shiny, you could practically see your reflection in it.

"Nice hair," Trinity said, as if reading her mind.

Josie turned and checked her reflection in the glass panes of her front door. One side of her head looked like someone had teased her hair straight up in the air. She licked one of her palms and tried to smooth it down, but it only made it look worse.

Trinity took a step toward her. "What's that from?"

Josie tugged harder at her hair, dragging her fingers through it. "What's what from?"

"That scar."

Josie's fingers found the silvered skin and traced its jagged form. It started near her ear and ran down the side of her face, along her jawline. "Not that it's any of your business, but it's from a car accident," she lied. "Are you always this intrusive? Like, even in your personal life?"

Trinity thrust one hip out, her lips twisted in a look of disgust, but said nothing. Josie looked beyond her to see a small blue Honda Civic parked curbside. She pointed. "That's what you drive? WYEP doesn't pay very well, does it?"

Trinity remained silent, so Josie tried again. "What do you want?"

"You were at Rockview."

"So?"

"So, I'd like you to go on the record and talk about what happened. I'm not getting anything from Rockview or Denton PD."

"Shocker."

"I'm serious. Tell me what really happened."

Josie folded her arms over her chest. "What makes you think something happened besides what was reported by the police?"

Trinity rolled her eyes. "Please. Don't treat me like an idiot. You know as well as I do the police always hold things back. You were there. Did you see the whole thing?"

This was how she did it. Slipping questions into conversation like they were old friends. Josie opened her mouth to answer and quickly stopped herself.

"Oh, come on. What have you got to lose? You were a witness. I'm only asking you what you saw."

"I could lose my job. I can't talk about Rockview."

"Did you know June Spencer?"

"Are you kidding me?" Josie shook her head and moved back toward the doorway, ready to leave Trinity Payne alone on the front steps.

"What about Sherri Gosnell?" Trinity called after her. "You must have known her. Your grandmother is a resident at Rockview. Sherri worked there for decades."

Josie stopped, half her body over the threshold, and turned

back to Trinity. "What are you trying to get here? June Spencer was being held prisoner by a sexual predator. She got rescued. She was messed up in the head. She had nowhere to go because her mom can't be located, and her uncle is in a coma. Rockview took her. The next thing anyone knew, Sherri Gosnell was dead. All of that's already been reported. I'm not sure what you're looking for. If you want a story, the real story here is how did Donald Drummond, who is on the sex offender registry, manage to take this girl and keep her with no one figuring it out?"

Trinity sighed. She glanced at her shoes. "Don't take this the wrong way," she said. "But that's not a story. I mean, it is—a terrible, horrible, tragic story—but people already know that the systems in place to prevent criminals from committing more crimes are broken. Take any ten crimes and you'll find that in eight of the cases, the perpetrator either had a lengthy criminal record or should have been in prison but got out on some kind of technicality. It's not news."

Josie narrowed her eyes. "You mean it's not the kind of news that's going to get you back on a big network show."

For a split second Trinity's face registered indignant shock. Then it was replaced by a more pragmatic look. Her brow crinkled and her lips pressed into a thin line. Then she said, "We're off the record here."

Josie rolled her eyes. "There is no record, Trinity."

"What's wrong with being ambitious?" Trinity said. "I mean, you're the youngest female lieutenant in Denton PD history."

"I'm a detective, which is an appointed position in our department. I was the only female lieutenant in Denton PD history and now I'm the only female detective in Denton PD history. I love my job, and I'm good at it."

"I love my job too, and I'm good at it."

Josie held up an index finger. "But you have to manipulate and harass people to be good at your job."

Trinity's eyebrows drew closer together. Her stomach growled loudly, and she covered it with one hand, as though that would silence it. She said, "The public has a right to know about what's going on in their communities. That is a fact. The press can be a powerful tool. Maybe the way I get the job done offends your delicate sensibilities, but what I do is important."

"Do you care about the public or do you care about being on television?"

"Both," Trinity said honestly, the word almost a shout in a feeble attempt to cover up the sound of her stomach protesting again.

Before she could stop herself, Josie laughed. The answer was so instant and brutally honest. Trinity had no illusions about the world or even herself. Josie couldn't admire the woman's thirst for celebrity or personal gain, but she certainly respected her truthfulness. She pointed toward Trinity's stomach. "When's the last time you ate?"

Trinity eyed her suspiciously. "That's not important right now," she said.

Josie pushed her door all the way open and gestured toward the foyer. "I won't talk to you about Rockview," she said. "But if you're going to harass me, why don't you eat some of my leftover lasagna while you do it."

Trinity's blue eyes narrowed. "You want something."

Josie didn't deny it.

"No one is ever nice to me. What do you want?"

"Just come inside," Josie told her.

Trinity's heels clacked as she walked slowly past Josie, eyes fixed on her as though she might attack at any moment. Chuckling, Josie stepped past her and led her into the kitchen. "Relax," she said. "It's just a little piece of information."

# CHAPTER 28

An hour later, Josie was armed with Ginger Blackwell's current address and Trinity had a nearly full stomach and a promise from Josie that if there was a connection between the Blackwell and Coleman cases she would be the first to know. Josie had warmed up Luke's creamy lasagna and made a pot of coffee while sharing her theory that Ginger Blackwell's case was not a hoax and that she had been set free, in large part, because of the intensive national coverage her case had garnered.

"She was raped," Trinity said around a mouthful of lasagna. "By multiple men, she thinks."

"You met her?"

"No. She only did press at the very beginning and wouldn't be seen on camera. Too traumatized. By the time I got the assignment she had stopped doing interviews. But her husband did a lot of press. Nice guy. Devoted to her. I felt badly for them. Especially when the police started to say it was a hoax."

"There are disappearances all over this country all the time," Josie said. "Why did her case get so much attention?"

"Her husband had a relative—a cousin, I think—who went to college with a producer at a major network. It was one of those 'I have a friend of a friend' situations, you know? Anyway, the cousin got in touch with his old college buddy, asked him to do a piece on her disappearance at the national level. It wasn't a hard sell. She was a gorgeous, small-town housewife who disappeared into thin air. People ate it up. The segment went viral and the other networks picked it up."

"If there is the slightest chance that her case is connected with Isabelle Coleman's, and if Coleman's case were to get national attention, do you think they'd let her go?"

Trinity shrugged. She swallowed her food and her face turned serious. "Or they could kill her and dump her body. If Ginger was telling the truth, and let's say it's some kind of trafficking ring, I think they only let her go because she couldn't remember anything. At least, that's what her husband said. He said they drugged her."

"Maybe they've drugged Isabelle too."

"Why do you think the cases are connected?"

"I don't. I mean, no reason. It's just weird that three women would be abducted around here, that's all."

"I didn't peg you for a conspiracy theorist," Trinity said.

"I'm not," said Josie. "I'm just saying it's worth checking out. What if Blackwell tells me something that does connect to the Coleman case?"

Trinity's eyes narrowed. "Does the chief know you're running your own investigation now? Why are you talking to me about this and not Denton PD?"

"They're pretty much at the limit of what they can handle right now," she told Trinity. "Besides, I'd like to have some actual leads before I take this to the chief."

"I don't believe you, but I also don't think the cases are connected. You know the deal: if you find a connection, I'm the first to know."

Reluctantly, Josie said, "Yes, that's what we agreed on. I

didn't forget in the last hour. But why don't you think there will be a connection?"

Trinity shrugged. "Look at June Spencer. Everyone thought she ran away, but she was in Donald Drummond's house. We have no way of knowing anything."

"Jesus. There are perverts everywhere. What if I'm right about the news coverage thing? Can you get national coverage for the Coleman case?"

Trinity leaned back in her chair and twisted a lock of hair around one of her index fingers. She stared at her empty plate thoughtfully. Josie had never seen a woman eat as much as Trinity Payne did, and she couldn't weigh more than one hundred twenty pounds. "I can try. I still have some contacts in New York. Coleman's perfect for the national news—a gorgeous, blond teenager with her whole life ahead of her—I'll see what I can do."

Josie was keying the Blackwells' new address into Google Maps when Trinity asked her, "Come on, tell me. Is it true that June Spencer killed Sherri Gosnell with a fork?"

Josie froze and shot Trinity a cutting look. "Trinity, please."

"Just tell me. When's the last time you heard of someone being killed with a fork? It must have been brutal."

Josie went back to Google Maps. "There was a lot of blood," she conceded.

"What do you think drove her over the edge?"

Josie shrugged. "I have no idea. I wasn't in the room when it happened. She was already in bad shape when she got to Rockview. Are you sure the Blackwells still live in this place?"

She had pulled up the street view of the address Trinity gave her. Trinity leaned over to glance at the computer screen. "I'm sure they're still there," she told Josie. "It took them forever to sell their house in Bowersville. I can't imagine them having moved again already. Good luck getting her to talk to you though."

# CHAPTER 29

The Blackwells had changed their name and moved to Phillipsburg, New Jersey. That was why Josie had been unable to locate them. Luckily for her, when Trinity covered Ginger's case she had promised Mr. Blackwell to continue trying to uncover evidence that Ginger's case was not a hoax, in exchange for knowing where they were going and what their new names would be. It was always a quid pro quo with Trinity.

Josie left early in the morning and drove straight eastward, fifteen miles over the speed limit, turning a four-hour trip into a three-hour trip. Trinity had given her a cell phone number for Ginger's husband, but Josie was afraid if she called ahead, the man would shut her down before she even had a chance to go to New Jersey. The element of surprise was best. She just hoped that the Blackwells—or the Gilmores as they were now known—were in.

Phillipsburg was just about the quaintest town Josie had ever seen. It reminded her a lot of Denton. Most of its buildings were grouped densely along the Delaware River directly across from Easton, Pennsylvania, but as Josie drove deeper into New Jersey, Phillipsburg's clean, quaint streets gave way to long, rural roads and farmland. It had a distinct country feel to it. The Blackwells had moved to the outskirts. Their large,

two-story Cape Cod with its gray siding and black shutters
lay along a rural road between two farms. Josie estimated a
good quarter-mile between the road and the house, all grass
cut to golf green standards. A long gravel driveway led to the
side of the house where the attached garage sat, its doors like
two eyes tightly shut. The area around the house had been
meticulously landscaped and lovingly decorated. It looked
like the perfect suburban family paradise.

She parked outside of the garage and walked to the front
door, ears tuned to the low, gravelly bark of what sounded like
a large dog coming from inside the house. The storm door
was accented with decorative steel bars. Josie tugged on its
handle but it was locked. The low bark continued from inside,
the sound so powerful she could almost feel its vibration from
where she stood. She rang the doorbell and waited. After a
few minutes, the heavier black door creaked open just wide
enough to reveal the white of an eyeball. "Can I help you?"

Josie pressed her face between the bars of the storm door
and spoke into the pane of glass. "Mrs. . . . uh, Gilmore?"

"She's not here."

"Well, actually I'm looking for Ginger Blackwell."

The eye blinked. The barking, closer now, rose in intensity.
"Who are you?" the woman asked, her tone strident now.

Josie had to shout over the barking. "My name is Josie
Quinn. I'm from Denton."

"Go away."

"I'm a detective with their police department—I mean,
I'm off duty now, but I'm a police officer. I just need to ask
you some questions."

The eye was so wide it looked cartoonish. "I'm calling 911.
I suggest you leave immediately. Do not come back."

The eyeball disappeared, and the inner door slammed shut
with the finality of a coffin closing.

"Wait!" Josie cried. She cupped her hands around her mouth and shouted into the glass. "Mrs. Blackwell, please! Just hear me out. Please. Another girl has gone missing. I need your help."

But she was certain she couldn't be heard over the barking. She waited a few minutes for the noise to die down and tried again, shouting once more into the heavy glass pane of the storm door in the gap between two of the steel bars. The barking began anew. She repeated the process several more times, waiting for a police cruiser to roll into the driveway at any moment. But it didn't.

After the fifth or sixth attempt to get Ginger's attention the door cracked open again. Josie's throat burned from trying to be heard through the doors; her voice was hoarse, her words tumbling out too fast. "Mrs. Blackwe—Please, another girl is missing, I need your help, I—"

The woman's tone was icy. "If you think I'm going to help the Denton police department, you're out of your mind. Go away before I call the police, for real this time."

"I'm on suspension!" Josie blurted in a last-ditch effort to keep the woman at the cracked door.

The eye stared at her warily, waiting as Josie plunged ahead. "Please. Just hear me out. I'm not here in my capacity as a police officer. I'm a private citizen. Some things have come to my attention lately, and I am just trying to figure them out. I—I read about you on the internet. You were abducted before I was a police officer. Trinity Payne—the reporter—she gave me your address. She told me you had changed your name, and she was very clear about the need to protect your privacy. She is the only one who knows I am here. I will never give anyone your address. I promise you, I will not disclose your new name or this place."

The door cracked open another inch and Josie could see the pale, lightly freckled skin of Ginger's cheek. Tiny lines extended from the corner of her eye. "Why were you suspended?" she asked.

Josie swallowed. She felt nervous, the way she had when she had to testify in court the first time. The assistant district attorney had fired off questions at her while the jury stared. She had felt like a bug trapped inside a glass. "It was a noise disturbance. Out by the old textile mill in Denton. You know, by the river, those houses that get flooded every year?"

"I remember," said Ginger.

"I'd been called to investigate a robbery nearby, so I was the closest. Otherwise patrol would have responded. So, I show up there—it's like one in the morning. One of the neighbors says he keeps hearing a kid crying, people fighting, that sort of thing. He knows none of his neighbors has kids. Tells me he has a bad feeling. So, I find the house that's the source of all the noise. It's a bunch of guys, maybe mid-twenties, mid-thirties—partying. They were pretty accommodating when I asked them to keep it down. I said I wanted to have a look around. I get out to the back, you know, near where the riverbank is—a few people from the party were out there—and there's this woman. Obviously a habitual drug user. She's got—she's got her daughter—"

Josie broke off. She still had trouble talking about it. The only way to even get the words out was to remember what the woman's face felt like against her elbow, the loud, satisfying crack of her teeth breaking. "The little girl was four. She was sick. Very sick. Burning up. Screaming and holding her left ear—an infection, they told me later—and her mother was offering her to every man at the party. Offering a 'good time' with her if she could get some drugs, or money for drugs."

"My God."

"I don't know what happened, but I lost it. I snapped. I—I hit her. Elbowed her, actually. She went right down."

A moment of silence stretched out between them. Josie noticed the door had opened further. Now she could see Ginger's face and her auburn hair. It was cut short and brushed forward in a chic, sophisticated look. Her face had thinned from the photos of six years earlier. She looked her age now. Her gaze was penetrating. "The girl?" she asked.

Josie closed her eyes, feeling the same flood of relief she felt that morning when she went to see the little girl in the hospital, and the pediatrician on call told her she was fine. She said, "Nothing more than an ear infection. She's placed with her aunt now, forever hopefully."

The door creaked as Ginger opened it wide enough for Josie to see inside. Beside the woman, its head well above waist level, stood the biggest dog Josie had ever seen. It took several seconds for her brain to process what her eyes were seeing. It stared at her silently with large, mournful brown eyes. Ginger's hand rested on the back of its neck. Even with the door between them, Josie felt a sense of primal fear so intense that her bowels loosened.

"He's a mastiff," Ginger said.

Josie couldn't take her eyes off the beast, and tried to make a joke: "What do you feed him? People?"

Ginger laughed, the sound genuine, and unlocked the door and pushed it open. "He won't hurt you. Come in."

Josie hesitated. The dog didn't move. Ginger's hand left his neck so she could hold the door open with one hand and beckon Josie in with the other. Instinctively, Josie's body backed away. She liked dogs, but the size of this one was intimidating to say the least. Her body screamed for her to get away even as her mind told her there was no threat at all.

Ginger's hand patted her shoulder. "Oh, honey, everyone reacts this way to Marlowe, but I'm telling you, he won't hurt a hair on your head. Unless I tell him to."

# CHAPTER 30

"My memory of that time is so...disjointed," Ginger said. "It's hard to tell what was real and what was just a nightmare. Sometimes I can see why it was so easy for the police to say it was all a hoax."

They sat in Ginger's well-lit living room. The furniture was rustic: stained cedar chairs and a couch with upholstered cushions the color of a blood orange. The floors were all hardwood, polished to a gleeful shine and covered with area rugs. There were potted plants and flowers everywhere. Josie felt like she was in a garden. Ginger's husband was at work, her daughters at school. She listened as Josie recounted what she knew about the Isabelle Coleman case. She didn't go into detail about June murdering Sherri Gosnell. Instead she only said that June had been recently recovered and that Josie believed she may have come into contact with Coleman at some point. She didn't mention the tongue piercing. Ginger listened intently and then promised Josie one hour, but no more than that.

Ginger sat straight-backed in one of the chairs. Marlowe sat beside her, and she absently stroked the back of his head as she spoke. He kept his eyes on Josie, an almost bored expression on his face. Occasionally, Ginger's fingers would knead the area just behind his ears, and he would close his eyes in pure ecstasy.

"I hate to ask you to relive it," Josie said. "Believe me. I'm just trying to figure out what's going on and if there are any connections between your case and the Coleman and Spencer cases."

"Where should I start?" Ginger asked.

"Let's start with what you *do* remember. Like that morning. Take me through your day."

Ginger's eyes drifted to a point over Josie's shoulder, like she was watching the memory play out on a screen behind Josie. "I got up. Had coffee with Ed before he left for work. He always left early, usually before the girls were even up. Our middle daughter had been invited to a sleepover. She hadn't slept out of the house before, and we were trying to decide whether to let her or not. I said yes because I knew the family pretty well, but Ed said no because he never trusts anyone."

At this, Ginger gave a pained smile. The mastiff turned and looked at her, perhaps sensing the change in mood. She gave the dog a sweet smile, and he huffed and turned his gaze back to Josie. Ginger went on, "My husband has good instincts—never trusting anyone with his girls. Anyway, we said we'd talk about it again later. I got the girls up and ready for school. I remember my youngest had buttoned her sweater herself that morning, and we were all exclaiming over what a great job she did. Then my oldest had to point out that she'd started on the wrong button so the whole thing was crooked."

She sighed and let out a small laugh. "Kids. Anyway, I took them to school, came home, straightened up a bit. Then I headed off to the grocery store. I took the long drive to Denton; the store there just has a bigger selection. I was going to make fried cauliflower that night for dinner. The kids love that."

Josie smiled. "It sounds delicious. While you were at the grocery store, did anything unusual happen? Did you notice anyone perhaps following you or lingering too close? Did anyone start a conversation with you—like, a stranger?"

This time, Ginger's eyes floated toward the ceiling. Josie could tell she was cycling through her memory of the trip to the grocery store, examining it anew for anything out of the ordinary. "No, no. Nothing. It was all very...normal."

"In the parking lot?"

"No. I didn't see anyone unusual. No one approached me. I loaded up my bags into the back of the car and drove off."

"And then you got a flat tire on the way home?"

Ginger's eyes sharpened and she peered intently at Josie. "No. I didn't have a flat tire. I know that's what was reported, but that's not what happened. There was a woman stranded on the side of the road."

Forgetting Marlowe for a moment, Josie scooted to the edge of her seat and leaned toward the other woman. "What?"

"Yes, in a black car, and before you ask, I don't know what kind. Honestly, I can't remember. It had four doors. It was black. That's all I remember."

"Okay," Josie said. "You said she was stranded. Her car broke down?"

Marlowe's long, sloppy tongue slid out of his mouth and swiped around his jowls. With a snuffling sound, he inched his front paws forward until he was lying down. He rested his face between them, eyes still on Josie. Ginger folded her hands in her lap. "Yeah. She was by the side of the road. She just had this look about her, you know? Like something was wrong and she couldn't figure out what to do?"

"What was she doing?"

"She was pacing and she kept putting her hand to her forehead. You know, like something was wrong."

"You stopped."

Ginger nodded. Her eyes took on a rueful, faraway look. "Of course. Why wouldn't I? A woman stuck on a rural road? In Bowersville? Did you know Bowersville hasn't had a homicide in fifty-three years? At least, they hadn't when we left."

"Yeah, it's safe." A lot like Denton, though Denton was a lot bigger than Bowersville.

"Anyway, I pulled over. She said her car just died."

"Died?"

"Yeah, I can't remember what else she said but that was it. Her car was dead. She needed a ride."

"Did you offer her one?"

Ginger grimaced. "I don't remember. I don't know. That's where things get . . . foggy, messed up. I'm sure I did. That's what I would do—what I would have done back then."

"It wasn't the woman from the hair salon? The one who came forward later to say she found your car unoccupied?"

Ginger shook her head. "No. I mean, I don't think so."

"Did she tell you her name?"

"I don't remember."

"Was it Ramona, by any chance?"

"I—I'm not sure. I don't think so. I don't remember her telling me her name. It's possible she did, but I really don't remember."

"What did she look like?"

"Like a cancer patient."

Josie couldn't keep the surprise from her face. She had to make a conscious effort to close her mouth. It wasn't the story she had expected.

"She was pale and she had on one of those, you know, turban-like things. Like a headwrap. A scarf. There was no hair sticking out, so I assumed she was sick. One of the girls' teachers at school had cancer; when she was going through chemo, her hair fell out and that's what she wore. This woman, she had sunglasses on. That's what I remember. She was average size, about my height. Maybe a little on the chunky side but some people gain weight during chemo, you know, because sometimes they give chemo patients steroids for nausea, or whatever. Anyway, who knows? Maybe that was just her natural weight. She wasn't huge. Just a little overweight."

"What was she wearing?" Josie asked.

Ginger's hands made a motion like she was pulling a coat on. "She had on a gray sweater. I can't remember what was under it." She laid her hands on her thighs. "And slacks—like polyester slacks, I think. I'm pretty sure. She was older."

"Older?"

"As in elderly. It was hard to tell but I would put her in her mid-seventies to eighty."

"Are you sure?"

Ginger nodded. "Yes. I remember her for sure. It's after that that it gets weird."

Marlowe whined softly. Ginger made a soft whispery sound in her throat and he stopped.

"Weird, in what way?" Josie asked.

Ginger's left hand searched out the fingers of her right hand. One by one, she squeezed the fingertips on her right hand. "Like . . . all I have after that are these . . . I can't—it's so hard to describe. It sounds ridiculous."

"Tell me."

Ginger's hands fanned out, palms up, like she was making an offering. "It's like clips of a video. Like, if you took a movie and you cut out small sections of it and then pieced it back together. Each clip is only a few seconds, sometimes just a flash or an image. Nothing sustained. The problem is that when I put them together, they don't make any sense. There's not enough there."

"Flash cutting," Josie said.

"What's that?"

"It's called flash cutting. In movies. I dated a pretty serious film student in college. What you're describing, it's a form of film editing." Josie could remember the boy vividly. She'd been enamored by his creativity but tired after she'd had to sit through film after boring film, pausing to discuss what clever thing the filmmaker, director or editing team had done and the overall quality of the film.

Ginger smiled at her. A genuine smile. "Really?"

"Yeah," Josie said. "It's a real thing. So, tell me about your flashes. What did you see?"

"It's so hard to piece them together, you know, in order."

"Then don't," Josie told her. "Don't try to put them in order, just talk about them as they come to mind."

Another smile, this one both genuine and full of trepidation. Marlowe lumbered to a standing position, turned in a circle and placed his head in Ginger's lap. She cradled his large, droopy face in her hands. Stroking the sides of his face with her thumbs, she spoke quietly. "I was walking through a wooded area—not walking, being marched. I could see my hands in front of me. They were tied together with plastic zip ties. There was nothing but trees. Not even a real path. Then this rock—it looked like the shadow of a man standing there. Well, not standing so much as leaning against the rock face. I thought it was a real man until we passed it and realized it was just the way the rocks looked from far away."

Something about this sounded familiar to Josie, but there were strange rock formations all over the forests of Alcott County—and beyond. They were like clouds; the more you looked at rocks, the more shapes you could identify.

"Then it ends," Ginger said. "Then I have flashes of men. Not faces, just men. Two- to three-second flashes of feeling hands on my body, seeing them on top of me, feeling them doing things to me. I think I was raped. Well, I know I was. They did a rape kit at the hospital after they found me. There was evidence there—evidence of... other men... more than one. Ed said they also found drugs in my system which would account for how disoriented I felt. That's why Ed and I were so furious when they said the whole thing was a hoax. I guess they thought I just went out and found a bunch of men to sleep with."

Marlowe whined again as Ginger's fingers massaged the fur behind his ears. She looked like she might cry. "Those flashes are dark. All the rest is dark. I have this recurring feeling of waking up, feeling truly awake but being in total darkness, panicking, feeling my way around some kind of box. A black box. It's so hazy though. Like I was drunk, or sick. Tired all the time and achy. Then the next thing I know, I'm lying on the side of the highway, and it was so bright I thought I had gone blind."

"The news reports said you were tied up."

Ginger nodded. "They practically mummified me in duct tape." She motioned toward her chest. "My whole upper body, but left my legs free. That was the other reason we were so angry when they said it was all a hoax. I mean, how could I have done that to *myself?*"

"Who said it was a hoax?"

"It was that district attorney investigator they appointed. There were some jurisdictional issues because I was found in Denton, but on the interstate which was state police territory. Ed talked to everyone involved. They all said there wasn't anything to go on."

Josie's brow furrowed. "But it's a big leap from nothing to go on, to hoax."

"Yes, it is. After several months, the district attorney's

investigator issued a report saying there wasn't enough evidence to suggest that anything criminal had happened at all. Immediately, the press started calling it a hoax. That was a much more interesting story than me being abducted and raped."

She closed her eyes. Josie saw a slight tremble in her lips. "It ruined our lives," she said finally, opening her eyes to let tears spill onto her cheeks. "People we had been friends with our whole entire lives turned on us. Neighbors, friends. We weren't welcome in our church anymore. People called me a whore, a liar. Our girls were teased at school. Ed lost his job. It was just unbelievable. That Trinity—she was the only reporter who believed we were telling the truth. Ed talked to her a lot. She did a piece about why it couldn't possibly be a hoax, but her producers wouldn't air it. People aren't interested in the truth, I guess."

"I'm so sorry," Josie said.

Ginger gave her a wan smile. "Ed talked to a lawyer. He wanted to sue the DA's office for defamation of character or something like that. The attorney said it would be a tough case to prove. Everything that we thought made it obvious that it was not a scam could be explained away. The results of the rape kit? I went out on a three-week bender and slept with a bunch of men. The duct tape? They'd say that Ed helped me do it."

"My God."

"Yeah, we were helpless. Powerless. I think that was worse than anything that happened to me in those three weeks. I don't really know what happened to me, I can't remember. But what happened to us when I was released, it was hands down the worst experience of our lives. We knew we had to move. Then Ed suggested changing our names. A fresh start. That has its issues as well, but all in all I think it was a good decision." She lifted a hand from Marlowe's head and waved it, indicating the room around them. "We're doing pretty well, I think."

"I'm glad," Josie said.

"I doubt any of this is helpful to you, but that's what happened."

"It was helpful," Josie assured her. She looked at her cell phone. "My time is almost up. I'll get out of your life. Let me give you my cell phone number though. If you remember anything else—anything at all—you can call me."

# CHAPTER 31

She lost track of how much time had passed. Her terror was a never-ending cycle of darkness and deprivation. When her stomach clenched from hunger, she couldn't tell if it had been hours or days since she had last eaten. Whether her eyes were open or closed, she saw nothing. Every inch of her small prison had been carefully catalogued; there was no way out. Part of her feared the return of the man, but another part of her longed for an interruption to the utter darkness. To the silence.

She began to fear the light more than the darkness: the chink of the door opening, the slice of his flashlight stabbing through her pupils like shards of glass. When she could pry her eyes open long enough to try to see him, she couldn't focus. He seemed to be everywhere at once, and nowhere at all. The center of a blinding sun. When he finally brought food, she ate it with her eyes closed, shoveling it into her mouth hungrily with both hands, squatting in the corner of the chamber like a wild animal.

All she could depend on was her sense of smell. By the third time he came to her, she could sense him before the door to her cell creaked open. His scent traveled along the dirt floor like a colorless mist, filtering through the cracks, jabbing her awake like the elbow of an unwanted visitor. He smelled of tobacco, detergent, and onions. If she ever got away from him, she would know that smell anywhere.

Sometimes he knelt beside her and stroked her hair. For once, gentle. But she didn't like it. There was something worse about that than the way he had dragged her through the woods or thrown her against the wall. She didn't like the way his breath quickened as he did it.

# CHAPTER 32

Josie's mind worked through the facts as she drove away from Ginger Blackwell's house. So Ginger had been drugged. Josie had taken enough statements from girls at the college in Denton who'd been roofied to know that Ginger Blackwell's abductors had used date rape drugs: Rohypnol, GHB, ketamine. It could have been any one of the most popular ones, or a combination. Any of them would lower inhibitions, sedate, and generally destroy any chance of her remembering what happened. That would certainly account for the flash-cut memories.

She wondered if the woman on the side of the road was involved. She must have been, otherwise she would have come forward after Ginger's disappearance. Although it was difficult to imagine a woman nearing eighty being involved in abducting women. Josie had seen news footage of the salon owner who had found Ginger's abandoned vehicle. She didn't look sick, and she certainly wasn't elderly. So who was Chemo Lady, and was she really sick or was the headscarf just a disguise to inspire sympathy in a passerby? If she wasn't involved, what happened to her and why hadn't she come forward?

Then there was the rock formation. The one that looked like a standing man. Josie vaguely remembered something like this from her childhood but couldn't remember how old she had been or where she had seen it. There was something there, at the edge of her consciousness, but she couldn't reach it. Mentally, she ticked through all the rock formations she and Ray had catalogued during their childhood. They used to use them as markers. *Meet me at Broken Heart.* The one in the woods behind Denton East High School that looked like a heart with one of its humps missing. *I'll be at Turtle at ten.* The one a mile behind Ray's childhood home shaped like a turtle's shell that they used to sit on and get drunk and fool around on in high school. *See you at the Stacks.* That one was used by lots of kids in Denton, in the woods near the old textile mill at the bottom of a rock face where several slabs of rocks had fallen from the side of the mountain, making large stacks of flat rocks. She and Ray had made out there too. She smiled to herself. There were many more, she knew; she just couldn't think of them.

They would be in her photos from high school though. She could look through them when she got home. From the cup holder next to her seat, her cell phone rang. Glancing down quickly she saw a selfie of her and Luke, their faces pressed together, all smiles. She reached down, pressed answer and then speaker, and said, "Hello, darling."

Luke's voice sounded tinny. "Are you in the car?"

"Yeah, what's up?"

"Where are you?"

"I, uh, drove to the craft store," she said.

"The what?"

"The craft store. You told me to take up knitting."

She could picture him shaking his head, that adorable little smile he got on his face that told her he was only half-serious about whatever it was they were talking about. "I said you should look into getting a hobby. I'm not sure you'll be satisfied with knitting. Although, hey, maybe you could do it with your grandmother."

"She crochets."

"What's the difference?"

A green sign to her right indicated the first Denton exit ramp was two miles ahead. She put on her turn signal and got into the right lane. "I'm not sure," she said with a laugh. "Guess I should find out."

"Will I see you tonight?"

"Of course."

"I got that file for you."

Her heart nearly stopped. The car drifted a little too far to the right, and she jerked it back into her lane. "You did?"

"Yeah. I photocopied it and brought it by this morning, but you weren't home. I left it on your kitchen table."

She slowed the car as she came to the exit ramp. At the end of the ramp she stopped for a red traffic light. "You copied it?"

He didn't speak. For a moment, she thought maybe the call had dropped. Then he said, "I didn't want there to be any emails or faxes or scans or anything of it that could lead back to me. I'm really not supposed to be doing this, Josie."

The light changed and she made her turn, heading toward home. "I know, Luke. I am really sorry to have even asked, but it means the world to me that you did this for me."

"Wanna hear something weird?"

"Always."

"There were four troopers who worked on Blackwell's case. You know, before the DA's office stepped in and took over."

"They're all dead!" Josie exclaimed.

Luke laughed. "No, Drama Queen. But they were all transferred within two years of Blackwell's case closing."

"Oh. Is that unusual?"

"Well, they were the only ones transferred. One guy had only just started his tour here. I just thought it was odd. Anyway, it's probably nothing. I've been spending too much time with you and your theories. Look, we never had this conversation, because I never got you the file, okay?"

"Of course," Josie said, pulling into her driveway. "Luke, I really appreciate this. I promise to repay you."

There was a lilt of flirtation in his voice. "Oh really? What kind of repayment are we talking about?"

"Your favorite kind." She hung up.

# CHAPTER 33

At home, she kicked off her shoes in her foyer, reveling in the feeling of her feet being free after so many hours in the car. Her leg still ached and throbbed, and her lower back was stiff from the long drive.

As promised, on her kitchen table was a large manila envelope containing the Ginger Blackwell file. Next to it lay a bundle of pink wildflowers, each one with four rounded petals and tiny yellow flutes at its center. Limestone bittercress. Her grandmother had taught her the actual names of most of the wildflowers that grew in rural Pennsylvania. These started blooming in March and were her favorite. Josie smiled as she picked them up.

She found a vase for the flowers, poured herself a glass of red wine, and sat down at the table. The Ginger Blackwell file was remarkably thin for a case that had garnered so much attention. She sifted through pages' worth of tips that had been faxed from Denton PD to the state police, ranging from vague (a brown-haired lady lurking outside of an elementary school in New York) to the bizarre (a woman claimed to have seen Ginger in a dream before). None were particularly useful, and all of them—at least, the ones that sounded sane enough to check out—had been investigated and dismissed. There were notes about where Ginger had been found and by whom. An Ohio driver passing through Pennsylvania on Route 80 had seen her struggling to stand up on the side of the road and stopped. He called 911 and the state police found her. The notes said she was "bound at the arms with tape."

Josie shuffled the contents of the folder until she found two photographs. One was of the area where she'd been found and the other was of Ginger sitting on a hospital bed. The photo sent a cold shock through Josie. Sure, it had been six years since Ginger Blackwell returned from her ordeal, but the girl in the photo looked like a terrorized shell of the woman Josie had met that morning. Her auburn hair was matted and shot through with dried leaves and small twigs, her skin was pale almost to the point of looking blue. Dull eyes peeked from above hollowed-out cheeks, her expression as vacant as June Spencer's had been.

She was naked from the waist down. Her upper body, from just below her hips to her neck, was wrapped so tightly with tape that the outline of her hands were only just visible as two small bumps.

"No way she did this to herself," Josie mumbled.

Josie paged through the rest of what was there, looking for fingerprint reports—surely they had tried lifting prints from the duct tape—but there was nothing. Ginger's statement was there, but there were no reports from investigators visiting all local oncology units to talk to female patients. Had they not investigated at all? Perhaps those reports hadn't made it into the file, or had been removed once the investigation concluded?

"Seriously?" Josie said to herself as she reached the end of the stack of pages. There were no medical records. She paged through the entire thing again. No log of the rape kit. No log of injuries. No crime lab results from the rape kit. No photos of Ginger's injuries. No photos of the duct tape, or of Ginger after it was removed. The cold fingertips of fear scuttled over her. This went beyond shoddy police work. You didn't omit the results of a rape kit in a sexual assault abduction case.

And then she finally realized what had bothered her from the moment she'd read about the investigation. Why would the police come out and say that Ginger's case was a hoax? Why not just quietly let it go cold without any leads if they wanted the problem to disappear? And what problem was that? What could the medical records or DNA results from the rape kit have revealed to warrant omitting them from the file?

The sound of her front door opening made her jump. Luke's laughter filled the room. He stood in the doorway. "It's me," he said.

She put a hand over her pounding heart. "You scared me."

"I'm sorry."

The last sip of red wine had sloshed over the contents of the Blackwell file. She rushed to the counter and got some paper towels to blot it. Luke watched her with a mildly amused look on his face. "You sure were engrossed in that file. Did you forget I was coming over?"

She got the last drops of moisture off the pages, although not the red stain, and stuffed the pages back into the envelope. "No," she snapped. "I didn't."

He stepped closer and hooked an arm around her waist, pulling her in. He smelled of soap and aftershave. "Did you like the flowers?"

She softened as his lips tickled her neck. "You know I did."

An hour later they were eating dinner in her bed. Luke had ordered fancy takeout from the restaurant that Solange, Dirk Spencer's ex-girlfriend, worked at and brought it with him, complete with plastic forks to go with the white foam takeout containers. She watched him devour more lobster ravioli than she could eat in a week.

"Do you know anyone in the forensic division?" Josie asked, catching him between mouthfuls.

"Where?" he asked. "You mean in the state crime lab?"

"Yeah, didn't you used to be stationed out by Greensburg?"

He nodded, putting his empty container on the nightstand and lying across the foot of the bed, one hand propping his head up while the other stroked her uninjured calf.

"Near there, yeah," he said. "Why?"

"So, do you know anyone in the lab?"

His fingers stopped moving. She looked up over her takeout container long enough to see a shadow cross his face. "What is it?" she asked.

"I might know someone there."

She wiggled her foot and inched her toes toward his chest, tickling his rib cage with her big toe. "Might?"

His hand moved further up to her inner thigh. "Well, I'd have to find out if they're still working there. Not to mention— again—that I shouldn't be pulling files, or strings, for you."

She put her takeout container to one side and stretched her body closer to his roving fingers. "I wouldn't ask unless it was really important."

His mouth followed his fingers with breathy kisses along the insides of her legs. "Is this about that Blackwell file?"

An involuntary moan escaped her lips. "Yeah. I need the uh, report, uh the … results of the …"

As his mouth reached her center, she lost her ability to speak. He lifted his head for a moment, a wicked grin on his face. "If I promise to ask about it, do you promise not to talk about the case for the rest of the night?"

She palmed his head and pushed his face back down. "Yes," she breathed. "Oh God, yes."

# CHAPTER 34

Luke left for work while Josie was still asleep but he had, at least, left some coffee on for her. Leaning against her kitchen counter, sipping it slowly, she noticed that all of the chairs had been pushed beneath the kitchen table. That the stack of mail she'd been riffling through yesterday had been piled neatly on top of the Blackwell file, which had been placed on her closed laptop. Everything in an orderly pyramid right next to the flowers he had brought her, the water topped up.

She knew she should be happy. Ray had driven her crazy with his perpetual messiness, but this irked her in a different way. This was her house. Her sanctuary. Her mess. Luke didn't get it. Sometimes he just didn't get *her*.

With a sigh, she retrieved a large plastic bin from her garage and pulled out an old photo album to see if she could find the rock formation Ginger had mentioned. By evening, nearly every surface in her spotless kitchen was covered with photos of her and Ray. The earliest one had been taken when they were almost ten years old. They were on his porch. Ray's mother had caught them laughing and snapped the picture. That was when Ray's family lived on the other side of the wooded area behind Josie's trailer park. Before his dad left.

They'd spent countless hours together exploring the forest but mostly hiding from their parents and avoiding their homes.

The next flurry of pictures were from high school. The two of them were always pressed against one another, Ray's arm slung across her shoulders and Josie turned toward him, her face looking up toward his. The memory of those years stung now. Never could Josie have imagined that Ray would hurt her like he did.

Josie found a photo of the two of them the day they'd made settlement on their house. Their faces glowed. They looked like two people deeply and wildly in love. They were meant for one another. She choked back tears as she snapped the album shut. That nagging voice in the back of her head asked for the thousandth time if she had been too harsh on Ray. She went over that awful night again in her memory and then the night she'd caught him with Misty. No, she had done the right thing. She might have forgiven his infidelity eventually, but that night with Dusty he had broken the most sacred kind of trust between them, the kind she could never forgive.

With a sigh, she took a second look through the pile of photos she had made of the two of them near the various rock formations in and around Denton, which had been taken by friends. She found every other formation in the city, it seemed, except the Standing Man. Had she imagined it? Why did Ginger's description sound so familiar to her? She tried calling Lisette both to check on her and to find out if she remembered the Standing Man, but the call went right to voicemail. She left a brief, cheery message asking her grandmother to call back.

Luke called just before nine, interrupting her mental catalog of her life and which part of it matched up with which rock formation. "What are you doing tomorrow?"

She laughed. "Gee, I don't know. Let me check my calendar. Oh, that's right, I'm doing nothing. Why? What's up?"

"My contact in the lab? She can meet you tomorrow at one. I figure if you leave around nine, you could get to Greensburg in time. If you feel like making the drive. It's almost four hours."

"I can't talk to her over the phone?" Josie asked.

"No, she wants to meet face to face. That was non-negotiable."

"Oh. Well, okay, I can make the drive. Are you coming with me?"

"I can't. Gotta work. I'll text you the address of the lab. There's a public park a few blocks away from it. You can't miss it. She'll meet you there. I know it's a long drive, but if you want the Blackwell results, this is the only way to get them. I'm already doing way more than I should over this, Josie."

There was no sternness in his voice, just a matter-of-fact reminder that he was bending rules to get her what she was asking for. "I know," she said quickly. "I'll go see her. Thank you. I really appreciate this." From the depths of the mountains of photos and photo albums on her table, she fished a pen. "What's her name?"

"Denise Poole. I'll text you the other information. I have to get back to work. I just picked up an extra shift."

He said the name so quickly, she barely heard it. "Denise Poole?" she confirmed, scribbling the name down.

"Yeah," he said, sounding uncomfortable. "She was my girlfriend. Look, I really have to go."

"You didn't tell me you had a girlfriend when you worked in Greensburg," she blurted.

"So?" he said. "What difference does it make? We broke up years ago. I mean, it's not like we're still married."

"Ouch," she said.

"I'm sorry," he said, without sounding it. "Listen, we'll talk tomorrow, okay? Gotta go."

She stared at the phone after he hung up. That stung. He was right, it wasn't a big deal that he and Denise Poole had dated before; obviously, Josie knew she wasn't his first. But it did bother her that he'd never mentioned her before. She'd talked about hers, but she didn't have much to tell. It was always Ray.

She called Lisette again as she tried to recall how long he'd been stationed in Greensburg for. The call went to voicemail again. Josie left another voicemail in a voice that sounded much too cheery to be believed. She tried again a little later. When she got Lisette's voicemail for the third time, she called the nurse's station.

"She's been really depressed," one of the nurses told Josie. "You know, since Sherri died. She still gets up for meals, but other than that, she's been in bed."

"Oh," Josie puzzled. "I didn't realize she was close to Sherri."

"I don't think she was, actually," the nurse mused. "But for some reason, the whole thing hit her really hard. It hit a lot of us hard."

"I know," Josie said. "Look, something has come up and I can't get over there tomorrow. Please, talk to her though. Tell her to call me."

"Of course."

# CHAPTER 35

The next morning Josie set out for Greensburg. GPS took her right to the park that Denise Poole had specified and Josie parked across the street, stretching her arms over her head before getting out of the car. She walked slowly toward the park, glancing furtively at the text Luke had sent earlier. *She said she'll wear a red scarf,* he had written.

The weather was warmer that day, inching upward of fifty-five degrees, and the park was busy with joggers and mothers pushing strollers and chasing toddlers around the playground area. There were benches on the periphery and Josie spotted Denise quickly. She sat alone, a Kindle in one hand, a cup of coffee in the other and a red knitted scarf tied loosely around her shoulders. She had dark hair, pulled back into an orderly bun, and was considerably bigger than Josie. Not fatter, just larger. A big-boned woman. But she was attractive, in an austere way, and stylishly dressed.

Josie sat beside her. "Miss Poole?"

The woman's eyes flicked from her Kindle to Josie's face with a hesitant smile. Josie noticed her eyes were light brown. "You must be Josie."

She put her coffee down and extended a hand, which Josie shook.

"Thank you for meeting with me," Josie said.

Denise motioned toward Josie's hand. "Nice ring. Luke didn't tell me you were engaged."

Josie stared down at the ring. Perhaps she should have removed it before coming to see Luke's ex-girlfriend. But why should she hide the engagement? Still, it made the moment slightly awkward. "Oh, yeah, thanks."

Denise looked back at her Kindle long enough to power it down. As she did, she muttered, "Enjoy it while it lasts."

"What's that?"

When Denise looked back up at her, her smile was stiff and pained. Her voice was laced with an almost patronizing sympathy. "He didn't tell you, did he?"

Josie said nothing.

"*We* were engaged," Denise said. "Funny that he sent you here to meet me but left that little part out. Listen, you seem really nice, and I know you're not here to discuss Luke, but you should know, he's a serial fiancé. He likes to be engaged. He likes the newness. Then it gets old, he loses interest, and moves on."

Engaged? Luke had called Denise his girlfriend. He'd never said anything about being engaged. Josie cleared her throat. "I'm only here for the Blackwell materials."

Denise reached over and patted her arm. "Of course. Must be important for you to ask Luke to call me."

Josie held her gaze. "I don't know if it's important or not. I haven't seen it yet."

Denise reached into her back pocket and pulled out a folded envelope, which she handed to Josie. "Then why did you need it?"

Josie shrugged. "I might not. If there is something important there, I'll know it when I see it. That's why I asked to see whatever you've got."

"I googled her. Ginger Blackwell."

"Yeah, so did I."

"Why would the police say that Ginger Blackwell's case was a hoax when the rape kit turned up evidence of three different types of semen?"

*Jackpot.* Josie resisted the urge to tear open the envelope in front of Poole. She said, "They believed the sex was consensual."

"Consensual sex with three different men at the same time?"

Josie shrugged. "Well, you know—desperate, lonely women will do just about anything for attention, or so I hear."

Denise frowned. "I guess there are women out there who would do that sort of thing."

Josie thanked her again and stood to leave.

"They weren't run through the state database," Denise said.

Josie said, "What do you mean?"

Standing, Josie could see that Denise was even taller than she had initially thought. Probably approaching six feet. She tried to picture Luke proposing to this woman or even locked in a kiss, but she just couldn't. Or maybe she didn't want to. Why hadn't he told Josie that Denise had been his fiancée? More importantly, why had Denise made Josie drive four hours to meet in person to tell her something she could have told her over the phone and give her test results she could have faxed or mailed? What kind of relationship did they still have that Luke only needed to make one phone call? Josie wasn't the jealous type, but the entire thing with Denise was strange, even by her standards.

"They collected the samples but never checked to see if they matched anyone already in the database. Any database. State or federal. They collected them but did nothing with them."

Josie stared at her.

Denise gave her another smile but it seemed strained, this time with a tinge of nervousness. "Why wouldn't they run them?"

"Because the whole thing was ruled a hoax," Josie said. "No point in wasting the state's resources on a crazy woman, right?"

Still, the fact that the results of the rape kit hadn't been checked against any database was both useful and not surprising. Something definitely wasn't right.

"You don't believe that. You wouldn't be here if you bought into the hoax idea. What's really going on?"

Josie raised a brow. "What?"

Denise crossed her arms over her chest. "You asked Luke to call me about getting these DNA results. He asked me to give these to you even though we could both get fired. Why?"

Josie couldn't answer that question, nor could she deny the feeling of dread building up inside her the more she found out about Ginger Blackwell's case and the shitty investigation following her recovery. Josie's off-the-books investigation was about to get them all into very deep water. She just hoped it would be worth the swim.

Josie sighed and decided to change tack. "There's a teenage girl missing in Denton," she told Denise. "Her name is Isabelle Coleman. I thought there might be a connection to Ginger's case."

Denise's brow crinkled. "Is there?"

"I don't know. I mean, if there is, I haven't found it yet."

"Why didn't you just make the request through your department?"

Josie's cheeks colored. "I—I couldn't."

"Why not?"

"I'm on my chief's shit list, and this"—she waved the

manila envelope in the air—"is a wild-goose chase. I figured if I found something useful I could get back in his good graces, and if I didn't, no harm, no foul."

"I see," Denise said in a tone that implied she didn't see at all. But if Denise had been so worried about Josie's motivations or about getting fired, then she would not have agreed—no, insisted—on this meeting.

"Listen," Josie said. "I really appreciate your helping me out, but I have to get home."

Denise narrowed her eyes. "Sure," she said, gathering her things. "I have to get back to work."

Josie turned and walked away from her. She was halfway to her car when Denise called after her, "Tell Luke I'll see him when I come to get the painting."

Josie stopped in her tracks and turned.

Denise gave her a breezy smile. "He'll know what I mean."

# CHAPTER 36

Driving home, Josie kept replaying the scene in the park in her head. What the hell painting was Denise talking about? Had Luke really made plans to see her again? Was he still harboring feelings for her? Josie dialed his number but it went right to voicemail. "It's me," she said tersely. "I'm on my way home. Ex-fiancée? Really? Pretty asshole move, sending me in there blind. Call me."

That done, she let her mind wander to the discovery that the DNA samples from Ginger Blackwell's rape kit had never been run through any database. Her instincts were right about the Blackwell case, despite what she'd told Denise about there being no reason for police to run them if they thought her case was a hoax. They'd secured the DNA samples the day of Ginger's recovery. They should have been run through the state and federal databases immediately after that. Instead, someone had held on to them long enough for her case to be dismissed, allowing the entire thing to be brushed under the carpet.

Her vehicle emitted a ding, letting her know she was low on gas. She watched the signs on the side of the interstate fly by until she saw a sign for gas at the next exit. Inside the minimarket attached to the gas station, she found the ATM and tried to withdraw money for gas and some coffee. Insufficient funds, it blinked back at her. She tried again. The machine must be broken.

In an empty stall inside the restroom, she pulled up the banking app on her phone to check her actual balance. Her paycheck came by direct deposit every two weeks, and her latest check should have been deposited that morning. But the app agreed with the ATM. No deposit had been made. She had no money. With a growl, she kicked the stall door, rattling it in its frame.

Outside, she dialed Ray's number and, for once, he answered right away. "Jo," he said, his tone telling her instantly that he had been expecting her call. A slow panic started in the pit of her stomach.

"What's going on?" she asked.

"You don't know?"

"I know that my paycheck didn't come in. I'm ... a couple hours away. I stopped for gas and just found out I have no money. What the hell is going on, Ray?"

"Why are you a couple of hours away?"

"Ray."

"The chief put you on unpaid suspension as of this morning."

"What?" she said so loudly it drew looks from other patrons moving in and out of the minimarket. She lowered her voice. "Why? He didn't even tell me. There are procedures. Ray, what the fuck?"

"It's because of what you said to Trinity Payne. About Rockview."

The panic rose to her chest and made her heart skip, giving her too many beats in too short a space. All of her savings had gone into her house, she had been living paycheck to paycheck for months now. She had a couple of credit cards, but how long could she live off them? She couldn't put her utility bills on her cards. "I didn't talk to Trinity Payne about Rockview. What are you talking about?"

"You haven't watched the news in the last twenty-four hours?"

"No, I haven't. What did she say, Ray? What did she say I said?"

He sighed. "I'll send you the link to the news report."

"Just tell me."

"That you confirmed that Spencer killed Sherri Gosnell with a fork and that there was a lot of blood."

Tha-thump went her heart. Tha-tha-tha-tha-thump. "Oh my God. Ray, you have to talk to the chief. I never said those things. Well, I said the thing about the blood, but I never confirmed the thing about the fork. Not explicitly. And none of it was on the record."

"What were you doing talking to Trinity Payne anyway?"

"I wasn't—I mean, not really. She came by my house. She's been harassing me since I got suspended. She wanted to know about Rockview, but Ray, I swear I didn't tell her anything."

"Listen, I can lend you money if you need—"

"I don't need money, Ray," she snapped. "I need my fucking job back. How can he do this? He didn't even tell me. He didn't even give me a chance to defend myself. I'm coming there. I'll be there in two hours."

"Jo, don't."

"He's not getting away with this."

"He told you to keep your head down, and almost the next day Trinity Payne is dropping your name on television."

Her voice was a full-blown shout. "I didn't tell her *anything!*"

Ray's voice was sad. "The damage is done, Jo. Coming here to confront Grizz is only going to make things worse. Two hours? Where the hell are you?"

"None of your damn business. I'll see you soon."

# CHAPTER 37

Her next call was to Trinity Payne, who picked up on the third ring with the words, "Did you talk to Ginger Blackwell?"

Josie could hardly get the words out. "You fucking bitch. How could you?" she spat.

Silence. Which meant she knew she was in the wrong.

Squeezing her cell phone so hard her fingers ached, Josie glared back at the people passing in and out of the minimarket who stopped to stare at her. "I know you heard me. How could you? You know what I said about Rockview was off the record."

"You said there was no record."

"You know damn well what I told you was in confidence. I never even confirmed there was a fork. How could you use that? Do you have any idea what you've done?"

Her tone was breezy. "Oh, please. Like anyone cares. So, I used a line or two from what you told me, and even then it wasn't very interesting. My producer didn't even want to run it."

"My *chief* cares. He put me on suspension without pay. Thanks to you, I can't even put gas in my car."

"I thought you were married."

The anger exploded in a flash of blinding light. For a moment, she couldn't take in any air. "I'm separated," she said through gritted teeth. "I pay my own way, and now I'm broke and jobless because you had to have your story. You are a manipulative, lying bitch, and unless you want me to rearrange those perfect television cheekbones of yours, you better stay the fuck out of my way. And that exclusive I promised you? Over my dead body."

She hung up before Trinity could say another word. Using her credit card, she bought enough gas to get her home. She didn't dare attempt coffee. Besides, her outrage was burning a hole straight through her stomach. She seethed the entire drive home, her hands cramping around the steering wheel as her brain furiously calculated how she was going to pay to live in the weeks to come. She could keep getting gas and food with her credit card, but she couldn't pay her bills. Or her mortgage.

Her beautiful house. Her refuge. She could go without utilities, she decided. She'd take whatever she would normally put toward gas, electric, and water and save her house. After that, she had no idea how she would survive. And no—no way was she asking anyone for money. Her grandmother had nothing to give, and Luke had given her enough already.

She was so consumed with thoughts of how she would make ends meet that she nearly missed her exit. As she pulled into the police department parking lot, she scanned the personal vehicles but didn't see the chief's Jeep. Of course it wasn't there. Ray would have told him she was coming and he knew better than to deal with her head-on.

She stormed inside anyway to find the place like a ghost town. Only Noah Fraley sat at his desk, a few others floating in and out of the common room on the second floor. Ray was nowhere to be seen. The door to the chief's office was closed—silent and impenetrable.

Striding up to Noah's desk, she put her hands on her hips and glared down at him. "Where's the chief?"

He stared back at her, surprised, his cheeks pinking. "He's out with everyone else on the Coleman case. Some lady called and said she thought she saw a blond girl walking down the side of the road out on Old Gilbert."

Josie raised a brow. She knew the road he was talking about. It wasn't far from Denton's Catholic high school. A lot of students used that rural road when they cut school to get to the strip mall a mile or so away.

"When's he due back?"

Noah shrugged. "Don't know. Guess it depends on whether the lead checks out, or not." He waited a long moment to see if she had any more questions. Then he looked at the chief's door as though it were the man himself, the side of his mouth hitched up in a pained expression. "Between you and me, the chief's being a real dick. Listen, if you need help, like with paying bills or whatever, I can lend you money. At least till the chief gets the stick out of his ass and puts you back on the payroll."

Had it been any other person offering to help her, Josie might have been insulted. Even the thought of Ray offering to help her with money made her hands sweat. But coming from Noah, the offer was not at all uncomfortable. She still wasn't going to accept it, of course, but she was grateful for it.

"Thank you."

Noah shrugged as though it was no big deal. "Want me to call you when he gets back? He's been sleeping here most nights. You could probably catch him."

But her rage had dissipated for the moment, placated by Noah's kindness. She didn't have the energy to keep it up until the chief got back. Maybe rage wasn't the best approach anyway. Maybe in the morning she would be more clear-headed, less prone to flip and say something that would get her fired for good. "No," Josie said. "I'll come back tomorrow." *It can wait,* she thought. "But thank you."

Noah's gaze floated back to his computer screen where Josie could see that he'd been logging in phone tips in the Isabelle Coleman case. There weren't many. "Sure thing," he said.

"Hey, Noah."

"Yeah?"

"Did they move June Spencer yet?"

He met her eyes once more. For the first time in the years she had known him, she realized he had tiny flecks of gold in his brown eyes. "No," he said. "Supposedly there's nowhere to move her to. The nearest psych unit is an hour away and they don't have any beds. The chief is trying to find a place for her at a facility in Philadelphia. But she hasn't been arraigned yet. She's down in holding till the DA decides what to do with her."

"I've never known the DA to move this slowly. She killed a woman with a fork, for God's sake! Why haven't they charged her yet?"

Another shrug—one that said "it's not my job to make these decisions"—and he went back to his computer screen.

"Let me know how the Coleman lead turns out," she said as she was leaving.

"No need," he called after her. "If it's her, you'll see it on TV."

# CHAPTER 38

It was nearly dark when she got home. She went straight upstairs without turning on any lights and thought about her water bill as she poured herself a hot bath. The accident at the Stop and Go seemed like it had happened years ago, but it had been less than a week and all the driving still made her back hurt. Before she lowered her aching body into the water, she checked her phone for a call from Lisette. Nothing, and straight to voicemail when she tried again. She'd have to head over to Rockview first thing in the morning.

There were also, noticeably, no calls from Luke. He would have seen her missed call from earlier and heard her angry message. Still, it wasn't unusual for him to be late, especially if he'd caught a difficult case toward the end of his shift.

As she eased back in the water, she let her mind slip between obsessing over Ginger Blackwell's possible connection to June Spencer and Isabelle Coleman, and the fact that the chief had royally screwed her for no good reason. It was all too much. These were the very scenarios that wine was made for, and she wished she had some left. Maybe Luke would bring some with him, as an apology. She could drink it down fast while she railed at him for not disclosing his true relationship with Denise and their secret meeting about some painting.

An hour later she lay in a nest of pillows on top of her bed, wearing only a T-shirt—one of Ray's old college T-shirts that she had taken with her when she left him—perusing the Blackwell file again. She reread the DA's report, which offered nothing other than "no substantial evidence" supporting Ginger's claims that she'd been abducted, unlawfully imprisoned or sexually assaulted. The DA himself had signed off on it. Josie searched for the name of the investigator assigned to review the evidence against Ginger.

"No fucking way," she mumbled to herself. "Jimmy 'Frisk' Lampson?"

James Lampson had been a Denton police officer when Josie was in high school. Back then he'd been on patrol, and kids at the high school had nicknamed him Frisk because he liked to pull over teenage girls, make them get out of their cars and frisk them for no reason. It went on for a couple of years before someone's parents finally complained. He got a slap on the wrist at first, but once Chief Harris took command he was out on his ass looking for a new job. Last she'd heard he was doing private security at the hospital.

Josie hadn't known until she saw his name on the Blackwell report that he'd taken a job with the DA's office. She had no idea how he'd ended up with the cushy investigator job there, but she could guess; his son was good friends with the DA's son—both of whom had played for Denton East's football team and both of whom had had reputations for sleeping with girls, dumping them and starting vicious rumors about them. She had no idea where those guys were now, but their fathers were still handling cases in Alcott County, and badly by the looks of it.

She thought of June still sitting in a holding cell at Denton's police department while the DA decided what to do with her. They were actively violating her due process rights. She should already be in a psych unit. Why was the DA's office dragging its feet? She wondered if Frisk was somehow involved and meddling in June's case the way he likely had with Ginger's and, if so, why?

Her cell phone startled her, sending the pages of Lampson's report flying across her bed. The ringtone sounded like bells chiming. Not Luke. Not Lisette. Not Ray. Someone who didn't call her often. The number was vaguely familiar, and as she answered she heard the tearful voice of Luke's sister.

"Carrieann?" Josie said, her heart in her mouth. There was only one reason that Luke's sister would be calling. She felt a cotton ball lodged in her throat. "Is he alive?" she choked out.

"Luke's been shot," Carrieann sobbed. "He's been . . . shot."

She had an image of Luke lying helpless on the side of the interstate somewhere, bleeding out and unable to call for help.

"Is he *alive?*" she asked again.

There was a sound like Carrieann wiping her nose and then she said, "Barely. He's in surgery now."

"Where? Where is he now?"

"At Geisinger. He lost so much blood. They had to life-flight him there for emergency surgery. Oh God."

That was an hour away. Josie could make it in half that time. "I'll meet you there," she said, and hung up.

# CHAPTER 39

Carrieann Creighton was one of the sturdiest women Josie had ever met: six feet tall and muscular in all the places most women were soft and curvy. She looked like a female version of Luke. They weren't twins. Carrieann was five years older than him and lived three hours away in a county so rural it only had one traffic light. Josie had only met her twice before. They'd gotten along well in spite of Luke's warnings that Carrieann could be tough and standoffish.

Josie found her in the small family waiting room outside the surgery wing, pacing in her faded, torn jeans, muddied steel-toed men's work boots and a denim jacket layered over a flannel shirt that had seen better days. Her blond hair, just starting to show the first strands of gray, was pulled back in a ponytail. Her face was drawn, her eyes red-rimmed. The moment she saw Josie she strode across the room, devouring her in a hard hug. Seeing Carrieann in distress made it more real.

During the ride to the hospital Josie had kept her hysteria at bay by cataloging all the questions she had. She was Josie the police officer, not Josie the police officer's fiancée. It was the only way to keep her foot on the gas, to keep moving forward, to keep her from pulling over and losing it completely on the side of the road.

Before her knees could buckle, she stumbled backward and fell into the nearest chair. Carrieann dropped into the chair beside her and reached over, squeezing Josie's hand in hers. It was odd and somewhat alarming to see her so affectionate, as though they'd been sisters-in-law for years, but she got the feeling it was more to comfort herself than to comfort Josie. Either way, she would take it. This was uncharted territory for her. The only two people Josie had ever truly cared about before Luke were her grandmother and Ray, and neither one of them had ever been in danger. Luke had come into her life like the air she needed when her shitty life threatened to suffocate her. She'd been surviving her suspension in large part because of him. She loved his good humor, his smile, his body—his body that was fighting to stay alive at that moment. She wished she hadn't left that message earlier. It seemed so trivial now. She hoped those words wouldn't be the last ones he ever heard from her.

"What happened?" she asked Carrieann.

Luke's sister looked around the room as though she had just realized they were there, alone among the vinyl upholstered chairs and old, discarded magazines. In one hand rested a balled-up tissue. She squeezed it. "They said he was in the parking lot at the barracks. He had just finished his shift. He was ambushed. Someone shot him twice. In the chest."

Josie closed her eyes. All she could think of was his heart. It was a kill shot. How was he still alive? Tears streamed down her cheeks in hot, salty streaks.

"Oh, hon," Carrieann said huskily as she slung an arm around Josie's shoulders and pulled her into an awkward side hug. "He's strong. He's going to survive this."

But Carrieann didn't believe that any more than Josie did.

It was just something you told yourself while you waited for an outcome that no one had any control over. "What caliber?"

"What?" Carrieann said.

"What caliber were the bullets?"

Most people would never think to ask, but Carrieann and Luke had been shooting targets and hunting game since they were old enough to hold a gun, which was younger than most people were when they first held a gun. "30-30," Carrieann said.

"A hunting round."

Carrieann nodded.

Nearly every household in rural Pennsylvania had a hunting rifle that took 30-30 ammunition. A hunter would know the immense damage the round could do to a human being; depending on the type of round, it could shoot straight through a person or it could fragment inside and destroy everything in its path. Luke was lucky to be alive. For now.

Carrieann said, "They said the shots came from the woods."

"Oh God."

It must have been close to the place they'd hooked up the other day. The barracks was surrounded on three sides by forest. Someone had intentionally hidden in the trees and waited for him to finish his shift. Him? Or any trooper, she wondered. She thought of the manila envelope on her kitchen table. The Ginger Blackwell file with all of its missing information. The other envelope in her car showing that Ginger had been raped, just as she had said. Had Luke been targeted because he'd been nosing around in the matter? It sure felt like it. Or was she reading too much into it again? No. She was sure that she wasn't. He had been picked off in the parking lot at the end of his shift. It was intentional.

Who could have known that he was nosing around in the

Blackwell file? Obviously, Denise had some idea that he'd been looking into it, but she seemed much more interested in him personally. Since he had accessed the physical file, it had to be someone in his barracks. They might not even know he'd passed it on to Josie or that he'd called Denise about the rape kit.

But if someone did know that he'd given it to Josie and that she was looking into the Ginger Blackwell case, was she next?

She looked around. She'd seen two state troopers at the entrance to the hospital and one outside the doors to the surgical wing, but that was it. Usually when a member of law enforcement was shot, their brothers in arms were everywhere. Standing guard. Keeping vigil. "Where is everyone?" she asked.

"Scouring the woods," Carrieann answered. "Trying to find the person who shot Luke."

But they wouldn't find him. Because it was one of them. He would know how to cover his tracks. He was probably out there with them right now, searching for himself. Everyone would be fooled. No one would expect that one of their own would turn on them. Unless the killer had help? Unless it was more than one person? She thought of the DA and Jimmy Lampson and their shady report on the Blackwell case. Then there were the four state troopers who were transferred soon after working on the Blackwell file. So they wouldn't ask questions? So the men responsible for Ginger's abduction would never be called to account for their crimes?

None of the Denton PD officers who had worked on the Blackwell case had been banished, and there were three law enforcement agencies involved in the Blackwell case. The state police, Denton PD, and the district attorney's office. Which meant that if law enforcement was either complicit or involved in Ginger Blackwell's abduction, there was no way of knowing exactly who was involved or how deeply it went.

"Josie?"

"Huh?"

"You okay?" Carrieann asked. "You look really pale."

Josie waved a dismissive hand, her mind running on overdrive. "Fine, I'm fine."

What if Blackwell's case was connected to the Coleman case, as Josie suspected? She thought about Ray repeatedly telling her to leave the Coleman case alone. Was Denton PD involved? What about the chief? Did he know who was behind the missing girls? Was that why he hadn't called in the FBI in the Coleman case? Was that why he had changed Josie's status from paid suspension to unpaid suspension right after she had brought him the lead connecting Coleman to June Spencer?

Carrieann clamped a sweat-damp palm onto Josie's forearm and whispered urgently, interrupting her thoughts. "It's the surgeon."

Josie looked up and, sure enough, a tall, burly man in blue scrubs and matching blue surgical cap was coming through the door. With a grim, fixed expression, he walked toward them. Carrieann's fingers tightened on Josie's arm. Together, they stood to greet him.

"You're here for Luke Creighton?" he asked.

Josie opened her mouth to speak, but her lips were so dry she could barely part them. Carrieann pulled Josie closer to her and spoke for both of them. "Yes," she said. "I'm his sister and this is his fiancée."

The man introduced himself. "I'm the attending trauma surgeon. My team is closing Mr. Creighton up as we speak. He is stable, for now, but there was a lot of internal damage. Two bullets to his chest." He pointed toward his right side, in the area just below the collarbone. "The first one missed his heart, but it fragmented once inside—both bullets did—and caused a lot of damage to the surrounding structures." He pointed lower and more toward the center. "The second bullet lacerated his spleen, so we had to remove it. We were able to remove most of the fragments and stitch up what we could. He is very lucky to be alive. We're going to move him to the ICU and keep him there in a medically induced coma until his body begins to recover from the trauma. I have to warn you though, his injuries are extensive and severe. He—"

"What are his odds?" Josie blurted. She couldn't take any more of the doctor's words. Severe. Trauma. Extensive. Fragmented. It was too much. All she wanted to know were his chances of survival.

The doctor grimaced. "I can't really give you odds."

"Guess. Your best guess. A percentage. Something. Anything. We won't hold you to it. We already know that he is in very bad shape. We knew that the moment he was shot. The only reason he's alive is because of you and your team. We understand that the rest is out of your control. But please. What are his chances?"

He stared at the two of them for a long moment, clearly uncomfortable with the scenario. Then he said, "Fifty-fifty."

# CHAPTER 40

They got to see him for ten minutes each, but no more, and that was about all Josie could take. Luke's large frame was dwarfed by the sheer amount of machinery needed to keep him alive. Tubes and wires seemed to extend from every part of him, IVs snaking from both arms, his hands and the crooks of his elbows. A large tube was jammed into his mouth and taped there. His blue hospital gown was haphazardly thrown across him and, from beneath it, zigzagging across his chest, were wire leads connecting to various machines. Multicolored numbers flashed across the monitors that surrounded them. On his head was a large blue shower cap. He didn't look like Luke at all.

She approached the bed slowly, afraid she might dislodge something important. It was freezing in the room, and she wondered if he was warm enough. But he was always warm. He'd often wake to open one of the windows in her bedroom in the middle of the night, only to have her get up to close it later. "Leave it open," he would whisper sleepily from the bed. "I'll warm you up."

The memory hit her hard like a baseball bat across her shoulders. An involuntary cry escaped her lips. Tears blurred her vision. She took a stumbling step toward the bed and tried to find a place on his arm where her hand would fit. She needed to touch him, to feel his body warm beneath her palm. She needed him to know she was there. The wiry hairs of his forearm were springy beneath her hand. His skin was cool and dry. She squeezed gently. More tears spilled from her eyes as she realized there was no way he could feel her touch. Not with all the artificial life-saving, vital-monitoring equipment attached to him and the remnants of the anesthesia from his surgery. She couldn't even imagine what they were pumping him full of to keep him under.

"Luke," she choked. "I'm here. I'm right here. I'm so—" Her voice broke, and she had to gather herself. "I'm so sorry that this happened. Please don't—please don't—"

She couldn't finish. She wanted to tell him she wasn't angry about Denise Poole and her stupid painting or about the closet door he had bought. She just wanted him to be okay.

But then the nurse was there, softly ushering her out of the room and out of the ICU altogether. The closing of the swinging door behind her sounded like her heart cracking in two. Wiping tears away with the sleeve of her jacket, she found her way to the small waiting room where Carrieann enveloped her in a long hug that crushed the breath out of her. She was glad when it was over.

People around them scrolled on their phones, slept on the chairs, or stared sightlessly at the television mounted in the corner of the room playing a late-night show on mute. Several state troopers stood along the far wall, near the windows. Josie eyed them warily as she found two chairs pushed together where she might be able to curl up on her side and get some sleep. She didn't recognize any of them, although she didn't really know Luke's coworkers.

She used her jacket for a pillow and curled on her right

side. Carrieann sat beside her at first, but after a few minutes she stood up and paced the room. Josie closed her eyes and listened to the rhythmic sound of her boots on the linoleum, until it lulled her to sleep.

She woke to daylight and a vibration beneath her head. Blinking awake, she sat up and spent several seconds trying to extricate her cell phone from her jacket pocket. It still had a charge, but there wasn't much left. She recognized Ginger Blackwell's number immediately, having memorized it because she didn't want to save it as a contact in her phone. Looking around, she didn't see Carrieann anywhere. A new group of state troopers lined the far wall. A new shift. Josie whispered a hello into the phone as she exited the waiting room.

"Miss Quinn?" Ginger's voice held none of the fatigue that Josie's did. She was clear and sharp, her words like spikes in Josie's temples.

"Yes," Josie said. She slinked down the hallway like she'd just stolen something, searching for a ladies' room.

"This is Gin—Are you okay? Can you hear me?"

Josie cleared her throat. She spotted the sign with the tiny stick figure in a dress down the hall and picked up her pace. "I'm fine," she said, trying to sound more alert and awake. "What's going on?"

"I had something to tell you. I remembered something. At least, I think I remember. I had a dream about it. Did you get my file?"

Inside the ladies' room, Josie bent to look beneath the stalls. Miraculously, she was alone, but she didn't know how long that would last. "I did. I have to tell you, Ginger, there's a lot of stuff missing."

"Missing? Like what?"

"Like the rape kit they took at the hospital. They took DNA from that. Do you remember?"

"Of course I do. It was horrible—very ... invasive."

Josie could feel her shudder through the phone. "I'm sorry. Let me ask you—do you know what it showed?"

Silence.

"Ginger?"

A rustling sound. Josie thought she could hear Marlowe whine in the background. "It showed—there was evidence. Corroborating my story."

"So they told you what the results were?"

"They did. One of the officers told us that the analysis of the rape kit showed ... I'm sorry. I can't."

"It's okay," Josie said. "I was just curious whether they told you."

"That's why we were so shocked when they started accusing me of orchestrating the whole thing. A few weeks earlier they had come to us and said the rape kit proved I was telling the truth ... about the men."

"The results weren't in the file, but I did manage to find a copy of them. But I need to know how far this goes. I'd like to see what the medical records say, which I guess we'd have to get from the hospital. If they still exist."

Ginger sounded relieved. "Oh well, my husband has the hospital records. He ordered a copy of them himself when the investigation started. Can I just email you the file?"

"Of course. That would be great." As Josie rattled off her email address, she heard the squeak of the door opening and turned to see a tall state trooper in full uniform walking through the door. He froze when he saw her.

Josie said, "This is the ladies' room."

Ginger said, "What?"

The trooper took a step back so he could study the sign on

the wall outside of the door. He gave her a sheepish smile. "Oh shit," he said. "I'm sorry."

"The men's room is across the hall," Josie told him.

Ginger said, "Miss Quinn? What's going on?"

Into the phone, in the steadiest voice she could manage, Josie said, "I have to go. I'll call you back later." But she could barely hear her own voice over her pounding heart.

# CHAPTER 41

The email came in while she was rooting through the mess of items under her passenger's side seat, trying to find a charger for her phone. By the time her phone chirped, she had found several half-finished water bottles, two dollars and seventeen cents in change—which she pocketed because she needed it—three granola bar wrappers, and a shoelace. She sat back in the seat with a heavy sigh. Closing her eyes momentarily, she rested her head against the seatback. The sun had come up while she was in the restroom and now it flooded through the windows of the vehicle, chasing away the bitter cold that had invaded overnight and leaving behind a perfect, delicious coolness. For just a few seconds she pretended her life was normal again. She was still a detective with the Denton PD. Still on the payroll. Luke was still safe and unharmed. Any minute now he would call to tell her something random and flirty, and they'd agree to get together later that night. Then they'd drink wine and make love, sleep and do it over again.

But thoughts of reality came crashing through the door to her mind, making her feel queasy. Her eyes snapped open and she pulled up Ginger Blackwell's email. There was no message. Only a PDF attachment. Josie downloaded it to her

phone and pressed open when prompted. The records from
Denton Memorial were voluminous. It took several minutes
for the whole of the PDF to load. As she waited, she reached
back down and fished beneath the passenger's side seat. Her
fingers brushed something that felt like paper. Anticipating a
receipt, she pulled it out to look at it and whooped aloud when
she discovered it was a five-dollar bill. At least she wouldn't
be subject to the humiliation of having to ask Carrieann for
money to buy a meal. Although she supposed the hospital
cafeteria would take her credit card.

Finally, the whole document was there. She wished she had
her laptop. Some of the nurses' notes were completely illeg-
ible. She scrolled through slowly and carefully as the sun rose
higher in the sky, infusing more heat into the car until she had
to roll her window down to breathe in the cool air. It was all
there. Ginger's version of events, disjointed though they were,
shortened and abbreviated into clinical medical facts. "Pt
reports memory loss secondary to sexual assault. Pt reports
assault by multiple males. SANE contacted." A SANE was
a sexual assault nurse examiner, specially trained to collect
evidence in a rape case and maintain a chain of custody. It was
all there. Everything had been done by the book.

The police file was incomplete, but all of the evidence was
there if you looked for it. Someone had made it difficult to find
the complete file, but hadn't tampered with the evidence or
destroyed it. So if anyone ever cried foul, all the investigators
involved could say nothing was amiss. No one would lose
their jobs or go to jail over the file because they hadn't done
anything wrong.

She closed the PDF, tossed the phone onto the driver's seat
and spent five more minutes digging before she found her
charger. She was just plugging it in so she could call Ginger
back when she saw a couple of troopers weaving their way

through the parking lot toward the hospital. They weren't acting suspicious or threatening, but she thought of the man who had walked in on her in the ladies' room that morning. Best not to be alone. Pocketing her phone, charger, and the five dollars she found, she headed back toward the hospital.

# CHAPTER 42

Tears leaked from the sides of her eyes as she waited for his touch again, wondering if it was going to be rough, or unbearably gentle. But it didn't come. Instead, the beam of the flashlight floated out of her eyes and to the ground as she heard him settle onto the floor. He stayed there so long that her eyes began to adjust to the dim light in the cell. The roof above them was stone, with tree roots snaking through the cracks. Condensation glistened in one corner. A large, black bug scuttled along one of the branches.

She turned her head. The man's boots were visible a few feet away, his knees pulled to his chest, his big, hairy arms hanging over them. She could just make out the gleam of his eyes fixed on her, sad and uncertain. He didn't know what to do.

Slowly, he crawled across the floor to her. His breath nearly made her gag as she willed her body to be still, and his hands slid around her throat. A wave of hysteria passed over her, her breath quickening. She lifted her arms to fight, but he was too strong.

The words choked in her throat. *Please don't.*

# CHAPTER 43

"I'll be in the cafeteria," Josie whispered to Carrieann as they passed one another in the corridor. It was just before the lunch rush and Josie's stomach growled loudly, clenching at the scent of food. She hoped to God her five dollars would be enough to sustain her.

The cafeteria was starting to fill up with men and women in scrubs and weary-looking family members crowding in and out, so Josie took a table near the back of the large room, her vantage point allowing her to pan the entire place as she ate her plate of fries. No one could sneak up on her. It was also near an outlet where she could charge her phone. Several feet away, a television played the morning news from WYEP. The sound was on but she was too far away to hear it, so she followed the headlines that trawled across the bottom of the screen.

HEROIN OVERDOSES HIT NEW HIGH IN
ALCOTT COUNTY
CORONER CALLED TO 3-VEHICLE CRASH IN
BOWERSVILLE
ROAD GIVES WAY IN COLUMBIA COUNTY

Josie wiped her greasy, salt-tipped fingers and picked up her phone. It was at thirty-eight percent. She tried calling Lisette again but the call went to voicemail. She left another message as worry began to gnaw at her gut. She would have to get over to Rockview at her first opportunity, but it wouldn't be today. She scrolled until she found Ginger's number and hit call. Ginger picked up on the third ring.

"Did you get the email?" she asked, not bothering with pleasantries.

"Yes," Josie said. "Thank you."

"Do you have everything you need?"

Everything she needed. What did she need? What was she going to do with the Blackwell file? Sure, she knew now that Blackwell hadn't staged her own abduction, but that didn't change anything. Knowing that Blackwell was telling the truth didn't bring Josie any closer to finding Isabelle Coleman. What she really needed was to find the Standing Man—and even then she might be no closer to finding Isabelle Coleman. But Ginger couldn't help her with that, so Josie simply said, "Yes, thank you."

Ginger said, "Well, there's just one more thing. You remember I said I had something to tell you?"

On the TV, the words "Top Story" appeared over a photo of Luke's face. It was his police photo, so his face was stoic and serious, his jaw looking more square than it actually was beneath his large trooper's hat with its sturdy chin strap. He looked handsome but so uncomfortable. Her heart skipped again, and she used a grease-stained napkin to pinch in the tears before they came. The screen changed to short video clips of law enforcement converging on the area around Luke's barracks.

"Search for State Police Shooter Continues," read the text. They would never find the perpetrator. She wondered how the faceless contingent of men behind Ginger Blackwell's abduction would keep the press off this. A few years earlier, in a barracks in northeastern Pennsylvania, two state troopers had been ambushed similarly in their barracks' parking lot. The news coverage had been constant and exhaustive and stretched nationwide.

"Josie?"

"Yes," she said, turning her mind back to Ginger. "I'm here. I'm sorry. You said you had something to tell me?"

Ginger said, "There might have been another woman that day. The day I was taken."

"Wait, what?" Josie said, more loudly and forcefully than she had intended. A few people at neighboring tables turned her way and stared. She gave them a sheepish smile and lowered her voice. "Are you sure?"

"I think so. I had a dream last night, after you visited. My therapist said some of my memories might come back in dreams. I always have this dream where I'm talking to the elderly woman, and the next thing I know I'm in blackness. This time, though, there was another woman in the dream."

"This was in your dream?" Josie said. "Not an actual memory?"

"Well yes, a dream, but it's also a memory. Speaking with the elderly woman was the last lucid memory I have before I was taken. I think this dream was a continuation of that memory. Maybe talking to you about it jarred it loose."

"Okay, so the woman in your dream, are you sure it wasn't the owner of the hair salon?"

"I'm certain it wasn't her. It was a different woman."

"So you think there were two," Josie said. "The elderly Chemo Lady you stopped for and the woman from your dream."

"Yes. I believe there were two," Ginger agreed.

"You're sure this woman in your dream was real?"

Silence. Then Ginger made a noise of exasperation. "Well I don't know for sure. Like I said, it *was* a dream. But it felt like a real memory to me."

"You've never had a dream about her before? Or a memory?"

"No, I'm sorry. You don't believe me, do you?"

Josie couldn't stake an investigation on a dream that may or may not be a memory, but she didn't tell Ginger that. Instead she asked, "What can you tell me about the new woman?"

"It's hazy. Very hazy. In my dream she was in her fifties. Short hair. Brown going gray. I can't... I can't see what she was wearing. Her face is... you have to understand, the memories are distorted. But I think she said her name was Ramona."

"Are you sure?"

There was a brief silence. "Well no, I'm not. I mean, the name Ramona has been swirling around in my head ever since you said it. But what makes me think maybe that was really her name, and that I was having a real memory, is that in the dream I talked to her and I said I never met anyone whose name was Ramona in real life. Then I started telling her about this series of books I read when I was a little girl. I loved those books, and the main character was named Ramona. I remember telling her how I tried to get my kids to read them but they had no interest. Too dated, maybe. She just kept smiling and nodding and I thought, she probably doesn't care. That part seemed so concrete, made it feel real."

Josie felt a prickle at the back of her neck. She got up from her table and, cradling the cell phone against her ear with her shoulder, gathered up her lunch tray and disposed of it. She kept her voice low as she made her way out to the elevators. She waited for an empty one and slipped inside, pressing the button that would take her back to the ICU. "But you said yourself that you'd been thinking about the name since you spoke with me. Then hearing it in a dream...the power of suggestion, maybe?"

"I suppose so, but I really think it was a memory. I really think she was there and that she called herself Ramona."

"Maybe she lured you, then. That doesn't account for what happened to the first woman—the sick one—but this Ramona would have been one of the last people to see you," Josie said, almost to herself. "In your...flashes, do you remember seeing her again or seeing any other women?"

There was a long silence and another sigh, then Ginger said, "No, I'm sorry. I don't. I remember blathering on about the name Ramona, and that's when I woke up."

"If this woman was real, do you think you'd recognize her if you saw her again? If you saw a photo?"

"I don't know. It's possible."

"In this dream, did Chemo Lady leave while you were talking to Ramona?"

"I'm sorry, I don't know. I can't remember."

"Did they have a conversation?"

"I think so, but I can't remember the particulars. I'm sorry. The whole thing was still quite hazy but I'm certain now there was another woman."

She'd stopped to help a sick woman and had then been approached by a woman calling herself Ramona. She had been abducted, drugged and assaulted. Held for three weeks until the pressure of the national press coverage became too great and her captors chose to dump her. Alive. Again, Josie was struck by the care these people took to avoid committing some crimes while actively committing others. It was like the evidence in Ginger's file, which had been scattered but not destroyed. Ginger had been abducted and assaulted but not killed. Instead of killing her, they'd dumped her and then took care to discredit her story. Why?

Because it was easier to discredit a stay-at-home mother of three than it was to beat a murder rap.

Still, they had taken a big chance in allowing Ginger to live and go free. Whoever they were.

"I'm sorry. You probably think I'm being ridiculous. Calling you about a dream," Ginger said.

The elevator lurched to a stop and the doors opened. Josie took her time walking down the hall, not wanting to finish the conversation in the ICU waiting room where many of the state troopers had gathered. "You're not being ridiculous," Josie assured her. "I want to hear anything you can remember, even if it came in a dream. Thank you."

"You'll keep me posted?"

"Of cour—" Josie faltered as a passing woman bumped shoulders with her, sending her phone flying and muttering a sorry as she hurried on. Josie retrieved her phone, her eyes locked on the diminishing figure. She wore scrubs like all the staff, with a faded black hoodie on top. There was something familiar about her, but Josie couldn't place her. Her hair was short: dirty blond with dark roots, and spiked. Josie could have sworn she'd seen tattoos peeking out from the collar of her top, but she had passed so quickly. There was something off about her though. Josie pressed the phone back to her ear. "Ginger, you there? Sorry, I dropped my phone. If you remember anything else then…"

"I'll call."

"Great."

They hung up and Josie stared after the woman. Then it came to her: she was wearing boots. Old, beat-up combat boots. The nurses in the hospital all wore either sneakers or those rubberized clogs. No one working an eight- or twelve-hour shift would wear combat boots, no matter how worn in they were. Josie took off in a dead run after her.

# CHAPTER 44

The woman turned her head at the sound of pounding feet and Josie saw the glint of a nose ring. When she saw Josie bearing down on her she set off in a sprint.

"Wait!" Josie hollered.

The woman zigzagged down the hallway, trying every door, looking for escape. Finally, she disappeared behind one. Josie caught up and pushed through the door to find stairs and the sound of the woman's feet pounding downwards. She raced after her, jumping down three steps at a time. Two floors down she caught up, snagging a handful of the woman's black hoodie and pulling hard. Within a few seconds she had the woman's cheek pressed into the wall, her arms behind her back, legs spread wide. Josie held her there. "Keep still," she said breathlessly.

"Let me go," the woman spat. "I don't even know you. Why are you harassing me? This is assault. I'll call the police."

"I am the police."

The moment the words were out of Josie's mouth her captive started struggling like her life depended on it. Josie held tight, bucking like she was on a mechanical bull in a dive bar.

"I know who you are," Josie bellowed into her ear. "Lara Spencer. Now stop. I need to talk to you."

Dirk Spencer's sister didn't give an inch. "I got nothing to say to you, bitch."

"I can help you," Josie said.

When Lara continued to resist, furiously, Josie said, "I know you're in trouble. I know June is in trouble. I want to help. I'm not really with the police. I'm on suspension. I'm trying to figure out what's going on and I need your help."

She stilled, but Josie could feel every muscle in her tensed. The moment Josie let go, she would bolt.

"I think I'm in danger too. My fiancé tried to help me find out why women are going missing around Denton, and he got shot for it. He's in the ICU, same as your brother. I think I'm next. Please."

Lara's muscles relaxed slightly. "Have you . . . have you seen June?"

"I saw them both, Lara. The car Dirk was in almost ran me over when it crashed. I was the last one to talk to him before he went into a coma. I saw June right after she killed that woman in the nursing home. I need to talk to you. I won't tell anyone you're here, or that you're you."

She relaxed a little more, and Josie slowly loosened her grip until she had released Lara completely, staying close though in case she made a run for it. Lara turned and straightened her clothes. Up close, Josie could see how thin she really was, a different woman from the one in the photo of her, June and Dirk that Josie had found on Dirk's fridge. The scrubs and hoodie hung on her. Her cheeks looked sunken in. Tattoos climbed up her neck almost to her chin. She said, "No one knows who I am anyway. I got fake ID."

"Oh. Well that's good, then."

Lara looked Josie up and down, assessing. "You got any money? I sure am hungry."

"Actually, I don't. I just spent my last five dollars in the cafeteria."

"You got any credit cards? They take those."

She hadn't wanted to use her card for a meal that only cost a few dollars, but then she remembered the baskets and shelves in front of each food station. She should probably get some snacks for later. She could leave them in her car. "Okay," she told Lara. "Let's go."

The cafeteria was now packed and Josie was grateful. No one paid them any mind at all as Lara greedily loaded up a tray with food: cheeseburger and fries, taco bowl, chef salad, yogurt and three bottles of iced tea. Josie bit back a protest as the cashier rang it all up and she reluctantly handed over her credit card.

Lara ate hungrily, her hood pulled low over her head, shoving food into her mouth like she was in some kind of eating contest.

"Put your hood back down," Josie hissed. "Having it up draws attention. When's the last time you ate?"

Hastily, Lara pushed her hoodie down and kept on shoveling food into her mouth. "Few days ago," she said around a mouthful of food.

Josie waited for Lara to slow down, surprised by how much the skinny woman could put away. Her eyes drifted back to the television on the wall. More news. It would go on for a few hours, refreshing every half hour until the afternoon when the daytime soap operas came on.

"How's Dirk?" she asked.

Lara shrugged. "He's shot up. Got a big tube down his throat. Machine breathes for him. How do you think?"

"I'm sorry."

Another shrug, as if to say, "Whatever."

If June had been anything like her mother, Josie could see why Solange had found her to be such a challenge. "Lara," she said. "What was Dirk doing in an SUV full of gang members from Philadelphia?"

"How do you know they were gang members?"

"Tattoos."

"Oh. I don't know."

"Lara. Be straight with me. This is serious. Your brother is fighting for his life."

Lara looked up at Josie, eyes flashing. "You think I don't know that? He's all I got. Him and June." She tapped a finger against her temple. "And I heard June ain't really there no more."

"Then tell me the truth so I can help you."

Lara gave her another appraising glance and her pinched expression told Josie that she didn't like what she saw. "What are *you* going to do?"

"I'm not sure yet. First, I need to know what I'm dealing with. Tell me what you know."

Lara twisted the cap off one of her iced teas and gulped down half the bottle. Wiping her mouth with the back of her hoodie sleeve, she narrowed her eyes. "I need cigarettes."

"You can't get cigarettes in a hospital."

"No, but you can get them down the road with that credit card."

"I'm not buying you cigarettes, Lara."

She chugged down the rest of the iced tea and went to work on the taco bowl, now eating with a prim slowness that made Josie want to scream. She could see why Dirk had fought so hard to get June out of her sphere of control. Josie waited patiently until she had finished and gulped down another half bottle of iced tea. She watched the WYEP coverage of Luke's shooting play again, followed by a story about Sherri Gosnell. The headline read: "Local Murder Victim Laid to Rest." The screen cut to the outside of the large Episcopal church on Denton's west side where people gathered in knots. Six men emerged from its red double doors, faces drawn, wearing suits and carrying Sherri's coffin. Next the screen cut to the graveside service, zooming in on the man Josie assumed was Sherri's husband, Nick Gosnell. He was barrel-chested and slightly overweight. Average height, with light-brown hair peppered with gray and parted down the middle. His goatee was also graying. From what she could see, one of his eyes was swollen and badly bruised, as though someone had given him a black eye. Had he gotten into a fight? Gotten drunk, fallen and hit his face? People did crazy things when they were grieving. Remembering the sight of Sherri's body, Josie was betting he'd gotten drunk and fallen down. His good eye brimmed with tears as he watched his wife being lowered into the ground. Josie felt a wave of sadness engulf her and pushed it away. She needed to focus.

She turned back to Lara. "Six years ago, a woman named Ginger Blackwell was abducted, held for three weeks, and raped by multiple assailants. She was drugged and dumped on the side of the road. The police made a half-assed attempt at investigating the whole thing before they declared it a hoax. I've looked at the file; it wasn't a hoax. Ginger didn't do it to herself. Today I talked to her and she told me that the last thing she remembers before being taken is talking to one, possibly two women on the side of the road. One was a woman whose car broke down. She looked like a chemo patient. She thinks there was another woman there as well, a younger woman who said her name was Ramona."

Lara sat back in her seat, folding her arms across her thin chest. The corners of her mouth turned down in a skeptical frown.

"Do you know what the last thing Dirk said to me was? When he was bleeding out in that SUV crashed into the side of a building?"

Lara didn't move, but Josie caught a flicker of interest in her eyes.

"He said one word: Ramona."

Lara said nothing.

"And your daughter? After she killed that nurse, she wrote something on the wall in blood. Do you know what she wrote?"

Lara's face darkened, her shoulders jerking just a fraction. This had not been released to the press, so Josie was sure that it was the first time June's mother was hearing about what actually happened at the crime scene. Still, she didn't ask. She merely stared at Josie.

"Ramona."

"So?" Lara said finally.

"Who is Ramona?"

"I don't know. I don't know no Ramona."

"Dirk and June know a Ramona, obviously. Ginger Blackwell believes that she met a Ramona before she was kidnapped."

Lara reached out and untwisted the cap on her final iced tea, but didn't open it. "I don't know who Ramona is, and I don't know why they know her name. Dirk didn't tell me everything. Said it was for my own good."

"What do you mean?"

She clammed up again, hugging herself and looking down at the table. "I already said too much. I'm done."

"Lara."

A piece of lettuce from the remains of her taco bowl suddenly distracted Lara. Thin fingers reached out and picked up her fork, using it to pick at the lettuce.

"Did June have a pink tongue barbell that said 'Princess'?"

Lara continued to push the lettuce around on her tray, but she shook her head slowly back and forth. "No," she mumbled. Then she made a huffing sound. "June wouldn't be caught dead wearing something pink, much less something that said 'Princess'."

"There's a girl missing right now," Josie said. "Her name is Isabelle Coleman."

As though her words had conjured Isabelle Coleman, the teenager's face flashed across the television screen above Lara's head. It was one of the many Facebook photos they'd pulled from her page. In this one she stood on the sidelines of Denton East's football field. It was night, but the stadium lighting lit the field. In the background glowed the scoreboard, showing Denton up by seven points. Isabelle wore a light-green jacket and smiled brightly, almost as if someone had caught her in mid-laugh. She was breathtaking. Beneath her photo the words read: "Search for Missing PA Girl in Second Week." The camera cut to a reporter standing beside a large video screen with Isabelle's photo on it. But it wasn't Trinity Payne. It was a man. A very familiar man.

"So what?" Lara said.

For a moment, Josie couldn't figure out what was going on. Where was Trinity Payne? Why was this world-renowned news anchor reporting for WYEP? Why would WYEP call Isabelle a "missing PA girl" when the entire viewing audience already knew exactly what state they were in?

Without taking her eyes from the screen, Josie said, "So I think that the Coleman case might be related to the Blackwell case, and as of my conversation with Ginger Blackwell this morning, I also think it's related to June."

But the man on the television screen wasn't reporting for WYEP. He was the news anchor for the national network morning show. That's why he was so familiar. WYEP was just an affiliate. In fact, the WYEP newscast had ended. Now the network morning show was playing. Trinity Payne had done it. She'd gotten the Coleman case national coverage.

"I told you I don't know no Ramona," Lara said.

"Yes, but you know something. You might not know that

you do, but you know something. I need to know why your brother was in that car. After he was brought here no one could find you. You've obviously been hiding. Why? What did he tell you? What was he planning to do?"

The anchor stopped talking and the screen cut to a montage of images and short videos: Isabelle in various photos, vehicles crowded around the Coleman home, searchers picking through woods around Denton.

With a sigh of resignation, Lara said, "I don't know what he was planning to do, that's the thing. He didn't tell me anything. He said that he couldn't tell me anything because it was too dangerous."

"What was too dangerous?"

Lara tossed her fork back onto the tray. "He didn't think June ran away. He was obsessed over it. She ran away from me before, but whatever. He thought something was wrong. I told him to do what he needed to do, but I just figured, you know, one day she'd show up. Anyway, one weekend he comes down to see me, and he says he thinks he knows where she is and what happened to her, but he wouldn't tell me. All he would say was it was a very dangerous situation. He thought he needed help."

"Like the kind a gang can offer?"

"Dirk went to school with this Hispanic kid—Esteban Aguilar. He's in charge of this gang now around my neighborhood. I didn't even know Dirk still talked to the guy or knew where to find him. I told him don't mess with no gangs. It's not a good idea. I said, call the police. Just call the police. He said he couldn't. So he goes to see Esteban. I don't know what they talked about. I just know that a few weeks later he calls me up and tells me that Esteban is going to send some guys to help him get June."

Another set of words appeared at the bottom of the

television screen, beneath another photo of Isabelle grinning: "New Cell Phone Footage from the Day of Abduction Released." Next came a video of Isabelle and another teenage girl in what looked like a bedroom. Josie recognized the other teen as Isabelle's best friend. She'd talked on camera to Trinity many times since Isabelle's abduction. Josie knew that the girl had stayed overnight at Isabelle's house the night before Isabelle went missing. She'd left that morning while Isabelle's parents were still home. The camera was tight on the girls' faces, blocking out much of the background. They were giggling and talking and making faces at the camera.

"I said, get her from where," Lara went on. "He said he couldn't tell me. He said he couldn't tell me anything. He just said that I would know if something went wrong because it would be on the news. He said if something went wrong, I should hide, and then he said 'under no circumstances' was I to call the police. He said the police were crooked."

Josie was listening to Lara's words, but she couldn't tear her eyes from the television screen. In the video, as she mugged for the camera, Isabelle made a face like she smelled something rotten. She lifted her hand to wave it back and forth in front of her nose. Her nails were long—acrylic nails like the kind you got in a nail salon. They were pink with yellow stripes. Suddenly Josie couldn't breathe.

Lara said, "He said the police were mixed up in it."

# CHAPTER 45

The stall door clanged open and Josie rushed toward the toilet, falling to her knees and vomiting up everything that her precious five dollars had bought her. Her body rebelled against her. Once everything was up, she dry-heaved until her abdomen contracted painfully. A woman who had been in the restroom two stalls over stood anxiously behind her. Josie could see her white sneakers beneath her dark blue scrubs.

"Honey, are you okay?" she asked.

Josie had no idea where Lara had gone; hopefully she was still at the table. She nodded her forehead against the toilet seat. "Something I ate," she breathed. "I'm fine."

The woman's feet left and returned again, closer this time. A paper towel appeared next to Josie's face. "Take this."

Josie thanked her and stumbled to her feet. The woman was young and blond and smiling sympathetically at Josie. Maybe it was the blond hair or her perfect skin, but she fleetingly reminded Josie of Misty.

"I'm sorry," she told the nurse. "I'm going to be sick again."

She turned back toward the toilet, leaning over it while her body convulsed, wishing she was alone to process what she had just seen and heard.

Ray. The man she had known and loved her entire life. He had lied about the acrylic nail. Why? There was no way he was involved in Isabelle Coleman's abduction, but was he covering for someone? Dusty? The chief? Were they all covering for someone, or multiple someones? How far did it go? Her head spun.

The nurse laid a palm on Josie's back, between her shoulder blades. "Do you need me to call someone, hon?"

*The FBI,* Josie thought.

"No, no," she told the nurse. "I'm fine, really."

She straightened, turned and headed for the sink where she splashed water on her face. In the mirror she could see the nurse hovering, still looking concerned. Josie forced a tight smile. "Really, I'm okay now. You don't have to stay with me."

The nurse pulled a cell phone from one of her scrubs pockets and looked at the display. "I really have to get back to work," she said.

"Go ahead," Josie told her. "I just need a few moments to compose myself. I'm fine now. Thank you."

With one last anxious glance in Josie's direction, she left the restroom. Josie splashed cold water on her face a few more times, rinsed her mouth with water from the faucet, and smoothed her hair down. The door swung open and Josie tensed, watching the mirror. But it was just Lara.

"What the hell was that?" she asked. She held out the granola and protein bars that Josie had bought with her credit card. "You sick or something?"

Josie took the bars from her and stuffed them into her jacket pockets. "Or something," she said ruefully. "Listen, do you have somewhere safe you can go, for today? Can you stay out of sight?"

Lara leaned against the sink next to Josie, her fingers fidgeting with the zipper on her hoodie. "Sure," she said. "What are you going to do now?"

Josie tore a paper towel from the dispenser beside the sinks and dried her hands. "I'm going to talk to my husband."

# CHAPTER 46

She found an area outside near the entrance, but far enough away from it that no one would overhear her. Immediately after Luke's shooting, the press had descended on the hospital, hungry for news of his condition, but now only two news vans sat across from the hospital's entrance, their occupants nowhere to be found.

Pacing back and forth, she dialed Ray. The call went to voicemail and she hung up without leaving a message. From the other side of the entrance, Lara stared at her. Josie had no idea where she'd found a cigarette, but she lifted one to her lips and inhaled. Josie waited three long, torturous minutes and dialed again. This time, he picked up on the fourth ring.

"Jo?"

The moment she heard his voice—so familiar, a voice that had been a source of comfort to her since she was nine years old—a sob rose in the back of her throat. She tried to keep it down, but her voice cracked when she said his name.

Ray's voice was filled with concern and a tinge of urgency. "Jo?" he said again. "Are you okay? What's going on? Where are you?"

She took in a long, shuddering breath. "I'm with Luke,"

she said, her voice shaking. "But I guess you know that, don't you?"

He completely missed the accusatory note in her voice. "I'm sorry, Jo," he said. "I saw it on the news. How is he?"

So he was going to act stupid, normal, like he hadn't lied to her face. "He's clinging to his life, you asshole."

He sounded genuinely confused. "What?"

"You and your...cronies know exactly how he's doing. Tell me, Ray. Did the shooter mean to kill him or just to wound him? Who did you send? Because whoever it was—they're not a very good shot."

His tone got slightly colder. It had none of the indignation she would have expected had he known nothing at all about who was behind Luke's shooting. "I don't know what you're talking about, Josie."

He never called her Josie.

"How many of you are involved, Ray?" she asked. "How far does this go?"

"I don't know what you're talking about."

"Who is Ramona?"

There was a beat of silence followed by a long sigh. "There is no Ramona."

"I know that's not her real name. Who is she?"

"I wish you would stop with this," he said. "I'm getting concerned about you. You're starting to sound crazy, Jo. You're not handling this suspension very well. Making up people with fake names, harassing the department when we're in the middle of an investigation. Even that stunt you pulled with Misty the other night. What did you say to her?"

"What?"

"She won't talk to me now. Won't take my calls. I don't know what happened, what I did. The only thing I can think of is that you said something to her, and after she had time to think about it, she decided she was finished with me. What did you say to her?"

"Don't change the subject, Ray. Do you think I give a shit about your stripper girlfriend right now? Didn't you hear me? Luke is fighting for his life. What have you gotten us into, Ray?"

"I—I don't know what you're talking about," he stammered.

He had an official party line, and he was sticking to it. She changed the subject. "Where's the Standing Man, Ray?"

His sharp intake of breath told her she'd hit on something important. When he spoke again, there was naked fear in his voice. "Josie," he said. "This is very important. You need to walk away from this. Leave it alone. All of it. I'm begging you."

She'd hit the right nerve. It was time to keep pushing.

"Why did you lie to me about the acrylic nail? I know it was Isabelle Coleman's. She's wearing the nails in the video her friend took of the two of them on the day she went missing."

"Listen to me, please. You need to stop this right now. Do you understand? I can't protect you."

"Protect me from what?"

His voice was barely audible. "Them."

"Who, Ray? How far does this go?"

"Far. Very, very far. You have no idea. I am begging you, Jo. As my wife. Please walk away."

His words were like barbs in her heart. Her voice cracked again. "How much do you know?"

"Enough."

"You know I can't walk away, Ray. I'm not built that way."

He whispered, "They'll kill you, Josie.

"Then I have to stop them. Where's Isabelle, Ray?"

"I don't know."

"Ray."

"I'm serious. I don't know."

"Did you know? When she went missing?"

"Not at first. I suspected that...that they were involved. No one said anything outright. Everyone kept looking for her. Then the searchers found her phone in the woods—I think it was purposely missed by our guys. I think...I think maybe someone was supposed to get rid of it, but they didn't do it in time. The chief started calling it an abduction. I think he knew where she was. I think a lot of them did."

"Where, Ray?"

"I can't tell you that, Jo. You're in too much danger as it is. I don't even know for sure."

"But you think they are behind her abduction."

He didn't speak, but she could hear him breathing.

"Ray."

"I don't know. I—I think they could be."

"Do they have her now?"

"No."

"Where is she?"

"I don't *know*," Ray said. "And I don't think any of them do either."

# CHAPTER 47

For a few seconds, Josie felt like she was suffocating. Searching around, she sat on the nearest bench, closed her eyes, and concentrated on her breathing. Something had been niggling at the back of her mind after Ray's reaction to her mention of the Standing Man. He knew where it was, obviously, though she had no memory of it from her shared time with Ray. But she knew she had seen it before, which meant she had to go back before Ray. She skipped over the horrors of her time with her mother, going back further to her time with her father. Her tiny hand in his as he led her away from a white house and into the woods to look for cardinal flowers. They were wildflowers that grew on long, weedy stalks, with red petals that looked like fingers and a stigma like a tiny periscope shooting out of the center. Josie loved them, almost as much as she had loved hunting for them with her father in the woods. There was only one place they'd ever found them.

She opened her eyes, took in a deep breath, and dialed Lisette again. Voicemail. Again, she dialed the front desk at Rockview. Again, a nurse told her Lisette was taking a nap.

"I've been calling for a couple of days now," Josie said. "She hasn't called me back. I'm getting concerned."

There was a beat of heavy silence. Then, "Well, hon, like I told you before, she has been pretty down since the business with Sherri, and without her here, Alton has been on a rampage, harassing the ladies like nobody's business. Nobody wants to come out of their rooms. Sherri was the only one who could keep him in check. It's like a funeral home around here. We're all traumatized, to tell you the truth. I mean, the way she was killed . . ."

Come to think of it, it was just like Lisette to take Sherri's untimely death to heart. Josie remembered the way Lisette had reacted to the newscast on Isabelle Coleman's abduction. "She's probably thinking of poor Sherri's mother," Josie mumbled.

"Oh well, Sherri's mom passed on a few years ago," said the receptionist.

"Did she?"

"Yep. Cancer got her. She was quite old though. Had some dementia too."

"Really?" Josie said.

"Yep. Do you want me to wake your grandmother up, hon?"

Something was emerging in Josie's mind, like a fogbank clearing. "No, no thanks. I needed to ask her something, but I just remembered what it was I needed to know. I'll stop by to visit her as soon as I can."

She hung up and used her phone to log in to the Alcott County Office of Property Assessment website. It took a few minutes to search the database, but she found what she was looking for. She was closing the browser when her phone rang. It was Ray. She sent it to voicemail. He called back immediately. Again, she sent his call to voicemail. She stood on shaky legs and sat back down immediately. She didn't know if the dizziness was from shock and anxiety or dehydration and sleep deprivation. Maybe all of those things.

Her phone chirped with a text from Ray. *Don't shut me out. Please.*

She turned her phone to silent, dropped it in her jacket pocket, and closed her eyes again. Even in the darkness behind her eyelids, the entire world seemed to spin. It was all too much. Luke near death, Ray a liar and now . . . a criminal? Because that's what he was now. She had no idea just how much he knew, but he knew enough to implicate himself in something big. Something horrific. If he was sitting on even the slightest suspicion of where Isabelle Coleman was being held, he was every bit as guilty as whoever was keeping her. The thought made her sick to her stomach.

She wondered if he expected her to lie for him, because she was his wife or because she was a cop? Or both? How could he? Ray had always been good and decent, honest and loyal. It was those qualities that made him a good cop. What happened to him? How had she missed it? Maybe she hadn't been paying attention at all during their marriage.

He had said that he suspected early on that "they" were involved in Coleman's disappearance, which meant he had reason to believe that his colleagues were involved in something bad before Coleman even went missing. How long had he known? Had he known about June Spencer all along? They had worked together side by side for five years. What had Josie missed? Or had he been privy to things she wasn't because he was a man? The good old boys' club. She searched her memory banks for a moment in their marriage when he started to act differently, but she couldn't think of anything. Their jobs could be stressful; sometimes you would catch a call or a case that left you on edge for weeks.

Nausea clenched her stomach again, but there was simply nothing left for her to expel. How had things spiraled this far? Three weeks earlier she had been a respected police detective in Denton, a town she loved, with a beautiful new house, and an exciting new relationship. Now she was suspended, broke, and quite possibly in mortal danger. Her soon-to-be ex-husband—her high school sweetheart—was a criminal, and her fiancé was barely alive, his insides shredded, and an innocent teenage girl was still missing. How did things get so bad, so fast?

Her eyes snapped open.

"June," she said aloud.

She pulled her phone back out and scrolled through her contacts until she found Noah Fraley's cell phone number. As she listened to the phone ring, she wondered if he too was involved. Sweet, shy, bumbling Noah? But yesterday she couldn't imagine Ray being involved either. She could trust no one.

"Fraley," Noah said after the sixth ring.

"Noah, it's me."

His voice dropped to a near whisper. "Hey, Josie. I'm really sorry about Luke. How . . . how is he?"

Her heart skipped and sped up again. She hadn't expected this. He sounded genuine, but she couldn't trust Noah any more than she could trust a stranger.

"He's in a medically induced coma," she said stiffly. "It doesn't look good."

"I'm really sorry. How're you holding up?"

Damn him. "Not good," she said, tears gathering behind her eyes. If he was involved, she couldn't let him know she was calling about June. She took a chance that Ray wasn't at the station. "Um, Noah. Have you seen Ray?"

"Nah. He's out with everyone else looking for Isabelle Coleman."

Josie looked toward the entrance. Lara was gone. "You're still logging tips?"

"No, I'm down in holding. Someone has to babysit June Spencer."

Relief flooded through her. She strode toward the entrance and made her way to the elevators. "They haven't moved her yet?"

"Nope. They're saying maybe tomorrow or the next day. That psych unit in Philly might have a bed by then. Want me to tell Ray to call you?"

"Oh no. Don't worry about it. I'll keep trying him. He does this from time to time. Doesn't want to hear me nag him."

"Well, he's an idiot," Noah said. "Want me to tell him that?"

She had to force a laugh. "Sure. You can tell him that."

They hung up just as she emerged from the elevators onto the ICU floor. She found Carrieann in the waiting room, her face ashen and tear-streaked. Josie felt a strange weightlessness, like she was made of nothing. Like her pounding heart would propel her right off the ground.

She walked up to Carrieann and gripped her by the shoulders. "What happened? Is he . . . is he . . . ?" She couldn't bring herself to utter the word, to even think it.

Carrieann seemed to stare right through her. "They found the shooter," she said.

"But is Luke okay?"

Carrieann nodded. "He's the same."

Her relief felt palpable, like a breath she'd been holding for five minutes rather than five seconds. "They found the shooter?"

"They arrested her an hour ago. The press doesn't know yet."

Puzzled, Josie said, "Her?"

Now Carrieann met her eyes. "Denise Poole. Did Luke ever mention her? She's his ex-girlfriend. She was always a little off, a little obsessed with him, but I never thought she'd try something like this."

The whole world seemed to narrow to a pinprick. Carrieann was still speaking, but all Josie could hear was a roar in her ears, like a bathtub faucet on full blast. A cold sweat broke out along her forehead and upper lip. She pushed past Carrieann and fell into one of the seats lining the walls. She tried to steady herself by focusing on the painting across the spinning room. It was a copy of a Renoir, she thought, with relief, so purposely out of focus. She wondered if this was how Ginger's memories looked in her mind, faces blurred and indistinct. She wondered about the painting Denise had mentioned.

Whoever was behind all this clearly had no idea that Josie had met with Denise Poole the day before, or Josie would be dead. She *would* be dead as soon as Denise gave her name as an alibi.

As the roar in her ears receded, Josie looked up at Carrieann, willing herself to focus. She couldn't give in to her emotions right now. She had to find a way out of this.

"I just can't believe it," Carrieann went on. "Denise. I just never thought she could do something like this."

Josie said blankly, "Because she didn't."

Confusion creased Carrieann's face. "What? What are you saying?"

Josie beckoned Carrieann closer and whispered, "I need your help. Now."

# CHAPTER 48

Three sharp knocks and a boy's voice called, "You in there?"

Another loud thump on the door and the hand on her throat relaxed. She sucked in as much air as she could. As painful as breathing was, it was a sudden and sweet relief. Another thump and hope filled her battered chest. She tried to call out, but her words were weak and barely audible, even to her own ears.

The voice came again, clearer now. "Dad, you in there?"

This monster had a son? She wondered how old he was and if he would help her. Surely, if he found her, he would help her, take her home.

The man picked up his flashlight and swung open the door just long enough for her to see a boy's slender frame in the ultra bright sunlight before she was slammed into darkness again and heard the lock click into place. Her hope disintegrated. New tears stung her eyes. The boy was so close. Rescue. Home. She dreamed of being back in the arms of her mother and sister. If only the man hadn't beaten her so badly, she could have cried out. She lay like a broken doll discarded on the dirt floor, listening for the boy's voice again.

"I just want to know what you've got in there."

# CHAPTER 49

Denton's holding area was a little-used group of cells in the basement of the police department with an emergency exit leading to the back parking lot. It was mostly reserved for drunk college students and drunks who needed to sleep it off. For prisoners who were being charged, Denton PD relied on the county's central booking office which was only a few miles away. It was much more secure, manned twenty-four hours, and the sheriff supplied transportation of prisoners to and from court. It saved Denton a lot of time and expense to send people awaiting arraignment to central booking rather than keep them in holding.

That June Spencer was still in their holding was extraordinary. Noah's claim that they couldn't find a bed for her in any nearby psychiatric units was bullshit; there had to be one somewhere. What made matters worse was there was no one to fight for June's rights; her uncle was clinging to life, her mother was in hiding. She couldn't even speak for herself.

Obviously, they were trying to delay her transfer. Another day or two and she'd likely have some sort of accident— maybe in transit—or perhaps she would find something to kill herself with. At least that's what they would claim. Then there would be no chance of June recovering enough to testify against any of them.

Josie had to get June out of there and to safety. She parked a block away from the police department in a pick-up truck she'd borrowed from Carrieann. She'd also lent her a Marlin ranch rifle. It was probably twenty years old and its wooden stock was nicked and scratched, but Carrieann had assured her that it would shoot someone just the same. Now it was hidden beneath Josie's jacket as she lurked in the shadows near the dumpsters in the back parking lot. Quickly and surreptitiously, she checked the display on her cell phone. "Any minute now," she whispered under her breath. It had gotten cold, almost to the point where she could see her breath. She silently hopped from one foot to the other, trying to keep warm as she waited.

Finally, she heard the doors around the side of the building bang open, shouts and footsteps and, soon, cars roaring to life. She listened as one by one they tore out of the parking lot. As planned, Carrieann had called in the false Isabelle Coleman sighting on the other side of the city. Everyone on shift would be sent out looking for her, leaving one person upstairs in the main lobby to greet any visitors and one person in holding to watch June Spencer. She didn't know if it would be Noah, but it didn't matter. She was leaving with June Spencer no matter what she had to do.

Josie knew one patrol officer who worked nights and always parked in the back lot, and she waited for him to exit through holding. As he strode toward his car, she slipped inside the door just before it slammed shut. She knew she'd be captured on CCTV, but that didn't concern her. She was already a dead woman walking. All she needed to do was get June, get out, and get her to safety.

She paused in the small hallway that led from the door into the holding area. Her heart pounded out a steady rhythm.

She opened her jacket and raised the rifle, holding it in both hands, the stock flush against her right shoulder. She paused for a moment to steady her breath and her trembling hands. She was about to break the law. She was about to seal her fate, throw away everything she held dear in life. But there was no other way; it was kill or be killed.

Still, committing a crime in her own station house was not something she ever thought she would do. She took one last shuddering breath and made her way down the hall. On one side was a row of cells: two small, two large. On the other side was a row of unused desks and an empty bench. Directly across from where she stood sat Noah Fraley, his feet up on a large desk, so all she could see was the mud-crusted tread of his boots. He'd been nodding off but didn't startle when he saw her, which was what she'd expected. She moved toward him, catlike, raising the rifle and sighting in on his center mass. Slowly, he unlaced his fingers from behind his head and brought his hands down, palms out toward her, a gesture of surrender. An uncertain smile played on his lips, like he couldn't quite be sure if what he was seeing was real or not.

"Detective Quinn?" he said in a worried, questioning tone.

She glanced quickly to her left and saw that all the cells were empty, save one. June was curled in a fetal position beneath the cot in one of the single cells. Like a dog. Someone had put a pair of sweatpants and a plain white T-shirt on her.

Noah stood as Josie drew closer. "Josie," he said, trying a different tack.

"Keep your hands where I can see them," she instructed.

"What are you doing?"

She motioned toward June's cell with her chin, keeping the gun steady on him. "I'm taking her with me."

He started to laugh, but then thought better of it. His face flamed red. "You're kidding, right?"

"Are you involved?" she asked. "Are you with them?"

He looked genuinely puzzled, but she held fast to her resolve not to trust anyone, not even Noah. "What are you talking about?" he said.

"Never mind. Just get your keys. Let her out."

"You can't . . . why are you . . . what the hell is going on here?"

"I know what's going on. I know about Ginger Blackwell. I know about June. I know about Isabelle Coleman."

By degrees, his face became more and more pinched. "You know what? Josie, I have no idea what you're talking about."

"I *know* about Ramona," she hissed.

No flicker of recognition.

She said, "It doesn't matter anyway. Maybe you really don't know what's happening in this town or maybe you're an excellent liar just like my husband. Either way, I'm taking June. Open the cell."

He took a few cautious steps around the desk toward her. From inside the cell, June stirred, creature-like, her beady eyes locking onto Josie. She reminded Josie of the animals at the zoo—a wild predator trapped in a cage. She hoped she wasn't endangering herself. She didn't want to end up like Sherri Gosnell.

"You don't have to do this," Noah said. "Look, why don't you take a moment? Go home. Sleep on this. I can meet you tomorrow. We'll talk about whatever is going on. Let me help you."

"Don't patronize me," she shouted.

June moved like a snake, slithering out from beneath the cot and over toward the cell bars. Noah stood between the desk and the cell. The keys to the cells were there on the desk, to his left. His gun hung on his right hip.

"Just let me help you . . . sort things out. We can go somewhere else and talk about things."

He thought she was crazy. He was trying to de-escalate the situation. He was treating her like a woman about to jump off a bridge.

"I'm not fucking crazy, Noah. You want to know what's crazy? I'll tell you what's crazy. Isabelle Coleman went missing twelve days ago. There are men on this police force who know where she is, or at least where she was, and yet she's still missing. What's crazy is that I found one of her acrylic nails by her mailbox that day you let me into the crime scene—a crime scene in the middle of the damn woods, a good quarter mile from that mailbox. What's crazy is that June Spencer is wearing Isabelle Coleman's tongue piercing, but June was missing for a year, which means that June was being held with Coleman at some point. Yet she was found in the home of Donald Drummond who's not here to tell us what the fuck happened because the chief shot him dead."

Her voice escalated. "What's *crazy* is that six years ago a woman named Ginger Blackwell was lured onto the side of the road and drugged by a woman calling herself Ramona and the police never even looked for her. What's crazy is that in the face of indisputable physical evidence they labeled it a hoax. What's crazy is that as soon as I found out about Ginger's case, my fiancé was shot. What's crazy is that his ex-girlfriend, who I was with yesterday, is being framed for the crime. What's fucking crazy is that there is some fucked-up shit going on in this town, and I am the only person who gives a shit. Now let her out of that cell!"

With each new nugget of information, Noah's face grew one shade paler, and his right arm dropped a fraction of an inch lower, toward his gun. Noah had never pulled his weapon in the line of duty, and he would be slow on the draw. His fingers brushed the gun's handle, but he hadn't even unfastened his holster. He didn't stand a chance.

Josie placed a shot into his right shoulder, the sound of the rifle deafening in the tiny room. Guilt assailed her, but she pushed it aside. By the time he hit the floor, she was already standing over him, unfastening his holster and disarming him, tucking his weapon into the back of her waistband. He lay on the ground, holding his shoulder, turning his head, straining to get a look at the blood blooming on his blue shirt. "You... you shot me," he gasped.

"It won't kill you," she said. "It's a .22 and I'm a good shot."

He didn't respond, his eyes gaping at the wound in disbelief. She had a minute, tops, before the desk sergeant made it downstairs. If Noah wasn't involved, then at least they wouldn't think he had helped her. If he was involved, then she was glad she had shot him. Snatching up the keys, she stepped over him and unlocked June's cell. The girl shuffled out, her eyes raking warily over Noah's prone frame. Using one arm to keep her gun up and at the ready, Josie led June out by the upper arm. She didn't put up a fight.

Before they left, Josie took one last look at Noah lying on the floor, blood oozing from the wound in his shoulder. Biting back an apology she pushed June out into the dark, cold night.

# CHAPTER 50

June sat in the front of Carrieann's pickup truck, staring out the window as the lit-up buildings of Denton proper gave way to the inky blackness of rural roads. Josie kept glancing over at her. She didn't know what she expected; the girl had viciously and violently killed a woman with a fork, and yet she was as meek and mute as an abandoned pup. A shiver ran through Josie's body even though the heat in the old truck was on full blast.

"I'm going to take you somewhere safe," she told her.

No response, and Josie had a sudden flash of how absurd that must sound to June. She'd been rescued from Donald Drummond by people who were every bit as evil as Drummond. Out of the frying pan and into the fire. No wonder she had snapped.

"I mean it," Josie told her. "This place is safe. It's a woman I know. She won't let anything happen to you. She'll look after you until..."

Until what? Until Dirk woke up from his coma? Until Lara could come out of hiding? Until they no longer had targets on their backs? When would June be safe? When would any of them be safe?

"Until I get things sorted out," she finished, limply.

June's dull eyes never left the window.

They still had an hour in the car before they reached Carrieann. Josie doubted she would get anything out of her, but she had to try. "June, I need to know. Did Donald Drummond take you?"

Silence.

"Or was it Ramona?"

June's head swiveled slowly in Josie's direction, her dark eyes flashing in the low lighting from Carrieann's dashboard. She looked into Josie's eyes just as she had in the nursing home.

"It was, wasn't it? A woman named Ramona. She picked you up or offered you a ride. Or maybe you met her before and she led you to believe she could help you get out of town. Maybe back to your mom or your friends in Philadelphia. Except she didn't take you there, did she?"

June continued to stare at Josie, unblinking, but her eyes were alive again. She was in there, somewhere.

"You saw Isabelle Coleman, didn't you?"

Nothing, the stare slipping back into a vacant deadness.

"No," Josie said. Reaching over, she touched June's forearm. "Don't go. I know you're in there. Please talk to me. I need to know what you saw. I need to know what you know."

But her head was turned back to the window, back to the nothingness flying past outside.

With the miles stretched out before them, Josie kept talking, peppering June with questions and reassurances, desperate for her to understand that she was on her side. Until, at last, exhausted and out of things to say, she fell silent and they drove the rest of the way with only the blast of the heater filling the cold void between them. As she pulled up on a remote mountain road near the hospital where Carrieann was parked in her SUV, Josie shot one last glance at June, but the girl's eyes were closed.

# CHAPTER 51

Josie unfastened her seat belt and turned her whole body toward June, lightly touching her forearm. "June, wake up. We're here."

June opened her eyes and looked straight past Josie, watching Carrieann walk toward her door with the wariness of a cat.

"That's my friend, Carrieann," Josie said. "June, I have to ask one last time: did you see Isabelle Coleman? Can you tell me anything about where you were held before you came to be with Donald Drummond?"

Carrieann rattled Josie's door. Josie wanted to keep trying to get more information from her, but it might take forever. Josie didn't have forever. Especially after what she had just done. With a frustrated sigh, she opened her door and got out.

"How'd it go?" Carrieann asked, glancing behind Josie. "That her?"

"Yeah, that's her. I shot someone."

Carrieann kept her eyes on June. "You kill him?"

"No."

Carrieann shrugged. "No worries, then."

Josie was trying to decide whether she was joking or not

when Carrieann stepped past her and climbed into the cab of the truck. "Name's Carrieann," she told June.

The girl stared back, unblinking.

"Where's Lara?" Josie asked.

"She wouldn't come with me. I'm going to meet up with her now."

"Carrieann, thank you for doing this. You don't have to—she could be dangerous," Josie said, lowering her voice so June wouldn't hear.

"You said that earlier," Carrieann reminded her, matching Josie's voice with her own whisper. "At the hospital. And I told you I'd do whatever it takes to find out what really happened to my brother. I'm not afraid of that girl."

"Maybe you should be."

Carrieann raised a brow. "I can be vigilant without being afraid. You stop worrying now. I'll handle this."

"Please be careful," Josie implored. "Don't let anyone see her."

"You got it." Carrieann gave her one last meaningful look. "I'll be back in the morning after I get these two stashed away on my farm. Don't get killed while I'm gone."

"I'll try not to."

Josie watched Carrieann drive off with June until the tail-lights of her truck disappeared into the night.

# CHAPTER 52

She had promised Carrieann that she wouldn't return to the hospital, but Josie couldn't leave without seeing Luke one more time. The nurse let her stay an extra ten minutes. It had only been a day, but he already looked thinner. She touched his cool skin and carefully avoided the mess of tubes and wires so she could lean in to kiss his cheek and whisper, "I'm sorry," before a nurse ushered her out.

Before leaving, she took a quick scan of the waiting room to make sure Lara wasn't in there, only to find two troopers sleeping in chairs and a handful of worried relatives. Josie was about to turn away and leave when the sight of Trinity Payne on the television caught her eye. She stood outside the Denton police department, hair whipping in the wind, microphone in hand. Along the bottom of the screen scrolled the words: "Prisoner Taken." Josie had to get close to the television to hear what she said.

"...there was only one officer on duty in the holding area this evening when a masked gunman stormed the back door, shot Officer Noah Fraley and kidnapped June Spencer..."

A masked gunman?

Guilt was a sharp pain in her chest. Noah had lied. She shot him, and he lied for her. If ever there was a sign that he wasn't involved, it was this one, perfect lie. But why had he reached for his gun, she wondered? Why hadn't he tried to convince her that he was innocent, instead of trying to handle her?

*You wouldn't have believed him,* a voice in her head confessed.

Then a horrible thought struck her. What if he had been reaching for his gun to surrender?

"Oh, sweet Jesus," she muttered to herself.

But it didn't matter. At the time, she had no way of knowing if he was an enemy or not. She had done what she had to do and June was safe.

Her cell phone vibrated in her pocket. She ducked out of the waiting room and down the hall as she pulled it out and looked at the display before answering.

"Ray."

"Where is June Spencer?" he asked.

"Last I heard she was in a holding cell in the basement of Denton's police building," Josie said.

"Are you really going to do this?"

"Do what?" she said, with a little more feigned innocence than she had intended.

"Lie," he growled, his voice growing louder.

She laughed. "Are you really going to do *this?* Lecture me about lying? *You?*"

There was a long silence. Probably while he catalogued the vast number of lies he had told in the last several years. Then, quietly, he said, "Are you fucking Noah Fraley?"

She let out a short, uncontrolled burst of laughter. She couldn't help it. The thought was so absurd. Then the implication of what he was asking sunk in. Was he really implying that she could not possibly accomplish anything unless she used sex to do it? "Maybe your little stripper girlfriend needs to use her vagina to get things done, but I do not."

"Jo," he said, voice softening for a moment.

"Why would you even go there?"

"Noah erased the security footage. He left a goddamn trail of blood from holding to the CCTV room. He erased it all—from the outside *and* the inside."

Her heart leapt. "Security footage of what?"

Again, he sighed. "You know goddamn well what."

"No, I'm sorry, I don't."

She could hear that he was speaking through gritted teeth. "This is not a game, Josie. I can't protect you if you take this much further. Tell me where June is. I'll go get her and take her back. They'll never have to know for sure that it was you."

"Who are 'they'?"

"You know I can't tell you that. It's for your own good. Please, Jo. This is serious. I know you're not good at backing off, but I'm telling you that your life depends on it."

A chill enveloped her entire body. The hand holding the phone to her ear trembled. "You think I can just forget about this? Stop asking questions and go back to my life like normal? What about the next time a teenage girl goes missing, Ray? I'm not backing away from this. I remembered where the Standing Man is, and I'm going there."

"Josie, don't. Jesus. Don't go there. You don't understand. They'll kill you."

She thought about the woman she elbowed for selling her four-year-old for drugs. She thought about Noah Fraley lying on the tile floor, blood blooming from his shoulder. About Luke in the hospital bed, and June curled up under her prison cot like a child. She had a sudden flash of memory of her mother, of all people. "You can't always be all roses and sweetness," she had always told Josie. "That don't get shit done."

"Maybe," she said to Ray. "Or maybe I'll kill *them*."

# CHAPTER 53

In the long, endless hours that followed she tried to move twice, but the pain in her chest was too great. She drifted in and out of a sleep filled with dreams of her sister; sneaking into her bed in the middle of the night, as she often did, snuggling and laughing all night until the daylight crept through the window. Each time she woke, she was devastated anew to find herself in this black nightmare, pain coursing through her body with every breath. She prayed for the boy. Surely the boy would find her and get help.

The next time the door slid open, the dull gray light of either dawn or dusk leaked into the chamber. From where she lay, curled towards the wall, she heard two sets of footsteps draw closer. One set heavy, the other set light. The boy. She didn't dare look over her shoulder as hope surged inside her again in the warm glow of the flashlight that shone down on her.

"I—I don't understand," the boy whispered.

The fear in his voice told her that he would not save her.

"This one's mine," said the man. "One day, you'll get your own."

Hot tears streaked her face and a large hand reached down and wiped one of them away. "Shhh, hush now," he whispered. "Hush now, my sweet Ramona."

# CHAPTER 54

Back in her own vehicle, Josie drove for an hour and a half in darkness, staying off the interstate, using only the rural roads to get to the turn-off to her great-grandparents' old house. They had owned twenty acres of land which they had sold to Alton Gosnell when Josie was five years old. Alton, and Alton's father before him, had owned roughly ten acres abutting the twenty acres that Josie's great-grandparents lived on. The property was near the top of one of the mountains on Denton's outskirts. It was remote and about thirteen miles from the center of Denton, but still considered part of the city.

Like the Colemans' place, her great-grandparents' old house was high off the road, at the end of a long, rutted driveway overgrown with grass and brush. She drove past the entrance to it three times before she found it. The Gosnells had erected two steel bars with a chain between them on which hung a "No Trespassing" sign. Once she saw it, she drove a half mile down the road to a wide area of shoulder. She pulled off the gravel and into the trees, her shocks protesting as she rode over a downed fence and a few small logs. She couldn't risk being seen from the road. Once her vehicle was safely nestled behind a grove of trees, she turned off the engine and climbed into the backseat. She had an emergency kit that had a blanket inside it. She retrieved the blanket and stretched out beneath it, Carrieann's Marlin in her hands.

She woke a few hours later to the thin light of day pouring through the windows. Slowly, she sat up and glanced outside. There was no movement near her car, no sounds except the insistent chirp of birds in the trees all around her. Her cell phone revealed six missed calls from Ray, three from what she knew was Misty's cell phone, and two from Trinity Payne. None from Carrieann, which was good. They had agreed to have no contact unless Luke took a turn for the worse. Josie didn't want to leave a trail back to her and June.

She checked her text messages. There were a dozen from Ray imploring her to call him, or at least to tell him where she was and he would come to her. She had slept through it all. Her exhaustion ran deep and it was tempting to crawl back beneath her blanket and keep sleeping. But she couldn't. Isabelle Coleman was still out there. These faceless men kidnapping and abusing young women had to be stopped.

Josie turned her phone to sleep mode, relieved herself quickly by the side of the car and snatched up the Marlin, picking her way through the forest toward the Gosnell property and on to the old chained-off driveway. By the time she found it, the sunlight had started to burn off the fog that swirled along the forest floor. A fine sheen of sweat covered her face, beads of it rolling down her back as she walked along the side of the driveway, ears pricked for the sounds of a vehicle or footsteps approaching.

Finally, she came to the overgrown clearing where her great-grandparents' house sat, its white siding now gray with dirt and grime. The center of the roof had caved in. A gnarled tree branch had fallen onto the floor of the front porch, causing the wood flooring to splinter. The Gosnells had bought the property but let the house fall into disrepair. Josie had only snippets of memories of being inside the house with her father and grandmother. She didn't have any emotional attachments to the place, but it seemed a waste to let it fall down.

She circled the house, glancing into the windows as she went. It was empty and dark, its plaster walls crumbling inside, the floorboards sagging. A chipmunk scurried over her feet, and she yelped in surprise, swinging the gun toward the edge of the clearing where the tiny creature had disappeared. Satisfied that no one was inside, she went to the back door and stared at the line of trees at the edge of the clearing.

She tried to pull the memory from the recesses of her brain. She couldn't remember where she and her father had gone into the woods, only that they had meandered from the house to the forest, hand in hand. She decided to start in the center of the line of trees, almost directly across from where she stood. As she walked, she panned left and right, eyes searching for the rock formation.

She thought once she stepped into the woods her body would remember where to go, like the way your hands learned how to hold a gun after you'd trained with it and shot it for years. But her memories of the woods behind her great-grandparents' house were like Ginger's memories of her abduction—indistinct and out of focus. She only knew she had seen the Standing Man before.

When she realized she had circled the same moss-covered tree three times, she started marking her path, using her car keys to carve an X into the trunks at eye-level. It felt like hours before she came to what looked like an actual path in the woods. Sweat dampened her armpits so she took off her jacket and tied it around her waist. The underbrush had been tamped down into a rut just the width of the average person's shoulders. It led downward into a small dell. As she traveled further down, one side of the leaf-strewn ground rose up into a rock face. Then she saw him. The Standing Man.

The closer she got, the sharper her memories became. It looked like a man in profile leaning up against the rock wall with one leg bent, knee jutting out, foot flat against the stone behind him. His chin dipped down as if he was looking at something on the ground. As she got closer, she saw that it wasn't a single formation but a series of small rocks jutting out in different places, creating the illusion. It could only be seen from a certain distance and angle. Once you passed him and looked back all you saw were random rocks sticking out of the wall. A few feet from the standing man was a small opening. It was only about three feet tall. She crouched down to look inside, but there was only darkness. She pulled out her phone and turned it back on. No service, it announced. Still, it had a flashlight.

The cave was small, only big enough to accommodate two people at most. It was cool and damp and filled with rocks. She was just crawling in when, outside, a twig snapped. She startled so abruptly that she hit the top of her head on the cave's roof. Massaging her scalp, she pocketed her phone and turned back to the entrance, sliding the Marlin around to the front of her body only to realize that the only way to hold it so that she could shoot whoever was out there was if she lay on her stomach.

Another twig snapped as she flattened her body to the ground, resting the barrel of the Marlin on some small rocks in front of her. Cheek pressed against the stock, she peered outside of the cave and waited. Her heartbeat pounded in her ears. Whoever was out there wasn't trying to be quiet. A pair of heavy, black, steel-toed boots came into view. Then a familiar voice hissed, "Jo!"

"Ray?"

The boots jumped back. Then Ray's face appeared in the cave's entrance. "What the fuck are you doing in there?"

She extricated herself from the cave and stood, but kept her hands on the Marlin, the barrel pointed toward the ground. Ray pointed to the gun. "And where the hell did you get that?"

Josie narrowed her eyes at him. "Don't you worry about what I've got."

He stepped closer to her. His face looked thinner, his skin sallow. "I'm worried about you," he said. "You need to come with me right now. Away from here. You can't be here, do you understand me?"

Her hardened voice faltered. She hated herself for it. "You know what, Ray? I don't understand anything anymore. I sure as hell don't understand a goddamn thing about what is happening in this town anymore."

She tried to step around him, but he moved with her, blocking her way. She poked him in the thigh with the barrel of the gun. "Get out of my way, Ray."

"Yeah, Ray," said a male voice to their left. "Get out of her way."

They both turned to see Nick Gosnell standing several feet away. He held a shotgun in his hands and it was aimed directly at Josie's head.

# CHAPTER 55

There was a tension-filled moment of awareness before the three of them acted simultaneously. Josie raised the Marlin, pumping a round into the chamber as she brought it up, and fired a shot at Nick. Ray pushed her out of the way, sending her shot wide. Nick fired back. Josie tumbled into the rock wall, hitting the back of her head. A bright light flashed across her vision. She tried to take a step but fell forward, the Marlin jabbing her in her side. Ray rushed Gosnell, and Nick's shotgun boomed again. The two men tumbled down the dell and out of sight, a whirling dervish of flailing limbs and the sleek black of the shotgun barrel. Josie's vision seemed to split, everything multiplying by two, and then returned to normal. She reached back and felt blood in her hair. She could hear Ray and Nick crashing through the underbrush in the distance. She tried to stand again, but her legs were made of jelly. She moved toward the noise on her hands and knees, the heavy Marlin slung across her back, until the sound stopped.

Ray.

There had been no more gunfire. Was Ray still alive? The thought made her sway on her knees. She could go back to the cave, maintain a defensive position there until she figured out what the hell was going on. She would be able to hear Gosnell coming from inside the cave, see his shoes. She'd shoot before he could move on her. Then she could get away. If she could just stand. She tried to stand. The forest around her spun. She sat back on her heels and shifted the sling to bring the Marlin around to her front.

By the time she heard the crunch of feet in the leaves beside her it was too late. Her hands fumbled with the Marlin but they were clumsy and unsure. Someone behind her lifted her body as if she weighed nothing. The cold metal of the Marlin's barrel pressed into the side of her throat. On the other side, the coarse material of the sling cut into her skin. As her carotids were slowly crushed, the spinning forest around her went gray, then black.

# CHAPTER 56

She woke to complete darkness. Reaching up, she gently felt her fluttering eyelids to make sure she was really opening her eyes. Little by little, sensation came back to her: a heavy pounding in the back of her head, the cold feel of concrete beneath her bottom, a smell like rotted wood and mildew. Her back rested against something soft. She turned slightly and pushed against it with one hand. Something hard clamped down on her forearm and she shrieked, writhing away and kicking with all her might. It took several seconds for her to register Ray's voice beneath her screams.

"Jo, it's me. It's *me*."

"Ray?" she called into the blackness.

Her hands searched all around her but all she felt was concrete. She heard a whistling sound and, too late, realized she was hyperventilating. She hated dark closed-in spaces. Her heartbeat thundered over the sound of her wheezing breath, her body flailed around in the darkness even though she willed it not to move—to be still, to calm down, to catch a breath. Then Ray's arms were around her, his breath hot on the nape of her neck. "It's okay," he told her. "You're safe. I'm here with you."

She wanted to scream at him to let go of her, but she couldn't find the words, just a sound like an animal trapped in a bear trap. A terrible keening that hurt her own ears. Her body still recoiled against his touch, familiar as it was. She knew it should be comforting, but it wasn't.

As if reading her mind, Ray said, "I know you don't want me to touch you, but you need to calm down, Jo. Pretend I'm Luke or whoever. Please, calm down."

The keening continued. Her mind screamed commands at her in rapid-fire fashion, none of which her body was able to obey. *Breathe. Stop struggling. Be quiet. Calm the fuck down.*

Ray loosened his grip on her but still held her against his chest. He rested his chin on the top of her head. "Shhh," he cooed. "Jo, everything is okay. Listen to my voice. You can still listen to my voice, right?"

He was right. The night that had ended their marriage—even before Misty came into the picture—had not ruined that for her. She calmed to a whimper, her breath slowing fractionally.

"I won't hurt you," he told her. "I promise you that. You know me, Jo. I would never hurt you."

Lies, all lies, but she listened anyway because she had to. Because his voice had once been home to her. She followed the sound of it back up from the rabbit hole of hysteria, clinging to it as though her life depended on it.

"I'm here with you," he continued. "I'm not going to leave you."

Her heaving chest slowed. The wheezing stopped. She could almost speak.

"You're not a kid anymore. You're not alone. The darkness can't hurt you, remember? It's only darkness."

He was right. The darkness couldn't hurt her. Neither could a small space. Or her mother. But there was a new monster outside the door, and he had already tried to hurt them. They were in the black box now.

Her voice was small. "Did he hurt you?"

"I'm okay," Ray said, although by the small catch in his voice, she suspected he was keeping something from her. Her hands began searching his body for injuries, but he caught them and held them fast in both of his. "I'm fine," he assured her. "Really."

She wished she could see him. She leaned back into him, and they sank to the floor together. "He took our phones," Ray said. "Not that there's any service up here. I tried kicking my way out, but it was a no-go."

"Where are we?" she asked.

"Gosnell's . . . bunker."

"Bunker?"

"Well, whatever you want to call it. He built this place out in the woods behind his house. Like one of those earth houses or whatever."

A structure in the earth. A hole in the ground.

"Have you been here before?"

"No. Yes. I mean, I've been to his house before, on the property, but I didn't—I never made it inside here."

She laid the side of her head against his jacket. The smell of blood and sweat mingled with the earthy smells of the tiny room. "Are you bleeding?"

"No," he said, too quickly. "I mean, yeah. I think he put a pretty bad gash in my leg, but I'm all right, Jo."

"What is this place? What does he use it for?"

Ray didn't speak for several seconds. The only proof she had that he was still alive was the rise and fall of his chest beneath her cheek. She wondered if he'd fallen asleep. "Ray?"

"He uses it for . . . I mean, I think he uses it to keep . . . you know, women."

Her tone was more strident this time. " 'Keep women?' "

His voice remained calm but sad. "Jo, when you came out here, what did you think you were going to find?"

"Is Isabelle Coleman here?"

"No," he said with absolute conviction.

"How do you know?"

"Because I know."

"We're going to die here," Josie said.

"No. I won't let that happen."

"Because you're such good friends? You can just ask him to let us go and he'll do it?"

He gave an exasperated sigh. "Josie."

"I want the truth, Ray. All of it. How much you know and when you knew it. I need you to keep talking to me, or I'm going to lose it in here."

# CHAPTER 57

"Last year," he began and she cut him off with a high-pitched, "Last year?"

"Do you want to hear this or not?"

"I'm sorry. Go on."

He took another tack. "You know after things went down between us, I was a little out of control, right?"

She could feel his discomfort in the tensed muscles of his body. Revulsion churned her stomach. "That didn't happen after we broke up. You were out of control long before that, and you know it."

"Jo, you know I'm sorry. I don't know how many times I can say it."

She didn't say anything because it was old territory. They'd been over it a thousand times. Ray remembered nothing from the night that had essentially ended their marriage, even before Misty came along.

"Jo, you know I didn't mean it—"

"Don't," she snapped at him. "Just tell me what happened."

He sighed. "Well, last year, me and Dusty and a bunch of the guys were out drinking. We were really tying one on, you know?"

"Yes, I do know."

"Jo."

"Just tell me."

"I was upset. I was upset about losing you. I knew…I knew things would never be the same. I saw it in your eyes every time you looked at me."

She shook in his arms, half with rage and half with the remembered trauma of that night. "You told Dusty to stay," she said.

"Dusty always stayed over."

"You got so drunk, you told him he could fuck me if he wanted—and he tried, Ray."

She remembered waking from a deep sleep to hands roaming all over her body, thinking it was Ray, and then as she floated closer to consciousness realizing that nothing about the person touching her felt like Ray.

"Dusty was drunk too, Jo."

"Not as drunk as you, and that doesn't excuse him. It doesn't excuse any of it. I was asleep."

She had sprung out of the bed, hitting and kicking Dusty so furiously that his cries brought Ray up the stairs. He had pulled Dusty away from Josie and, in that moment, she had been relieved. But then she saw his face. His blank eyes. Like he was looking at her but not seeing her at all. They flashed with anger. He had gone after her, calling her a bitch and a whore and accusing her of cheating on him with Dusty. It was at that point that Dusty, standing naked on the other side of the room, had said, "Dude, chill. You told me I could fuck her."

"Jo, you know I never would have said that if I wasn't drunk."

"But you were that drunk, Ray. Drunk, angry, jealous, out of control. Just like your father was with your mother."

She felt him tense but he said nothing. She was angry with

him for what happened, but she hated him because he didn't remember. He had flown into an explosive rage then, punching Dusty hard enough in the mouth to draw blood. When she told them both to get out, Ray had turned and punched her too. Just like that. He'd hit her so hard she hit the floor.

"You promised you'd never hurt me," she whispered into the darkness.

"Jo, I'm sorry. I don't even remember telling Dusty he could... I don't remember fighting with either of you. I don't remember any of it."

"But you remember Dusty telling you about this place?"

"He didn't tell me, really."

"Then what happened?"

"The guys were trying to get my mind off you—our problems and all—and they asked Dusty if he had ever taken me to see Ramona. Dusty got real weird, like he didn't want to talk about it. You know Dusty and I—we've been friends a long time. We don't have many secrets from each other. So I asked him, who's Ramona. He got real uncomfortable. Like, I could tell he really didn't want to tell me. But the other guys, it was like they smelled blood, you know? So they really egged him on, but he wouldn't talk. Then one of the other guys says, 'Fuck it, let's take him to see her,' and they... they brought me here."

He paused for breath. She could feel his muscles twitch beneath her. He went on, "Well, not here, like back here, but to the Gosnells' house. It was late, and I didn't know whose house it was at first. Like, I had met Nick a couple of times. He fixed the john at the station house once, and I met him at Dusty's parents' house before when he was doing some plumbing there. But I didn't really know the guy. Anyway, the guys get me out of the car, and we knock on the door to the house and Sherri Gosnell answers. They said they were here to see Ramona."

"*Sherri Gosnell* is Ramona?"

Again she felt him shake his head. "No, Ramona is like a code word. Like, you come to the house and ask for her and they bring you here." She felt him lift one hand to indicate where they were.

She thought of Ginger's words and shivered. "To a black box like this?"

"I don't know," he said. "I couldn't . . . I couldn't go through with it. Sherri told us to wait and she would get Nick. Then he came out, and he was smiling like he was all happy and it reminded me of that guy at the body shop when we were kids. Remember him? He used to offer girls rides to the mall. Like, why is a grown man with no kids giving thirteen-year-olds rides to the mall, you know? Like, he was a perv."

Josie swallowed the acid that rose in the back of her throat. "I remember him."

"Well, that's exactly how Nick looked. So he says come on back and leads us out into the woods. In the dark. He had one of those battery-operated lanterns. So we're following him, and I ask Dusty what the hell are we doing, and he says Nick's got girls. I said what do you mean and he just says, you know, Nick keeps girls back here, and if you know the code word and you're willing to pay for it, you can come and do whatever you want with them. I asked where does he get the girls and Dusty got all mad at me and told me to shut up and stop being such a pussy."

"Never mind that you're all cops," she muttered. "So, what happened next?"

"Well, we get down to the bunker. I can see there's a door, but before we go inside Dusty gives me this whole thing about how once I go in, there's no turning back. He kept calling it a brotherhood, like, you can't rat people out. He said if I said something to the wrong person, it could get me killed. Or you.

He kept asking me, are you sure you want to do this, or maybe you should just ask out the stripper at the club."

"You chose Misty."

"No. Yes. No, no. I mean, it wasn't about Misty. The truth is…"

He trailed off and she felt him raise his chin and blow out a long stream of air. "I was scared, okay? I had a bad feeling. Why did he need to threaten me? And there was no light coming from the place or anything. It was just weird. It was weird that you needed a code word. I didn't really want to know what was on the other side of the door, 'cause if I knew then I would have to do something about it, and—"

"You're a pussy?" she said pointedly.

"Jo, come on."

"It's true, Ray. You knew something was wrong from the moment they took you there, but you chose to do nothing. Don't act like you're some big martyr. Walking away without doing anything makes you every bit as bad as those other guys who came in here and…and…" She couldn't say it.

"It wasn't like that."

"Really? What was it like, Ray?"

"I didn't really know how bad it was. All I really knew was that this guy was running a brothel out of his backyard bunker that a lot of cops had visited. No one wanted to get busted."

"Sure," she said sarcastically.

He was silent for several moments. She tried to wait him out, but she couldn't take it any longer. She said, "What did you do?"

Ray sighed. "I said I wasn't ready for it, and I walked back to the car. I waited for them there. Then they took me home. We never talked about it again."

"You and Dusty?"

"No. We never discussed it. Well, until Isabelle Coleman went missing."

"You thought Gosnell took her?"

"I didn't know. After a week or so and no sign of her, I had to ask him."

She kicked out in frustration. She wanted to push away from him, but his arms were the only thing keeping her from being sucked into the abyss. "Ray, if you thought Gosnell had her, why didn't you just come up here and bust her out of here? If you thought Gosnell was holding women against their will, why didn't you *do* anything?"

"Because . . . Because you don't understand how deep this goes. It wasn't that simple. If she was really here, and he had taken her, and all the guys on the force knew about it, do you know what that would mean?"

"Do all the guys on the force know about this place?"

"I don't know. A lot do. A whole lot. And it's not just here. It's not just police either. I think . . . I think Gosnell's been at it for a long time."

Disgust rose in her. "His wife knew. She helped him. How could she do it? All those women." Suddenly June's vicious fork attack seemed too good a death for Sherri Gosnell. It all made sense.

"Yeah," Ray agreed. "I think she lured them. Sometimes, anyway."

"So you just asked Dusty outright?"

"Well, yeah, basically. I asked him if he thought Gosnell had anything to do with Isabelle Coleman going missing. He told me to shut my mouth and stop asking stupid questions."

"But when we talked on the phone you made it sound like you knew she wasn't here. Like she was but she wasn't anymore. What the hell, Ray?"

"Dusty came to me. A few days ago. He said Gosnell told him that he had her but that she got away."

Every muscle in her body tensed, a slight quickening. If she got away, she might still be alive.

"That was when everyone went crazy, like looking for her around the clock. We started getting all these tips, sightings of her walking along roads or in the woods. It was different than when she first went missing, you know? Like all these guys were freaked out that they would get busted so it was more important to find her than before."

She shuddered. "What were they going to do when they found her?"

She felt him shrug. "I have no idea."

Josie had some ideas. "And the chief, is he—?"

"I don't know."

"He hasn't said anything?"

"No one says anything, Jo. I mean, Dusty said something to me but that's it. It's not something anyone talks about."

"Ray."

"Yeah?"

"What happens to the girls when Gosnell is done with them?"

# CHAPTER 58

It was impossible to tell how long they'd been there, but it seemed endless. Ray had felt his way around most of the tiny cell and found a toilet in one corner which they used to relieve themselves. They were both thirsty and starving. The only water was the toilet water, but they agreed they weren't that desperate yet. Josie still had the granola bars in her jacket that she had bought at Geisinger. There were four in all. They each ate one and resolved to save the other two for later. They clung to one another and talked until they could no longer stay awake.

Josie had no idea how long they slept, but she woke to Ray shivering uncontrollably. She had fallen asleep with her head in his lap, and now her skull bobbed as his legs shook. Her fingers searched his body, reaching up to his face. Cupping his cheeks in her palms, she got onto her knees and leaned in close. "Ray," she said. "Ray!"

He moaned.

A surge of adrenaline shot through her like it had just been injected directly into her heart. Every sense sharpened. His ragged breath sounded deafening. Why was he shivering? He said he wasn't badly injured.

"Oh my God, Ray!"

Of course he said that. He'd lied. He was trying to keep her calm. She felt for the zipper on his jacket and slipped her hands inside, walking her fingers over every inch of him until she found the wound. When her fingers pressed into the tender, torn skin, he cried out. It was on his left side, closer to his back than his front. She knew from her training there wasn't all that much on the left side of your abdomen, which was why he was still alive. But he was going into shock. She couldn't tell how much blood he had lost. Or how much time he had. Her T-shirt would work well as a bandage. She took her jacket off, tossed it to the side and pulled her T-shirt over her head. Shivering in just her bra and tank top, she balled the T-shirt up and pressed it against his wound.

"Jesus, Ray."

By feel she switched places with him, leaning her back against the wall and lowering him down so that his head lay across her lap. She felt for the shirt, making sure it was firmly pressed against his torn flesh and then laid her jacket across his chest. One hand stroked his hair as hot tears rolled down her cheeks and landed on his face and neck. With her other hand she found them and gently wiped them away. He was burning up, his skin on fire. She wished she could see him, see his face. She cursed the darkness yet again, and she cursed Nick Gosnell for putting them here.

"Ray," she said loudly. "I need you to talk to me. I need you to stay with me. Ray!"

He moaned again, uttered a few incoherent words. She said his name again and again, each time her tone more strident. His words became clearer. "Need to talk . . . you about . . . and Misty . . ."

They were few, but his words hurt. She couldn't bring herself to be cruel. "I know," she croaked. "You want to marry her and live happily ever after. Ray, it's fine. I'm okay with it. You have my blessing. Please stop worrying about that."

He relaxed a bit, although his body still trembled. She gathered him into her and held him as tightly as she could, trying to still him. "Stay with me," she whispered to him. "Stay with me."

It was impossible to tell how much time had passed. But eventually Ray's body went still. She felt his throat for a pulse and cried out in relief when she found one—thready, but there. It took a few moments to extricate herself from beneath him. She took her jacket back, balled it up and put it beneath his head and took a few minutes to feel her way around the cell. The walls seemed to be made of concrete—cinderblocks maybe. There was a slab of wood on hinges which was pressed against the wall, like one of those baby-changing tables that hung on the walls in women's bathrooms, only this one was adult-sized. She considered trying to pull it out and get Ray onto it but decided it would be more work than it was worth in the dark. Plus, moving him could prove fatal at this point. Finally, she felt seams in the wall which could only be a door. There was no knob and what felt like rubber furring strips sealed the bottom of it. Still, she got down on her hands and knees and pressed her mouth against the bottom edge where she might be most likely to make herself heard.

Then she screamed her head off.

She screamed until her throat was raw and her voice hoarse. First she screamed for help, and when it didn't come she called Gosnell every name in the book. A far-off groaning answered her. The breath froze in her lungs. There was another woman.

"Oh my God, Ray," Josie whispered over her shoulder. "There's someone else here. He's got someone else."

Not Isabelle Coleman. Who, then? Someone reported

missing, perhaps, who remained missing because of the police department's deliberately lackluster efforts to find these types of victims. Anger flared white-hot inside of her, and she began her onslaught anew.

She screamed and beat against the door until she could barely move, taking breaks only to check on Ray, whose pulse was becoming more and more difficult to find. As she slumped against the door, chest heaving, sleep hovered around the edges of her consciousness. She fought against it, not even realizing that she had lost the battle until she was startled awake by the noise of something scraping across the floor outside her cell. She lifted her head from the ground and pressed her ear to the door. Footsteps. What sounded like furniture moving.

"Ray," she hissed over her shoulder. "Someone's coming."

Her hands flailed in the darkness until she found some part of Ray's body. A knee. She followed it to his throat, her fingers sinking into the flesh, searching for a pulse. Where his skin had been fiery earlier now it was cold.

"Ray."

She felt the other side of his throat. There was nothing. She found his parted lips, her cheek hovering over them, hoping to feel a soft exhalation of air. Nothing.

"No—Ray!"

She could not keep the hysteria out of her voice. Oxygen pressed out of her lungs, escaping faster than she could take it in again. Dizziness swept over her. This could not be happening. This was a nightmare. She would wake up any second and she'd be in her big, beautiful bedroom. Luke would be in her kitchen cooking scrambled eggs, and Ray would be leaving angry messages on her phone, telling her to leave Misty alone. She would return to work with the men she had known for five years, and they would all be good men. Honest men who knew nothing of Gosnell's bunker.

Ray had hurt her. Wounded her deeply in that vulnerable place in her soul that she had never shared with anyone else—not even Luke, not really. But he was so much a part of her reality, it was hard to imagine living without him. He had always been there—only a phone call away. He was a liar, a cheater, a criminal and, she had to admit, a coward. But he had always been hers. He had been hers since they were kids. He was a part of her identity. Good or bad, she wasn't ready for this.

"Ray," she gasped, cupping his face in her hands and pressing a kiss to his unyielding mouth. "Please don't leave me. Not like this."

She laid her body over his, taking in his scent for the last time, willing him to wake up, wrap his arms around her one more time, tell her he would protect her, tell her he wouldn't let Gosnell or anyone else hurt her. But she was alone in the dark. More alone than she had ever been in her life.

How was she back here again? Alone in the closet, paralyzed by her own fear, terrified of what waited for her on the other side of the door. With her mother—drunk, hateful, spiteful—she knew what to expect. But what about Gosnell? She knew he was violent, that he had no problem hurting women. He'd killed Ray. She held on to that because it made her angry, and she needed her anger for when that door finally opened. She imagined herself as a fire, starting out slow and growing until she lit up the whole room. When he opened the door she would burst—an explosion of grief, hate, and anger. Her hands held on to Ray's lifeless body as her mind held tightly to her rage. Now, she had to wait.

# CHAPTER 59

When the door to her cell finally scraped open Josie lifted her head from Ray's corpse, disoriented and blinded by the soft, hazy light that crept in, and scrambled to her feet, swaying on unsteady legs. One hand covered her eyes. She squinted and then blinked rapidly, trying to bring Gosnell's looming figure into focus. He was just a black, man-shaped shadow filling up the doorway. His voice boomed inside the tiny space, "He dead yet?"

She didn't speak, trying to take in the room around her between the colored light spots that assaulted her eyes. The walls were cinderblock, as she had suspected, but painted red. The wooden fold-down slab was just as she had pictured it. The toilet was a grime-covered white. She purposely kept her gaze away from Ray's prone form. She didn't think she could bear it. If she saw him—what Gosnell had done to him—she would lose control and have nothing left to fight the man who stood before her.

His shadowy hand beckoned. "Come on, then," he said.

"No." Her voice sounded like a door creaking.

Gosnell's black form moved closer. "What did you say to me, girl?"

She gathered what little saliva there was in her mouth, swallowed and said, "I said, NO."

His laughter was like a foul smell filling up the tiny space. "Girls don't say no to me, honey."

He came at her then, faster and more agile than she anticipated. Or maybe she was just weaker and more dazed than she thought. She struck the soft flesh of his torso but it had no effect as he grabbed a handful of her hair and dragged her out of the cell. The wound at the back of her head threatened to pull open and tear her scalp apart. She screamed in spite of herself, her feet scrambling to keep up with him. Outside the tiny cell, he tossed her and she landed on something high and soft. A bed, she realized once she had a chance to take in her surroundings—a king-sized, four-poster bed.

The room was large and oblong, with the bed taking up one corner of the rectangle. From it, Josie could see the entire length of the room. It was windowless and decorated like a living room; couches lined one wall with at least three small end tables, and small lamps sat on each, casting a soft, golden glow over the room. The floor was covered in an old brown shag carpet. Along the same wall as the bed, to her left, was a door slightly ajar, revealing a toilet and what looked like a shower curtain. A bathroom. The wall across from the couches held four doors, each one wallpapered in an outdated floral purple and white print to look as though it was part of the wall. Only the seams and the lever handles on each one gave them away. Mortise locks atop reinforced steel panels were affixed beside each door handle. Above them were sliding deadbolts.

Four doors.

Her heart stopped, beat twice, skipped and then kicked into overdrive. Four doors. That meant there could be four women there at any given time, possibly more if they were sharing cells. How many women had Gosnell kept over the years? How many women were here right now?

She blinked, trying to get the soft blur of the room to come into sharper focus. Gosnell was on the other end of the room, leaning over a small refrigerator that she hadn't noticed. Next to it was a heavy exterior panel door. That must be the exit. On the other side of the fridge was a white cabinet with glass doors holding what looked like vials of medication and unused needles. The sedatives.

He turned and sauntered back to her, a beer can in his hand. He opened it with a snap that sounded oddly muted. There was a strange absence of sound in the place. As if every noise was instantly absorbed by the walls and the earth beyond it. No wonder her screams had been useless. As he came closer, into the circle of light cast by the bedside lamp, she saw just how dark and ugly his black eye was. It looked even worse than when she'd seen it on television.

"Did Isabelle Coleman do that to your eye?" she asked.

The leering smile playing on his face collapsed. Anger flared in his eyes. He took a long swig of beer and looked her over, as if deciding what he wanted to do to her first. She never felt such revulsion in her life. It was like a thousand insects trying to crawl out of her skin. He held the can of beer in one hand and, with the other, loosened the belt of his jeans. Did she have the strength and stamina to rush him? Her eyes panned the room again, looking for weapons. She could use one of the lamps, perhaps. They didn't look heavy, but the cords could wrap around his disgusting fat neck. Gosnell was big though—husky and round and probably strong with it. She realized she would have to get him talking if she was going to have time to figure out just what the hell she was going to do, and how she was going to do it.

"Did Sherri watch?" she asked.

The fingers fumbling for his zipper paused. He smiled at her. "What?"

"Your wife. She helped you. Did she like it? She brought you the girls, right?"

"She brought me girls because that's what I told her to do. She didn't like to watch. I made her watch sometimes, but she didn't like it. She knew better than to say anything. Sherri was a good girl."

His hand moved away from his pants and motioned toward the wallpapered cell doors. "How about you? Do you like to watch?"

Her head turned in the direction of the doors. When she looked back at him, she noticed his face was flushed. He looked excited, hungry. He put his beer down and came to the foot of the bed. One of his hands touched her ankle, his fingers sliding under her pant leg to touch bare skin.

"Don't fucking touch me," she said, kicking at his hand.

He moved quickly for a large man, climbing onto the bed and straddling her. The weight of him on top of her crushed her hips. She tried to buck him off but she was too weak. He held her wrists in his hands, squeezing so hard she could feel them bruising.

"I said, don't touch me," she gasped.

"Nobody tells me what to do," he said.

*Get him to talk,* a voice in her head commanded. Against every fiber in her body screaming to fight, she forced herself to relax a bit. He smiled down at her, his hands still gripping her wrists.

"I do whatever I want," he said proudly. "Not just in here. Out there too. I never pay for anything anymore. Never get a speeding ticket. I punched some guy out in a bar last month and never even got arrested. Cops came and saw it was me and let me go." He laughed. "Guy needed seven stitches in his face.

Get my taxes done free. There's one bar I drink at—always drink for free there. Everywhere I go, it's like I'm a king."

"Because they want to keep coming back"—she nearly choked—"for more?"

He rocked back and forth on top of her, grinding into her. She couldn't keep the repulsion from her face, which only made him laugh. "Well, sure, but mostly because they're afraid of what I got on them. They all got wives and girlfriends and families and shit." He let go of one of her wrists and pointed toward the door to outside. Josie could just make it out over his shoulder. "There," he said, pointing to a small black camera affixed to the wall above the door. "My camera takes their picture as soon as they walk in. I have a record of who comes and how many times and what they do while they're here."

He took hold of her free wrist again and pinned her hands to the bed above her head. His breath was hot and smelly against her cheek as he laid himself on top of her. "And no one wants to be the one who takes me down."

She turned her face away from his, so she didn't have to see his beady eyes. *Just keep him talking.* As one of his hands reached down into the waistband of her pants, she forced out a question. "Where did you come up with it?"

"Jesus Christ, you talk a lot," he complained. He sighed heavily, sat back up and let go of her hands. She immediately held them up in front of her. The relief she felt at having a bit of distance between them was palpable. "My dad," he said. "It's kind of a family business." Her waistband momentarily forgotten, he reached down into his undone jeans, working his hand inside of them.

Josie thought of Alton Gosnell nestled safely and comfortably inside Rockview, just a few doors down the hall from her grandmother, and wanted to retch. So his father had started it. Taking his larynx seemed the least Sherri could do. "And your mom?"

His hand froze. A shadow passed over his face. After a few seconds he heaved himself off her and retrieved his beer. Josie scrambled up onto her knees.

Gosnell said, "She didn't help. She didn't know how to act. My dad had to put her down."

"But you didn't have that problem with Sherri," she prompted.

His smile returned, faintly. "Sherri was a good girl." The shadow returned. "Then that little cunt killed her."

"June Spencer?"

"I let her out. We had the new one anyway. There wasn't enough room. Sent her up to Donald. Then she goes and kills my Sherri."

So June *had* been here.

"Was Donald one of your"—she searched for the right word, every choice making her cringe, and settled on—"regulars?"

He sipped the beer, suddenly in no hurry to get into her pants. He was enjoying this, she realized. Bragging about his sick enterprise. "Yeah, he was. Took a liking to June. When her time was up, he asked if he could take her. I told him he had to pay me for her. Two thousand dollars he offered. I took it. Easier than digging a hole."

A fresh wave of dizziness washed over her. So, he killed them. What else would a man like Gosnell do with his chattel? "Was she the only one you sold?"

"Yeah. I didn't need to get into all that. I make enough here with my girls."

He started to leer at her again, his hand working harder inside his pants this time, so she said, "It must have been hard. Losing Sherri like that."

His face colored with anger. The beer can hurtled toward her face, glancing off the wall beside her head. He leveled a finger at her. "Shut up already, would you?"

He took a breath, turned away from her, and stumbling, headed back to the fridge, next to the cabinet of vials and needles. Josie wondered how drunk he was and forged onward. "Sherri administered the drugs, didn't she? To your girls? She was a nurse. She would have been used to giving needles."

He took another beer from the fridge and slammed the door shut. He snapped the beer can open. "I said, shut up. You fucking talk too much."

"Where did you get the drugs?" Josie asked, trying to keep him talking so he wouldn't touch himself anymore—or, more importantly, her. "You must have needed a pretty steady supply. Your regulars—you had to have a doctor or a pharmacist, maybe more than one, as regular clients. Who's your supplier?"

He ignored her, chugging his beer down but keeping one eye on her.

"You can't do it, can you? Administer the drugs without Sherri?"

This beer can, fuller than the last one, hit her shoulder as she tried avoiding it and landed on the bed, its contents spilling onto the sheet. "You don't listen for shit, do you?" he growled.

"What will you do now?" she pressed on. "You and Sherri never had kids. There's no one to help you carry on the family business."

Shaking his head, he went back to the fridge to get another beer. "You better shut up about my wife," he muttered.

"What happened? She couldn't have children? Or she didn't want to have children with you? Or was it you? You couldn't give her children?"

Josie narrowly avoided the full beer can as it smashed into the wall above her head, leaving a gash in the drywall and spraying liquid all over her. He advanced on her, again pointing accusingly. "I told you to shut the fuck up. You don't know what you're talking about. Sherri had a tumor when she was nineteen. They had to tie up her female parts. There's not a goddamn thing wrong with me."

She felt a small kernel of sympathy for Sherri, which was quickly pushed aside by fear and disgust as Nick freed his penis from his pants and pumped it a few more times. He climbed onto the bed. On her knees, Josie shrank back, away from him. "I'll show you how good it works," he said. "No more talking. Now you're gonna do what I tell you."

She hoped he couldn't see her trembling. She was staring into his good eye. She would have to let him get close again. It was the only way. If he couldn't see her, he couldn't catch her. From a drawer in one of the end tables he pulled a length of rope, which he used to tie her hands to the nearest bed post at the head of the bed. She struggled, fingers flying at his face, trying to reach his eyes, then balled into fists trying to hit any soft or sensitive target she could. He slammed her head into the wall until she stopped, stars floating in front of her eyes. Then he finished tying her wrists and started yanking her pants down. A gateway in Josie's mind creaked open. The place she went when bad things happened. She hadn't needed it for many years. She never thought she'd need it again. As Gosnell climbed on top of her once more, she stepped through it.

A pounding on the door froze them both in place.

# CHAPTER 60

"Nick Gosnell," a loud male voice boomed from the other side. It sounded familiar, but she couldn't place it.

He glanced back at the door. The pounding intensified, rattling the door in its frame. "What the fuck?" Nick muttered.

"Gosnell," came the voice again. "Answer the door. I know you're in there."

He looked back and forth from her to the door, as if trying to decide what to do.

"Gosnell, get out here right now, goddamn it!" the voice growled. It was then that she knew who it was. The chief.

Nick zipped his pants up as he moved toward the door and stopped at the refrigerator, reaching deep into its recesses for something her addled brain couldn't process right at that moment. Then she heard the sound of a round being racked into a chamber. A pistol. He opened the door a crack. Daylight flooded in.

"Help you, Chief?" he said.

Chief Harris's voice came back low and furious, the way he sounded whenever one of his officers did something monumentally stupid. "I know what's going on up here, Gosnell."

Nick said, "I'm not sure what you're implying, Chief."

She saw Nick lose his footing momentarily and then brace his body against the door. The chief was trying to get in. "Let me in, goddamn it."

Nick said, "I don't know what you're playing at, but you better get the hell out of here. This is private property."

The struggle with the door continued. She could hear the chief throwing himself against it. "I'm the police, Gosnell."

"The law don't have no jurisdiction here. Get off my land."

"You're in my town, Nick. You think I didn't know something was going on? I couldn't prove anything until today."

"If you got something on me, where's your team? Why'd you come alone?" Nick taunted, trying to keep a handle on his pistol and keep the chief from bursting through the door.

"There's only two people in this town I know I can trust. One of 'em's me and I'll bet my kidney you've got the other one in there. Now let me in!"

Josie's heart sailed. "Chief!" she screamed.

The door snapped off its frame as the chief burst through, shoving Gosnell to the side and onto his back. He lifted his department-issue Glock 19 and swept it across the room. Josie had a glimpse of the chief's furious red face in the second it took for him to turn and spot Gosnell on the floor. Gosnell kicked the chief's knee with a booted heel, causing the gun to go off, the shot missing Gosnell high and wide. The chief fell, nearly toppling onto Gosnell as he rolled away and found his own gun, whipping it back toward the chief. The chief fired again. The bullet grazed Nick's arm, sending slivers of the fabric from his shirt flying. Gosnell fired and the chief went down.

"Chief!" she shrieked again, but he lay face down and limp.

She pulled desperately against her restraints until she wore away a layer of skin on her wrists. She couldn't hear above all the screaming, screaming like someone was stabbing a woman to death. It took Josie a moment to realize it was her before she stopped. She heard Gosnell moving around, muttering every curse there was under his breath as he propped the door back in place and surveyed the mess. Now her only hope was to get her hands free.

Then he was behind her, pushing her against the wall so he could untie her. She screamed again. "Will you shut the fuck up," he barked.

But she wouldn't. She couldn't. The chief was clean, and Gosnell had shot him right before her eyes. He could be dead. Luke, Ray, the chief. How much more was this man going to take from her?

"You're going back in there with your boyfriend until I get this shit cleaned up," he told her.

She started to kick at him until she realized that it was to her advantage for him to untie her. She would have a few precious seconds to try something. He was larger than her and armed. She was shackled and injured. She couldn't put herself in a position where he could overpower her or injure her so badly that she couldn't fight back or escape. She needed the upper hand.

She heard Ray's voice then, as surely as if he were standing at the foot of the bed. *Calm down, Jo. The darkness can't hurt you.*

She stopped struggling and took a long, shuddering breath, allowing Nick to free her hands. He reached for her hair again, his preferred method of moving women from place to place. Without hesitation, she reached up with both hands and grabbed the sides of his face, as though she was going to draw him in for a kiss. For a split second, his face registered delighted surprise. Then she drove her thumbs into the soft orbs of his eyes, holding onto his head while he howled and bucked and swung his arms, desperate to get away from her.

He fell away, off the bed and onto the floor. She leapt over him, landing painfully on her knees, and found his gun discarded on the floor. She stood, pain shooting through both her kneecaps, and trained the gun on his writhing form. He held his palms against his eyes. "My eyes!" he screamed. "My eyes!"

"Gosnell," she shouted.

"My eyes! You bitch. My eyes!"

"Stop moving," she told him as she stepped closer to him.

"You fucking bitch!" he shrieked.

"This is for Ray," she said and fired a shot into his left kneecap.

More howls. His hands scrambled for his obliterated kneecap. He curled onto his side. Following his jerky movements, she placed the barrel of the gun against his right kneecap—steel against bone—and fired again. Blood and bone sprayed up into her face. She used her forearm to wipe it away. The sounds coming out of him were like nothing she had ever heard before—not from a human—but she was dead to it. "That was for the chief."

She kicked him, rolling him until he was flat on his back, grinding her heel into the crushed knee closest to her. She leaned over so that she might be heard over his cries. "This is for the girls," she said and fired a shot into his groin.

She tossed the gun away and ran to where the chief lay, face down. She touched his shoulder and he coughed. "Josie," he choked.

She dropped to her knees. "Chief!"

"Don't move me," he said, his voice raspy. Every word seemed a monumental struggle. She strained to hear him. "I think the bullet severed my spine. I can't feel anything. It's hard to . . . hard to breathe."

She lay down next to him, her face inches from his, so he

could see her eyes. He tried to smile, but a tear slid out of his eye and rolled off the bridge of his nose. They stared at each other for a beat. The relief that Josie felt was subsumed by the grief that was already overwhelming her. Nothing would ever be the same again.

"Listen," he whispered. "This is important."

"Chief," she squeaked.

"Trust Fraley. He's clean. I'm promoting you to chief. You're reinstated and promoted. Don't...don't trust anyone else. You'll...you'll have to bring in...new—"

"I'll bring in new people," she promised.

"Watch your...watch your back."

"I will."

His eyelids fluttered. "Call..."

She touched his cheek gently. "Chief?"

"FBI."

"Okay, I will."

His eyes opened wide and he held her gaze with a penetrating intensity that made goosebumps erupt over her entire body. "Get them," he said. "Get them all."

Then he exhaled for the very last time.

# CHAPTER 61

She covered the chief with a sheet from the bed as reverently as she could in the godforsaken hellhole they were in. Nick's body had gone completely still amongst the wide and extensive blood and bone spatter all around him. She let herself sob for several minutes beside her mentor, holding her knees to her chest and rocking back and forth like a child. She wailed and keened and let herself feel the unfathomable loss she had just experienced for a few private moments. Then she wiped her tears away and hauled herself to her feet. She found her pants and put them back on. Then she surveyed the room. She had to think. She had to be smart about this.

First things first. She had to open the doors. Dread was a heavy brick in her stomach. She didn't know which door Gosnell had taken her out of so she would have to check each one. She started with the closest one and worked her way down. Much to her relief, the first cell was empty, although it looked as though it had been recently vacated. A crumpled blanket lay on the wooden cot, and a discarded fast food bag lay on the floor. When she opened the second door, she saw Ray's boots and closed it again. She couldn't bear to see him. Not like that. Not yet.

She sucked in a breath and opened the third door. Empty. Behind the fourth door a thin, waifish form curled cowering in the corner of the cell. She balled herself up tighter when Josie stepped through the door. "Hello?" Josie called. The woman shot upright and scurried away from her, one pale thin arm covering her eyes. "No more," she said, her voice hoarse. Josie didn't think it possible but the rage she felt toward Gosnell for all the horror he had inflicted on so many innocent young women burned even hotter.

"It's okay," Josie said. "You're safe now. I'm not going to hurt you."

Josie waited several moments. Finally, the woman lowered her arm and blinked, taking Josie in. It wasn't Isabelle Coleman. This woman was likely in her mid-twenties, with short dark hair and a pointy chin. "Who are you?" the woman asked, the question sounding like an accusation.

"My name is Josie Quinn. I am a detect—" she stopped, tears rolling unbidden down her cheeks. She glanced back to where the chief's body lay. Then she continued, straightening her posture and raising her chin proudly. "I'm the new chief of police in this town, and I've come to get you out of here."

# CHAPTER 62

The woman stood on shaky legs, skeletal in an ill-fitting lace bra and underwear. "Wait here," Josie told her and quickly retrieved a blanket she had found in the empty cell. She held it out to the woman. "Here."

Still eyeing Josie with suspicion, the woman slowly wrapped the blanket around her shoulders. "What's your name?" Josie asked.

"Rena," the woman said, voice cracking with a sudden burst of emotion. "Rena Garry."

Josie held out a hand to her. "Rena, we have to get out of here. Now."

The woman's eyes flashed with understanding. She gripped Josie's hand and followed her out of the cell.

"It's not a pretty sight out here," Josie said. "Look straight ahead toward the door. Don't look down."

Josie tried to rush her past Nick Gosnell's ravaged body, but Rena stopped, pulling insistently on Josie's hand. Josie tugged back. "Please," she said. "We have to go."

Rena stood over him, staring. "This is him," she said. "He was here every day."

"This was his place," Josie confirmed. "Listen, we really have to—"

Josie's eyes were drawn to the chief's body. Struck by a thought, she dropped Rena's hand. "Just a second," she told her, but the woman's eyes were fixed on Gosnell's body with fierce intensity.

Josie left her there long enough to search out the chief's cell phone, which she found in his back pocket. As she strode back toward Rena, she realized that she couldn't exactly call 911. Who would she call? The chief had told her not to trust anyone. Not that there was even a cell phone signal on the mountain, she thought, looking at the screen. She'd have to go to Gosnell's house and use their landline.

She grasped Rena's hand once more. "Please," she said. "We need to get out of here."

"Did you do this?" Rena asked.

Josie looked down, really seeing what she had done as if for the first time. Through someone else's eyes. Gosnell's eyes pulpy caved-in messes, blood streaking his face. The front of his jeans shredded, blood pooling all around him. The jagged edges of bone sticking out from his left knee. The space where his right knee used to be. Bone splinters, tissue, sinew, and blood all around him. Close-range shots and devastating damage.

"Yes," she said. "I did."

She watched as Rena spit on Gosnell's body. Then she said, "Let's go."

Josie nodded, pocketing the chief's cell phone and pulling Rena toward the door, only stopping to snatch up the chief's gun in the corner. She put it in the waistband of her jeans, and pushed the mangled door aside. Daylight flooded around them, nearly blinding them. Rena threw an arm up over her eyes again and Josie looked down at her feet. "You have no shoes," she said.

"I don't care."

Josie laced her fingers through Rena's, and together they plunged into the light.

# CHAPTER 63

The Gosnell house was small and sparsely furnished. The back door led into a kitchen that looked like it hadn't been updated since the seventies. Josie left Rena sitting with a glass of water in front of her at the yellowed formica table that took up most of the room. The rest of the house was empty. She breathed a sigh of relief. They were safe for the moment, but it was only a matter of time before someone came by. They couldn't stay long.

From the living room window, the chief's Jeep was visible. She hadn't found any keys in his pockets, which meant he had probably left them in the vehicle. She could always load Rena into the Jeep and leave with her. But she needed to preserve the scene. Protect it. The last thing she needed was one of Gosnell's sick customers coming by and destroying evidence.

The chief had said to call the FBI, but she didn't know anyone from the FBI. Luke might, but he couldn't help her right now—at the very least she hoped he was still alive. Denise Poole probably knew someone, but she was likely in custody by now. That left only one person—one person who had a unique ability to help Josie protect and preserve the scene, even though calling her went against every fiber of Josie's being.

She returned to the kitchen and found the landline. It took three tries to get the number right—she was going by memory. Finally, her call was answered.

"Hello?" the woman on the other line said.

"Trinity?" Josie said. "I need your help."

"Who is this?"

"It's Josie Quinn."

There was a sharp intake of breath. "Where the *hell* are you? No one has seen you for two days. Or Ray. And someone at the station said the chief took off and no one can reach him either."

Two days. She had been in that cell with Ray for two days. She wondered if Luke was still alive. She couldn't bear to ask. She couldn't lose him too. She would never survive it. She squeezed her eyes shut. "I'll tell you where I am—where we all are—but I need your help. Do you know anyone in the FBI?"

"Sure. There's an agent in the Philadelphia office I'm friendly with. I . . . wait. What the hell is going on?"

"I need you to call them. As soon as we hang up. Also, I need you to get Noah Fraley."

"He was just discharged from the hospital," Trinity said.

"Great. Get him and bring him with you."

"Bring him where?" Trinity asked.

"I'll tell you," Josie said. "But you have to do exactly as I say. No exceptions, no deviations."

Josie pictured one of Trinity's perfectly groomed brows arching. "What's in it for me?"

"The story of a lifetime."

# CHAPTER 64

They had a few hours of daylight left, by Josie's calculations. She was worried about what would happen when it got dark. She didn't want to be in Gosnell's house in the dark, but turning on the lights before help arrived would be risky. If any of Gosnell's associates showed up Josie would be forced to defend herself and Rena.

"How long till they get here?" Rena asked, quaking, from the kitchen table. She had tucked her knees against her chest, toes curled over the edge of the chair. She kept tugging the corners of the blanket tighter and tighter around her. It wasn't cold in the house, but Josie knew she was in shock.

Josie stood in the doorway. She had opened the curtains in the living room so that from where she stood she had a partial view of the driveway. "It might be a few hours," she said honestly.

Rena frowned. "I don't understand. If you're the chief of police, why do we have to wait hours for help to come? Why did you ask for the FBI?"

Josie hung her head. "It's a long story," she said. "Which I am happy to tell you while we wait. But first I need to know, how long were you in that bunker?"

Rena's body began rocking slowly back and forth. "I have no idea. What's the date?"

"March twenty-third."

One of Rena's hands snaked out from beneath the blanket and covered her eyes. "Oh my . . ." she squeaked.

"When did you—when is the last date you remember?" Josie asked softly.

"October. It was October fifth. I was at the hospital. Oh my God. I can't . . . I can't believe it. I knew it was long. It felt like forever, but the drugs . . . So much is a blur. I don't . . . I don't . . ."

Hysteria raised her voice two octaves. Josie crossed the room, pulled out a chair and sat down next to Rena. "Hey," she said softly. "You're safe now. Rena, it's going to be okay. Why were you at the hospital in October?"

Rena didn't speak for a long moment. When she looked up at Josie, tears streaked her thin face. "F-f-for rehab. I . . . I'm an addict, okay?" She extended an arm and, for the first time, Josie noticed the track marks pitting the soft flesh in the bend of her elbow. "It was my third time. I had checked myself in. I drove myself there, did two weeks until my insurance stopped paying, so I left. I was looking for my car in the parking garage and this lady came walking past me. She asked if I needed help so I said yeah, I'm looking for my car. And that's the last thing I remember."

So, similar to Ginger's story.

"I'm sorry," Josie said. "I'm so sorry. Do you remember anything about the woman?"

"She was dressed in scrubs, like a nurse. Older, like, maybe in her sixties. She said her name was Ramona."

So, Sherri Gosnell had lured her.

"What hospital?" Josie asked.

Rena told her, but Josie didn't recognize the name. "It's in a small town outside of Pittsburgh," Rena added. Then her eyes widened. She looked around frantically. "Oh my God, where am I? Where the hell am I? Is this still Pennsylvania?"

"Yes," Josie said. "You're still in Pennsylvania. But you're about a hundred and fifty miles away from home."

"Oh my God."

"I'm so sorry, Rena," Josie said. She got up to check the living room window. Nothing yet. Relief warred with her anxiety. Trinity and Noah couldn't get there fast enough.

Behind her, Rena said, "So now you tell me. Tell me where I am, and how you found me."

# CHAPTER 65

Daylight was fading by the time Josie and Rena heard the first crunch of tire over gravel outside. They'd drunk every bottle of water in the fridge and raided the Gosnell's cabinets, finding some potato chips and crackers to chew on. Josie could tell by the way Rena picked at the chips that she had even less of an appetite than Josie did, but both their stomachs growled with hunger and Josie urged her to eat, if only to pass the time. "I don't know when we'll have a chance to get real food. Once the FBI arrives, things are going to move pretty quickly," Josie told her. They ate what they could. Josie's throat felt dry and scratchy from talking, but it kept her anxiety away, kept her from thinking about Ray and the chief lying dead and cold and alone in the bunker.

They both sprang up from the table when they heard the cars. More than one, Josie realized as she darted into the living room. She watched as the first rounded the last curve of the Gosnells' driveway and came into view. Her entire body unwound with relief as Trinity Payne's Honda Civic pulled up alongside the chief's Jeep. Behind it were two black Chevy Suburbans and one boxy white van with the FBI logo emblazoned on the side of it above the words Philadelphia Field Office Evidence Response Team.

"They're here," Josie called to Rena, her voice losing all trace of calm. "They're here!"

Rena sat back in her chair in the kitchen. "I'll be right back," Josie told her.

Josie never would have thought she'd feel such joy at seeing Trinity Payne, but she had to work hard not to fall into her arms as she emerged from her Honda. She stood a few feet back from Trinity, trying to smile but already feeling her composure cracking. Her shoulders quaked as all around them FBI agents began to alight from their vehicles and jog over.

"Thank you," Josie told Trinity.

For once Trinity's face was devoid of its usual eagle-eyed scrutiny. "You don't look so good," she replied.

The passenger-side door of the Honda opened and Noah stepped out. His right shoulder was heavily bandaged and his right arm rested in a sling. He looked pale and exhausted, bags hanging below his eyes. "Detective Quinn," he said.

"Noah," Josie choked. She wiped tears away with the backs of her hands. "I'm sorry I shot you."

He managed a weak smile. "All is forgiven," he said.

A tall male agent in a charcoal-gray suit stepped up beside Josie. He was easily six foot four, and thin as a rail. He was nearing sixty, his short hair a drab gray. Trinity looked from him to Josie and said, "This is Special Agent Marcus Holcomb. He'll be heading up this investigation."

Josie shook his hand. "Let me show you what we've got."

# CHAPTER 66

Josie spent two hours on the scene with Holcomb, leading his team to the bunker and giving him her version of events. As she grew more and more exhausted, Holcomb suggested that she let his team transport her to the hospital to be checked out and then to a hotel to get cleaned up, eat something, and get some rest. He put a female agent with her. Josie was grateful for the company. The last thing she wanted was to be alone.

Once at the hotel she thought she wouldn't be able to sleep, but after a shower and two painkillers she fell into a dreamless slumber. They let her sleep until early the next morning, but then it was time to get back to work. The FBI needed to know everything she knew in as much detail as she could give. The female agent set up an impromptu interview area in the hotel room, recording Josie's lengthy statement while Holcomb remained at the Gosnells', overseeing everything.

Josie was told that Rena Garry had been transferred to Geisinger Medical Center under guard. Josie was allowed to contact Carrieann to let her know that she was safe and to arrange for the FBI to take custody of June and Lara Spencer. There had been no change in Luke's condition. Josie was relieved, but disappointed. She needed Luke now, more than ever.

Noah and Trinity were allowed access to Josie at the hotel. It was Noah who told her that they still had not found Isabelle Coleman. "There are some graves up there," he said. "Some relatively fresh ones, but none fresh enough to be Coleman."

Josie shivered. "Gosnell and his father have been at this for decades. Noah, there could be a hundred bodies up there."

Noah sat down beside her at the foot of her hotel bed. "I know," he said. "Listen, I didn't get the chance to tell you, but I'm sorry about Ray."

She stared at the threads of the carpet beneath her sneakered feet. Maroon, mauve and more shades of pink than she could count. "Ray knew," she whispered. "He knew they were doing something bad up there, and he didn't try to stop it."

"But he was still your husband," Noah offered.

All she could manage was a stiff nod.

"Josie," he said. "There are a couple of things. Gosnell had videos—"

"I know," she said. "He told me."

She glanced up in time to see Noah's grimace. "Holcomb wants us to review them with him. We need to ID as many of the men in them as possible. If this goes as far as you think, it's going to be a delicate operation rounding up all these assholes without tipping them off first."

"Did Trinity run the story I suggested?"

"Yeah. She had to get her producer and the station to agree, but Holcomb worked that out pretty quickly."

Josie smiled. "Wonder what he promised her. Trinity doesn't do anything for nothing."

Noah shrugged. "She's not so bad."

The story that Josie had suggested was that both Gosnell and Chief Harris were alive and well and assisting the FBI in an investigation into a cache of illegal drugs found on Gosnell's property, including a meth lab being run out of the old house on the back end of the land. Josie had suggested they take footage of the FBI appearing to search Josie's great-grandparents' old house. It was far enough away from the bunker that it might keep Gosnell's regular customers from panicking. The fake story would keep Gosnell's associates from coming onto the property but also keep them from fleeing. Still, Josie knew there would be a lot of nervous men in Denton and the surrounding counties. Based on what Ray had told her, they knew without watching any tapes that Dusty was involved.

"Did Holcomb get Dusty?" she asked.

"He's cooperating fully," Noah said. "I think he's trying to work out some kind of deal. Holcomb barely said two words and he was rolling over like a goddamn dog in heat, ready to give everything up."

Revulsion rippled through Josie's body. "What a creep."

"Yeah. I never liked that guy."

"I don't even think his own mother ever liked him."

Noah laughed. The sound was alien after the few days she had had, and yet it felt good to hear it. Noah nudged her leg with his. "Dusty already ID'ed all the culpable Denton PD officers. Holcomb had them all picked up this morning. You're officially interim chief now. You outrank everyone anyway, even without Grizz promoting you. Everyone else is still operating as though it's business as usual. We're a little short-staffed, but things are being handled. I've got teams trying to locate Isabelle Coleman around the clock."

"That's good," she said. "Hey, did you talk to Holcomb about going to see my grandmother?"

"He can give you one hour, but that's it. He wants to review these tapes immediately. Once that's done you can go back and spend more time with her."

"An hour? Is he kidding?"

"No. I can take you by Rockview on the way to the station."

"Ray's mom? The chief's wife? Do they know?"

Noah's chin dropped to his chest. "I know you wanted to tell them yourself, but it couldn't wait. They kept calling. They knew something was up."

Josie squeezed her eyes shut, "Not Holcomb. Please, God, tell me you didn't let Holcomb tell them."

She opened her eyes and Noah met her gaze. "No," he said. "I told them myself."

"Thank you."

"You ready to get to work?"

Josie took a deep breath, bracing herself for what was to come. Reliving her ordeal for Lisette's sake, breaking the news of Ray's death to her, watching the videos, and finding Isabelle Coleman. "Yes," she said.

# CHAPTER 67

"You said they found bodies up there on the mountain," Lisette said. She stared at Josie from the recliner chair in her room, her eyes as wide as Josie had ever seen them. One of her hands fidgeted with a balled-up tissue.

"Yes," Josie said. "Noah said they found graves, but none fresh enough to be Isabelle Coleman. Gram, did you hear me? Gosnell killed Ray."

Lisette nodded and pressed the tissue to the corner of each eye. Maybe she was having trouble processing it. Maybe it was too much, too big to take in all in one go. Life without Ray was unfathomable. Josie had still needed him, she realized. Maybe not on a daily basis, but he had carried her past, her demons with him. Only Ray knew everything; he had been there through most of it, and without him she had to carry it alone. The only way Josie was able to function was by focusing on what needed to be done next. Talk to Lisette, then meet with Holcomb. For now her list was never-ending, and she was grateful.

"I'll go with you to the funeral," Lisette said. She reached a hand across to where Josie sat on the edge of her bed and Josie took it. "I'm so sorry, Josie."

Josie swallowed the lump in her throat. "Thank you."

It was kind, but Lisette seemed far more upset about what Nick Gosnell had been doing on his property over the years than she was about Ray's murder. She let go of Josie's hand and sank back into her chair. Second by second, her eyes took on a thousand-yard stare. Josie had the feeling her mind was somewhere else entirely.

"Gram," Josie said softly. "I have to go soon. They're only giving me an hour. I have to go... go look at videos. Identify all of Gosnell's customers. Will you be okay until I can come back?"

"Sherri must have been horribly abused," Lisette said as if she hadn't heard Josie.

Josie sighed. Perhaps the Gosnells were safer emotional territory than Ray right now. She glanced at the clock by Lisette's bedside. She had fifteen minutes left. "Yes," Josie responded. "On the way over Noah told me he had talked with the medical examiner about Sherri. She said Sherri's autopsy showed many old fractures. Ribs, arms, legs, even a skull fracture. Typical of a victim of domestic violence."

"It's so sad," Lisette said. "She never said a word."

"It would have been pretty difficult for her to socialize," Josie said. "Given what her life at home was like."

"She never said a word," Lisette said again. "Just went about her work. She wasn't unkind, just... she was just... there."

Josie tried to imagine what Sherri's home life had been like. In many ways, she reminded Josie of June Spencer in her catatonic state. She simply went through the motions of living. But she supposed that for Sherri, living with a monster like Nick Gosnell, life had been all about survival. Just getting through each day alive or without being beaten must have felt like a victory. Josie wondered if she had ever gotten any true joy out of life. She was torn between feeling sympathetic for Sherri and feeling enraged that the woman had been such an active participant in his evil enterprise. She wondered just how much culpability Sherri had. There was no denying that Nick had abused her, but the lengths she had gone to help Nick were simply incomprehensible.

Lisette's voice took on a sudden fierce intensity. "That son of a bitch, Alton Gosnell. Look what he created. You know they never did find his wife. He said she ran off, but I guess now we know what really happened to her."

"They'll find her on the mountain, I'm sure," Josie said quietly, not wanting to upset her grandmother further by sharing what Nick had told her about his mother.

She heard what sounded like a sob and quickly added, "I'm coming to question him, Gram. The moment we're done with these videos. Nick implicated him and I am not letting him get away with anything."

Josie heard sniffling. Then Lisette said, "Good. I'm glad. He shouldn't get away with a damn thing." She lowered her voice. "He's very sick though. Some kind of infection, they said."

"That doesn't concern me," Josie said coolly.

There was silence. Then, "That's my girl."

# CHAPTER 68

Josie couldn't stand Special Agent Holcomb. She had been relieved to see him at the Gosnell property and she was happy for the FBI presence, but Holcomb's personality left much to be desired. It was about as colorful as his short, drab hair. Maybe he had seen too much in his long career, especially working for the FBI's Civil Rights Division which investigated police corruption and human trafficking, but he didn't seem angry or impassioned enough for her.

"Maybe that's what we need. Someone who will be clinical. Detached," Noah had tried persuading her after a day in Holcomb's company, the three of them trawling through videos from Gosnell's bunker, trying to identify all the men in the videos. They would ID the men first so they could arrest them quickly. Later, the FBI team would work on identifying all the women and then matching them to the remains that were already being recovered. There were nearly two decades' worth of videos, and they only got through about five years' worth that first day. Holcomb fast-forwarded through all of them. He was only interested in catching stills of the men's faces at that point. Later, for the sake of prosecution, someone would have to go through each and every video thoroughly. He stopped the video every few seconds, demanding to know if Josie or Noah could put a name to the face, and grew impatient when they hesitated.

Even on fast-forward, the videos were horrific. Both Josie and Noah had to take several breaks, escaping outside into the fresh air, letting the rain wash the horror away if only for a few seconds. Holcomb had only gotten up twice. Once to eat and once to retrieve a cup of coffee—for himself, none for them. Then he had wordlessly recorded each name they gave him on a legal pad with the same expression Josie imagined he employed when making his grocery list. It irked her.

By the end of the third day they had a solid working list, and Holcomb left them to put together warrants and teams to execute them. "This has to be done quickly," he told them. "We'll want to pick them all up in a short span of time. We don't want them tipping each other off. I want every last one of these scumbags."

It was the first thing Holcomb had said that Josie could get on board with.

The moment he left, Josie turned to Noah. "How many people are searching for Isabelle Coleman right now?"

"I have a dozen people out right now."

"Then let's go talk to Alton Gosnell."

Noah frowned and looked at his watch. He was one of the few men that Josie knew who still wore a watch instead of relying on his phone for the time. "Right now? Don't you want to rest? It's been a long three days."

"No. I don't want to rest. Let's go."

# CHAPTER 69

Alton Gosnell was so ill that the nursing staff did not want to let Josie anywhere near him. She was not to be deterred. "I don't care if he's in the middle of a goddamn heart transplant. I want to talk to him," she told the director of nursing at Rockview.

"Miss Quinn—"

Noah, who stood behind Josie, said, "It's Chief Quinn. As in the chief of police."

The director forced a weary smile. "Chief Quinn, Mr. Gosnell has an extremely high fever. His heart rate is up, and his blood pressure is down. As you are probably aware, he has a stoma and speaks using an artificial larynx. In his condition, any type of...interview would be extremely stressful. I simply cannot allow it."

Josie put a hand on her hip. "I'll be sure to pass along your recommendation to the families of the women he raped and killed. It's not an interview. It's an interrogation. If he's about to die, then it's especially urgent that I speak with him. There is still a girl missing in this town, and I'm damn well going to find her."

"You can't just walk in here and start making demands.

You may be the chief of police, but you can't just do whatever you want."

Josie's voice was low and tense, a wire pulled taut to its breaking point. "I've had just about all I can take of people getting in my way. This man left a mass grave on his property. Do you understand that? They're unearthing the bodies of young women—ten so far—and they're still going. Ground-penetrating radar shows there could be as many as sixty more buried up there. Mr. Gosnell may speak using an artificial larynx, but he can still speak. Those women don't have that luxury anymore. I'm their voice now, and I have a lot of fucking questions. Now, you can get out of my way, or I can have you arrested and charged with obstruction of justice."

"You can't—"

"I can and I will. Don't test me. Maybe it won't hold up in court, but that's not really my problem, now is it? That would be your attorney's problem."

Josie motioned toward the hallway behind the woman and stared her down, daring her to stand her ground. After a long, tense moment, the director stepped aside, wordlessly. At Josie's back, she called, "He's in room—"

"I know where he is," Josie snapped without looking back at the woman.

Alton Gosnell was propped up in his bed, wearing a faded blue pajama top. The few strands of white hair left on his head floated upright. His skin flamed red. When he breathed, his stoma whistled. The sound of fluid in his lungs sounded like a coffee pot percolating. The room smelled of stale urine and sweat. His dark eyes followed Josie and Noah as they entered the room. Noah stood on one side of the bed, Josie on the other. Noah went through the motions of introducing them and reading him his rights. When Noah asked if he understood the rights as he had read them, Alton's right hand lifted and pressed the artificial larynx to his throat. "You arresting me?" the robotic voice asked.

"We're just here to talk, Mr. Gosnell," Noah said. He waved a copy of the Miranda warning in the air. "I just have to read this before I talk to people about crimes."

Alton nodded sagely. They had agreed beforehand that Noah would do most of the talking, since a misogynist like Alton would be more likely to talk to a man than a woman. That, and Josie wasn't quite sure if she could trust herself to be professional.

"Mr. Gosnell, I'm sorry about the death of your son," Noah began. Neither of them was sorry, but they had agreed that it was a place to start.

Alton shrugged. "He was weak. Stupid."

Noah and Josie exchanged a look. Noah dove in. "Stupid? It seems he was running quite a successful business up there on your property. From what we can tell, he was doing it for decades."

The gnarled hand pressed the larynx into his throat. "Got caught though, didn't he?" Alton eyed Josie. She refused to feel uncomfortable beneath his leering gaze, almost identical to his son's. He was old and infirm. He couldn't even walk. He could leer all he wanted, but he couldn't hurt her. "They never caught me."

"Your son implicated you in his crimes," Josie said.

The man laughed silently. Then he pressed his device against his throat again. "You can't arrest me now. I'm too old, too sick."

Josie didn't care if the guy disintegrated when they slapped the cuffs on him, he was going down. She opened her mouth to say so, but Noah jumped in. "What was the difference? Between you and Nick. Why didn't you ever get caught?"

Gosnell's eyes traveled back toward Noah. "I didn't bring

nobody else up there. It was just me. I didn't sell 'em, and I sure as shit didn't keep 'em around. When I was done with 'em, I put 'em down."

"Put them down?" Noah prompted.

Alton said nothing. Noah tried a different tack. "What did you do with them after you put them down?"

"Plenty of land up there," Alton said. "Especially after I bought the property behind us."

"Where did you take them from? Why didn't people notice?"

Alton shook his head. "Never took one from the same place twice. Drove as far as I could, picked one I didn't think would be missed, waited till no one was around and I took her. Back then we didn't have cell phones and goddamn cameras everywhere. It was easier back then, and I sure as shit never took as many as my boy."

"How many do you think are out there?" Noah asked.

"Don't know. Never counted 'em."

"Do you remember the first time you, uh, put one of them down?" Noah asked.

Alton stared straight ahead. If his breathing wasn't so labored, Josie might have thought he was dead. Noah said, "Mr. Gosnell?"

Perhaps he was remembering. His eyes glazed over, and a look that could only be described as euphoric came over his crimson face. Josie felt sick. He was, she realized, a genuine serial killer. He had operated for decades unchecked, unfettered, with enough private land to hide his crimes for all that time. Not only was he completely without remorse, but he had enjoyed his crimes. Josie knew from the resurrected town lore about the Gosnell family that Alton's wife had supposedly run off when her son was only nine, which meant that Nick had been raised almost solely by his father, who had shaped him in his image. Two generations of serial killers. Like father, like son.

Lisette's voice, fierce and tremulous, sounded from the door. "You tell them the truth, Alton."

Startled, Noah and Josie looked at her. She stood leaning on her walker, her tiny frame seeming to fill up the entire doorway. Her eyes were aflame, and they were trained on Alton Gosnell with a savage intensity. Josie had never seen that look on her grandmother's face before. Her sweet, loving grandmother.

"Gram?" Josie said.

Lisette thrust her walker into the room, wielding it like a weapon. She banged into Gosnell's bed, jarring it. Gosnell's euphoric reverie gave way to annoyance. He flicked her a dirty look. Pressing his artificial larynx into his throat again, he said, "Shut up, Lisette."

She shook a finger at him. Her entire body shook with rage. "You think I don't know what you did? I figured it out. I know it was you. I know what you did to my . . . my . . . Ramona. Now you tell the truth, you sick bastard."

At the name Ramona, Josie felt all the color drain from her face. "Gram?" she said again, her voice weakening as she looked over at a woman she barely recognized. This woman was not her grandmother. This was a different woman. A woman with hate in her eyes and vengeance quivering through her body. The only thing that seemed to stop her wrapping her fingers around Gosnell's throat was her walker.

Gosnell laughed noiselessly again. Then he looked at Lisette and pressed his device into his throat. "She was perfect. You did a good job making her, Lisette. I hated putting her down. I would have kept her forever."

Tears streamed down Lisette's cheeks but she refused to acknowledge them, letting them fall to her shirt. She said nothing.

"You think I didn't know?" he said to her.

Still, she remained silent.

"It was that army boy, wasn't it? The one who boarded with your family for the summer? I saw you in the woods with him once. Gave it to you good, he did."

Lisette gasped. Noah remained completely silent and still, letting the whole thing play out. Josie's voice was little more than a whisper. "Gram, what is he talking about?"

Lisette kept her eyes on Gosnell. "I was a girl," she said. "Only thirteen. My parents rented out a room in our house to make extra money. One summer we had a soldier on his way from one place to another. He stayed a few months. He wasn't that much older than me. I thought I loved him. After he left I realized I was pregnant."

"What? Dad was your only child."

"He was, as far as anyone knows. My mother told everyone that she was pregnant. As soon as I started to show, they kept me home. Told everyone I was sick. I gave birth at home to a beautiful baby girl. My mother passed her off as her own. My sister. Little Ramona."

Gosnell mouthed her words. *Little Ramona.*

Josie's voice trembled. "How long did she...did she live?"

"She was eight years old. I was hanging wash at the side of the house and she was playing there in the yard. Running around, chasing butterflies. Then she was gone. Just like that." She glared at Gosnell. "He took her."

"Wild animals ate her," Gosnell said.

"The only animal that got her was you," Lisette shot back.

More silent laughter shook his body.

Lisette said, "I searched the woods for her. My father searched with me. For days. We had the law up there looking too. Then, after about a week, we found her clothes there in the woods. Torn up. Police said she must have been attacked by a bear, or coyotes. They probably dragged her off. They tried to find her body for a few weeks but couldn't. We buried an empty coffin." Her voice choked in her throat. In a whisper she added, "An empty little coffin." She took a moment then to wipe her tear-streaked face with the back of one of her sleeves. "My mother was happy to brush the whole thing under the carpet. I never believed a wild animal got her, but what else could have happened to her? Back then we didn't have Megan's list and all those things. People didn't talk about sex crimes or child molesters. I just knew in my heart something bad happened to her, and it wasn't an animal that did it. I was in those woods my whole life and never even saw a coyote. When you told me about Nick and about the women, I knew. I knew the kind of man Alton is—you don't hear the things he says to the ladies here. It wasn't a stretch that the apple didn't fall far from the tree."

Like father, like son.

Goosebumps rose along Josie's arms.

Lisette jarred the bed again with her walker. "What did you do to her, you son of a bitch?"

Gosnell looked away from her. His smirk disappeared. He had an almost pained look on his face. "She was my first," he said. "I wanted to keep her, but after a few days of people searching for her, I realized I couldn't. So I put her down. Kept her somewhere no one would find her and left the clothes so everyone would think a bear got her. I thought for sure they would come for me. I waited."

"Did you hurt her? Did you touch her?"

His eyes glazed over again. "Not the way you think," he said. "There was no time. My wife—she was still alive. My boy was there always asking questions. I couldn't risk it. Every time I went to see her, one of them ruined it."

Josie moved over to Lisette and put a hand over her grand-mother's forearm. "Gram," she said.

"But she was the first one I took," Gosnell went on. His eyes lit up. "And I never got caught. Then I knew I could do it."

*I knew I could do it.*

Josie knew from the bodies being unearthed on the Gosnell property and the videos that all of the Gosnell victims were teenagers or older. If Alton's appetites ran along the same lines as his son's then eight-year-old Ramona would have been a victim of convenience, not necessarily chosen based on his sexual desire. He knew she was illegitimate, and she was easily plucked from the neighbor's yard. The perfect test subject.

"How long?" Josie asked. "How long were you thinking about taking a girl before you took Ramona?"

"A long time," he said. "Since I was a teenager. I wanted to do more things, but that came later with the others. I kept the name alive for my son. That first perfect kill. I told him he needed to find his own Ramona, and he did, but then he perverted the whole thing. Couldn't keep his mouth shut. I told you he was stupid."

So that's where it had come from. Nick had simply appropriated the name for his little business venture even though it disappointed Alton. Perverted was an interesting choice of word. Josie tried to imagine Alton as a young man, nursing abduction and rape fantasies for at least a decade. What a thrill it must have been for him just to take the girl. To finally take a step toward making his sick fantasies a reality. That he had gotten away with it likely opened the floodgates for more of his twisted urges to come alive. Then he had killed his wife and started teaching his son how to rape and murder women and dispose of their bodies.

"Where is she?" Lisette asked. "Where is my daughter?"

"She's up there," Alton said. "She's up there on the mountain with the rest of them."

# CHAPTER 70

"Gram, how come you never told me about your daughter?"

They sat side by side on Lisette's bed. They held hands but stared straight ahead at the open door where staff and other residents walked up and down the hall, not sparing a glance into Lisette's room. The hustle and bustle of Rockview went on just as normal. The emotional earthquake Josie had just experienced in Alton Gosnell's room belonged only to them. She and her grandmother. The last surviving members of their family.

"It was ancient history," Lisette said. Her voice sounded heavy and exhausted.

"Now, I know that's not true," Josie said. "She wouldn't have been ancient history for you."

A few seconds passed by. Lisette squeezed Josie's hand. "It was so long ago, and my parents worked so hard to put it in the past and keep it there. You have to understand how it was back then. You couldn't get pregnant out of wedlock. There weren't single mothers. My mother wanted to send me away. There was a home for unwed mothers in Philadelphia. I was supposed to go there to give birth. Ramona would have been adopted—hopefully. Maybe she would have lived if I had done what they wanted. But I couldn't give her up. I knew I wouldn't be able to do it. I wore them down. They came up with the idea of passing Ramona off as theirs. But they never really accepted her.

"For a time after she disappeared, I actually wondered if they'd taken her away. But they missed her when she was gone. Then I knew that it wasn't them. Still, when we found her clothes, they were eager to lay her to rest. They wanted to go on as if she'd never been there. She wasn't talked about. I think my mother was relieved."

"Gram, I'm so sorry."

"Eventually I accepted that I would never know exactly what happened to her. I understood that she was dead, although I used to have fantasies about her being alive, coming to find me one day. Those passed with time. I even accepted that I would never lay her body to rest. But I have never accepted the loss."

"I don't know how you could."

Lisette turned and looked at Josie. She smiled—the smile of a woman in excruciating pain but trying to remain upbeat. "Then there was you. A little girl. I was so happy."

Josie smiled back. She moved closer to Lisette and fit her head into the crook of her shoulder. Somehow, it still fit as perfectly at twenty-eight as it had at eight. "Did Dad know about her?"

"No. No one knew but me and my parents. I never told anyone."

"What happened to the father?"

"I don't know. I never heard from him after that. I heard he was deployed overseas to fight in Korea. I always imagined he died in the war. It was easier that way."

"June Spencer wrote her name in Sherri Gosnell's blood," Josie said. "That's why you were so upset, why you wouldn't return any of my calls. Did you know? Did you suspect Alton?"

Lisette shook her head. "Not right away. I didn't make the connection. It was simply the mention of her name. It brought it all back like it was yesterday. I'm sorry I couldn't face you. I knew you were dealing with a lot and I didn't want to burden you with this."

"Oh, Gram, you could never burden me—not with anything."

Lisette squeezed her hand. "But then when you came the other day and told me what you'd been through and what you found. Then I knew."

"I'm going to put Alton Gosnell in prison."

She had already arrested him after his confession. Unfortunately, he was in such bad shape he would have to be moved to the hospital instead of the county jail. Even though it was pointless, and she didn't actually have the manpower, she planned to have him moved and then put an officer outside of his hospital room. If for no other reason than to remind him that he had finally been caught.

"He'll never make it to prison," Lisette said. "He's too sick. But now I know. I know what happened to my sweet Ramona."

Josie felt useless and powerless in the face of her grandmother's grief. She felt even more helpless than she had in Nick Gosnell's dark cell. She was a doer. She thrived on action. But she knew from her own grief over Ray and the chief's deaths that there was nothing to be done. There was no way to mitigate or ameliorate her grandmother's grief. It existed like an entity, and it would be with Lisette until she took her last breath. Still, she asked, "Is there anything I can do, Gram?"

"After you find the Coleman girl, you go back to that mountain and you find my Ramona. Find her for me, Josie."

# CHAPTER 71

Josie stood at the window in the chief's office—her office now—and stared down at the street below, littered with news vans, reporters, giant mobile satellite dishes, and onlookers. Holcomb's teams had carried out their raids the day before— the day after she, Noah, and Lisette had gotten a confession from Alton Gosnell—and the news had broken wide open about what had really been going on at the Gosnell property. Noah had hired some local teenagers to erect temporary barricades to keep them a safe distance from the station house. Someone had even installed a Porta Potti on the sidewalk. The press was there to stay, that was for sure. For once Josie didn't feel uncomfortable with them there. They were pushy and intrusive, but they were also the watchful eyes she needed while the FBI and what was left of her staff sorted out this unholy mess.

Josie watched as a woman in a tight black dress and blue bolero sweater broke through the press barricade and sauntered toward the front doors, her four-inch heels clacking on the asphalt. Trinity was showing off. Josie had made it clear that Trinity was to have access to Josie and Noah at all times and that she was authorized to enter the building through the employee entrance on the other side of the building. Now she was just rubbing her elevated status in the faces of all her colleagues.

Josie turned away from the window and picked up the phone on her desk. She checked her temporary cell phone but there was no more news from Carrieann, no change in Luke's condition. Hopefully, tomorrow would bring better news. She sighed. At least Denise Poole had been released from custody, the charges against her dropped. Josie dialed Rockview and waited on hold while they went to find the director of nursing. After a few minutes, she picked up, sounding out of breath and harried. Without preamble she said, "No, Mr. Gosnell hasn't been moved yet. The hospital doesn't have any beds. Believe me, I'm doing what I can. Hopefully we can get him over there tomorrow."

She hated the idea that her grandmother would have to spend one more second under the same roof as that monster. She knew Alton couldn't hurt a fly in his present condition, but that wasn't really the point. She had implored Lisette to come and stay with her until things settled down, but Lisette was not to be deterred. "I'm staying put," she had told Josie. "I want to watch that son of a bitch die."

Apparently, Lisette had been deadly serious. "We keep finding your grandmother outside of Mr. Gosnell's room," the director of nursing added.

"What do you mean?" Josie asked.

"I mean, we caught her outside of his room a couple of times, just standing there, staring at him. I don't think it's healthy. Last night, one of the night shift nurses found her inside his room, standing over his bed."

Josie said nothing. What could she say? Alton Gosnell had killed Lisette's daughter and gotten away with it. She was not about to apologize for her grandmother wanting to confront the man again, and she was not going to offer to talk to Lisette. What would she say?

The other woman blew out a sigh. "I'll call you as soon as he is moved. I promise. I want this over with just as much as you and your grandmother."

"Thank you," Josie said, and hung up.

Down the hall she found two clean mugs in the break room and filled them with coffee, adding sugar and powdered creamer. Now that she was chief, she would have to get the department to spring for half-and-half. She carried the steaming mugs down the hall into the viewing room that adjoined the only interrogation room the Denton PD had. On a high-definition flat-screen television, Noah watched FBI Special Agent Marcus Holcomb interrogate Dusty Branson.

Noah swiveled in his chair as she entered. He smiled and accepted the coffee with his left hand. His right arm was still in a sling. Josie knew he had forgiven her for shooting him, but every time she looked at him she felt guilty. She smiled for him even though she hadn't felt much like smiling for the past week. "Anything new?"

"Holcomb's going in for the kill soon on Luke's shooting," Noah said.

Holcomb had been working steadily at Dusty for hours. He had already gotten Dusty to tell him how Sherri and Nick Gosnell had abducted Isabelle Coleman. They'd spotted her at her mailbox and followed her back up her driveway, pretending to be lost and asking for directions. Dusty wasn't sure what exactly had transpired, but at some point Coleman realized that the two weren't on the up and up and fled into the woods. Nick went after her, overpowered her and dragged her back to the car. It was an impulsive abduction. Gosnell rarely took women from the area, Dusty told Holcomb. Usually, Nick and Sherri took a weekend trip to a nearby state—Ohio, New

York, New Jersey, Maryland, even as far as West Virginia, Dusty said—and kidnapped girls from there. They almost never took girls within a hundred miles of Denton so as not to arouse too much suspicion. They tried to target girls who were troubled and estranged from their families so they were less likely to be missed—runaways, drug addicts, prostitutes. Coleman's abduction—like Ginger Blackwell's six years earlier—had been an aberration, a major deviation from their standard operating procedure. Only Dusty and a small handful of others had known that Coleman was in Gosnell's bunker.

Then, a few days after Sherri's murder, Gosnell had called Dusty in a panic. Isabelle had escaped. The first escape ever. Gosnell had put it down to him being off his game after Sherri's death. Plus, Sherri hadn't been there to administer the date rape drugs so it was likely that Isabelle had become much more lucid and capable of defending herself. She had run off into the woods and hadn't been seen since.

Josie knew from what Ray had said that the department had been searching for her around the clock for days before the showdown in the bunker. Even after that, they had kept up the search in the chief's absence, but to no avail. Now that nearly all of Gosnell's clients and accomplices in law enforcement had been arrested, the Denton PD was considerably lighter on staff. Josie planned to use Trinity to make a public appeal for every citizen who was willing and able to join the search.

Dusty had also given up two other Denton officers for the shooting of the gangbangers and Dirk Spencer. He said Spencer had managed to find out about "Ramona" from a bar he started frequenting after June's disappearance. It had taken him a while to get the barflies there to talk about Gosnell's enterprise, let alone give up its location, but eventually some-one did. Somehow, word got back to some of Denton's police officers that Spencer was planning to raid Gosnell's bunker with the help of his city friends, and they had managed to head him off. There was a dirty cop at Luke's barracks, as Josie had suspected, who helped cover up the police involvement in the shootout. That cop had also suggested framing Denise Poole, since he knew about her past relationship with Luke and her stalker-like tendencies.

What Holcomb hadn't yet managed to get out of Dusty was who had shot Luke. On screen, Holcomb stood at one end of the table, one hand on his hip and the other smoothing down his tie as he stared at Dusty over a pair of reading glasses. His suit jacket rested on the back of his chair. Even on television, he towered over the table in front of him. Dusty looked like a small child sitting across from the agent.

"Sit," Noah said, pulling her from her thoughts.

She took the chair next to him, sipping her coffee. "Turn it up," she told Noah.

Across from Holcomb, Dusty slouched in his seat. A shock of greasy hair fell into his eyes but he didn't push it away. He wore only a plain white T-shirt, and Josie could see the yellow pit stains creeping from his underarms. His hands waved as he talked.

"It was that guy I told you about earlier—the one who helped us cover up the shooting with the gangbangers," he told Holcomb.

Holcomb looked down at the notes in front of him and rattled off the name of a state trooper.

"Yeah, him. He saw the Blackwell file in Luke's truck. Like, in an envelope. So he called Nick, and Nick called me."

"Why would Nick call you?"

Dusty shrugged. "I don't know."

"You were a frequent customer."

The coffee burned a hole in Josie's stomach.

Dusty shrugged. "Well, yeah. Sure, I guess. We talked about it. By that time I had a few calls from guys on Denton PD and a guy I know in the sheriff's office. People were concerned, you know?"

"Names, Officer Branson, I need names," Holcomb said.

Dusty rattled off a bunch of names, and Holcomb wrote them down. Then he continued, "Who made the decision to shoot Trooper Creighton?"

"No one made the decision. I don't know. We talked about it—"

"You and the men on this list?"

Dusty nodded. "Yeah. We talked about it and agreed that someone needed to, you know, take him out."

Noah put his coffee mug down and reached over to squeeze Josie's forearm.

"Who shot Trooper Creighton?" Holcomb asked.

"Jimmy Frisk."

Holcomb again looked at his notes. "James Lampson?"

"Yeah. He's an investigator with the DA's office. He's been in tight with Nick for decades. Used to be a cop in Denton."

# CHAPTER 72

Josie followed Noah out of the room. She couldn't listen to any more. Lampson had already been arrested in the FBI raids the day before. He would be punished. That's what mattered.

Noah joined her in her office, leaning casually against the doorjamb. Again, she stood by the window, staring out but seeing nothing this time. "I'm fine," she said over her shoulder.

"Okay," he said, even though they both knew she wasn't. She wouldn't be fine for a long time. None of them would.

She turned away from the window and sat behind the desk.

"Any word on Luke?" Noah asked.

"They're going to try bringing him out of his coma tomorrow." A genuine smile crossed Josie's lips. "He's doing well though. They're very optimistic. I'll want to go and be with him."

"Of course."

They heard Trinity's heels clacking on the tile moments before she pushed past Noah and plopped down in one of the guest chairs on the other side of Josie's desk. The same chair Josie had sat in a little over a week ago to beg the chief to bring her back on, even temporarily. "Your coffee sucks," she said. "When are you getting new staff? This place is a ghost town.

Oh, and that FBI douche wouldn't let me in the viewing room. Did Branson give up Luke's shooter?"

Noah told her because Josie couldn't find the words. Trinity gave a low whistle and pulled out her cell phone. "Not yet," Noah reminded her. "Wait till he's charged, okay?"

"He's already in custody, but whatever." She rolled her eyes but dropped her cell phone back into her purse. "Who else did Branson give up?"

Noah said, "Couple of guys in the State Police, one guy at the sheriff's office, the DA, Frisk. Most of the guys involved— law enforcement, anyway—were from here. The rest of them were just locals including a doctor, a pharmacist, and a bartender."

"That sounds like the beginning of a very bad joke," Trinity said. "This is insane. You realize that, don't you? I mean this thing is huge."

"Huge, but exclusive," Josie said.

"Oh really?" Trinity said incredulously. "It sure doesn't seem like it was exclusive."

"They didn't let in anybody," Josie clarified. "Gosnell required absolute secrecy and loyalty. Nobody wanted to be the person to blow the whistle. Turning Gosnell in meant turning themselves in. Any one of them might have been able to cut a deal and testify against the rest of them—if they lived long enough to do it—but their friends and colleagues would have gone down with them."

"But surely someone tried to put a stop to it. I mean how did this go on for decades? How did so many people get away with it for so long?" Trinity asked.

Josie said, "Gosnell was all about intimidation and once he had people in his pocket who were willing to cover for him, he was unstoppable. Some of the men we identified on the tapes as Gosnell's clients killed themselves. Maybe they wanted to say something but couldn't." She thought about Ray and how he hadn't wanted to know because knowing would force him to act. He had known he wasn't strong enough to take on Gosnell and his accomplices. "But they couldn't live with it either."

"Some of Gosnell's clients had unfortunate accidents," Noah put in. "That probably weren't accidents at all."

Trinity stared at him open-mouthed. "Holy shit."

"If I wasn't living it, I wouldn't believe it," Josie said.

"What else did Branson say?" Trinity asked. "Did he say anything about Isabelle Coleman?"

Josie told her what Dusty had revealed.

"So she's in the woods somewhere?" Trinity asked.

Josie shrugged. "I don't know."

"Hopefully she didn't get eaten by a bear," Noah put in.

Trinity turned to regard him. "That's not funny."

His cheeks colored. "It's not a joke."

From down the hall, Holcomb called for Noah and he shuffled off, leaving Josie alone with Trinity. "Can you make a public appeal?" Josie asked her. "We could use help with the search. I've only got twelve people out there. It's all we can spare right now."

"Of course," Trinity said. She pulled out her cell phone and started firing off emails at machine-gun speed. Josie swiveled in her chair and stared back out at the gray sky. It had been overcast and occasionally rainy ever since she left the Gosnell property. She wondered if she'd ever see the sun again. It was a silly thought. Of course she would. But would Isabelle? Was she still alive? "She's still alive," Trinity said, as if reading Josie's mind.

Without turning, Josie said, "I hope you're right. The odds are not in her favor."

A tap on the door drew both their attention. Noah stood there, a pinched look on his face. "Boss?" he said.

Josie couldn't get used to him calling her boss, but she didn't correct him. He seemed to enjoy it. "Yes?" she asked.

"Someone just called in another missing person. It's Misty—Misty Derossi."

# CHAPTER 73

Josie stared at Noah. "What?"

"Misty's been reported missing."

Trinity looked from Noah to Josie and back again. "You've got another missing girl?"

"She's not a girl," Josie said. "She's a stripper at Foxy Tails."

"The stripper who was seeing your late husband?" Trinity asked.

Ignoring the question, Josie asked Noah, "When was she last seen?"

Noah looked down at the notepad in his hand, flipping pages as he spoke. "Well, she worked her regular shifts last week. Then she called out sick the first few shifts this week. After that, she was a no-show. Her boss says she'd never done that before. Cell phone goes right to voicemail. Her best friend is away on spring break. She says she talked to her four days ago and she sounded strange. She's called Misty several times a day since then but like I said, all calls go right to voicemail. She's not answering texts either. The best friend had one of Misty's coworkers go by her house but there was no answer, and her car's been in the driveway the whole time." Noah said.

"Sounded strange how?" Josie asked.

"Like strained, like something was wrong. Also, her dog is missing. The coworker says it always barks like crazy when she comes over, and when Misty's coworker knocked, there was no barking."

"She has a dog?" Josie and Trinity said in unison.

Noah gave the two of them an amused look. "What? Strippers can't have dogs?"

Josie rolled her eyes. Trinity, who had pulled out her own notepad and pen, asked "What kind of dog?"

Noah smiled. "A chi-wiener."

"A what?" Josie said.

"A chi-wiener. Half chihuahua and half dachshund. It's small and yappy, according to the friend, and Misty is obsessed with it."

It had never occurred to Josie that Misty could be in danger. She had sent Noah to break the news of Ray's death to Misty as soon as they'd finished watching the videos with Holcomb. She hadn't wanted Misty to find out second- or third-hand; she was capable of extending the woman that courtesy at least. But Noah hadn't been able to locate Misty either at home or at work. Josie had told him to let it go. When Misty was ready, she would surface. They didn't have the time or the resources to track her down.

But now both her best friend and her boss had reported her missing.

The chief's words came back to her. *Get them all.* Had they missed someone? Missed something? Had Gosnell or one of his accomplices done something to her before Josie called in the FBI? Josie had no warm feelings for Misty, that was for damn sure, but she didn't want her to be another casualty of one of Gosnell's conspirators.

"We need to check her house first," Josie said. She grabbed her jacket from the back of her chair. "Let's go."

Misty Derossi lived alone in a huge Victorian in Denton's historic district. As Josie, Noah, and Trinity ascended the steps to the large wraparound porch, Josie bit back a disparaging remark about how Misty paid for the house. Noah went from window to window, peering inside each one. "It looks dark," he noted. "No barking, just like the best friend said."

"Well, if the dog's not here, then that looks more like she took the dog and left," Josie said, hoping that Misty had simply left town. But the fact that Misty hadn't taken her car gave Josie a bad feeling. June Spencer and Isabelle Coleman had both disappeared while on foot. "We need to find out where she would go if she thought she was in trouble. Has anyone checked...Has anyone..."

Noah's face softened. "I checked Ray's house. You know his mom has been there all week? She's planning his funeral. Misty's not there."

Josie nodded, unable to speak over the lump in her throat.

"So, where else would she go?" Trinity asked.

Noah rattled the doorknob and pushed against the door frame, testing it. "Well, that's just it. She doesn't have many friends."

Josie swallowed another sassy remark.

"Her parents live in South Carolina, moved there ages ago. The friend says she called them, and they haven't seen her in five years. We checked with all her coworkers, and no one has seen her. The friend says if she needed a place to stay, she'd come to her."

He stopped talking and looked the door up and down like it was a puzzle he couldn't figure out. Trinity said, "You didn't ask if the best friend had a key?"

He blushed and pulled out his cell phone. "She's out of town, but she said she didn't have one anyway. Misty was

very private. But maybe she knows if Misty has one of those
hide-a-key things—"

Josie pushed him out of the way and drove her heel as hard as
she could against the door, just below the locking mechanism. It
took three kicks, and the door swung inward. She stepped over
the threshold. When Noah and Trinity didn't follow, she glanced
behind her and found them staring at her, open-mouthed.

"What?" Josie snapped.

"Boss," Noah said. "You can't . . . we need a warrant. That's
breaking and entering."

"If she's lying in there wounded or dying, I'm not wasting
time waiting for someone with a key," Josie said. The glare
she shot them left no room for argument.

The house was completely empty. It was also immaculate.
The three of them moved from room to room with a strange sort
of reverence. It looked like it belonged in a magazine. Expensive, ornate antique furniture, perfectly matched, adorned every
room. Some rooms looked so perfect, Josie felt like they should
be cordoned off. Misty could open her house for tours. Josie
thought of her own house and felt like someone was driving tiny
spikes into her heart. While beautiful, it lacked all of the charm
and style that dripped from every tasseled lampshade and every
perfectly plumped cushion of Misty's house. Hell, Josie didn't
even have furniture, and even if she did, it wouldn't be as finely
coordinated, as expensive, or as neatly kept as the pieces in
Misty's home. Josie tried to imagine Ray in this house with his
perpetually muddy boots tracking dirt through every room. Or
leaving his pit-stained undershirts over the back of the couch
all the time, or leaving empty beer bottles around the house—
sometimes even in the bathroom. Josie couldn't picture it. Of
course, now she would never have to; she would never know
whether Misty could tolerate him. Emotion rolled through her
like the tide, and then receded. She was here to work.

"Obsessed, much? Holy shit." Trinity's voice came from the kitchen. Josie followed it and found the reporter standing in front of Misty's very modern refrigerator. "Look at this," she told Josie and Noah.

The fridge was covered with colorful pages cut from magazines. Each page showed a room that precisely matched a room in Misty's house. "She's copying from these magazines," Trinity added.

From behind the two women, Noah remarked, "It's kind of sad."

Maybe it was, maybe it wasn't, but it made Josie feel slightly better. Awkwardly, she clapped her hands together. "Well, we should go. Obviously, she's not here. There aren't any signs of struggle. Nothing looks amiss. It looks like she took her dog for a walk and never came back."

Outside, Josie instructed Noah to call someone to fix the door and pull one of their officers from the Coleman investigation long enough to make some official inquiries into Misty's whereabouts. She turned to Trinity. "You think you can get this on the afternoon broadcast?"

Trinity's brow crinkled. "We *are* talking about the chick who stole your dead husband from you, aren't we?"

Josie resisted the urge to lash out. "My husband had an affair with her. Our marriage ended. But she's still a citizen in my town and she's missing. Given what I saw up on that mountain last weekend, I'm not taking any chances. So I'd like to make an appeal to the public. Please."

Trinity stared at her a moment longer, almost as if she could see how much it burned Josie to ask.

"No more Ginger Blackwells. No more June Spencers. No one falls through the cracks," Josie promised, mostly to herself.

# CHAPTER 74

That night, Trinity made a sincere and urgent request to the citizens of Denton to gather to search for the two missing women. Her face was now on the news practically every time Josie turned it on. Even national news shows tapped her for their ongoing coverage of the madness taking hold of central Pennsylvania. As Trinity gave her report, photos of Isabelle and Misty appeared to the right of her head. Beneath their smiling faces the word "Vanished" appeared. Then it was replaced by the Denton PD tip line number.

Josie watched the broadcast from beside Carrieann in the ICU waiting room. The doctors had reduced Luke's medication hours earlier; now they just had to wait and hope he woke up on his own. They took turns sitting by his bedside until the nurses kicked them out during shift change so they could bring their incoming replacements up to date.

The two women sat silently side by side, staring up at the television, watching Trinity Payne's special news bulletin about the missing women and the rest of the unfolding events in Denton.

"Boss?" Noah appeared in the ICU waiting room doorway.

Josie's heart jumped into her throat. If Noah had driven

all the way to the hospital it couldn't be good news. Had they found Isabelle Coleman? Was she dead? She excused herself and went out into the hallway with him. "What's wrong?" she asked.

He held up a plastic baggie with a cell phone inside it. "I thought you might want this."

She stared dumbly at the phone, completely confused. All she could think about was Isabelle Coleman. "I don't get it. Did you find Coleman? Or Misty?"

Now it was Noah's turn to look baffled. "What? No." He shook the baggie. "The FBI found your cell phone. They're done processing it. I thought you might want it back."

Slowly she reached out and took the bag. She'd been using a temporary, department-issued cell phone. Only Lisette, Noah, Trinity, Carrieann, and Holcomb had the number. With everything going on, her actual cell phone had been the furthest thing from her mind. But as she took it out, she remembered all the photos of her and Luke she had on it and was grateful that Noah had come all this way to return it to her.

She looked up at him. "Thank you," she said.

With his good hand he reached into his jacket pocket and pulled out a charger and cord. "You'll need this," he said.

Impulsively, she rocked up onto her toes and kissed him on the cheek. His face turned fire-engine red. "What was... What was that for?"

"For being one of the good guys."

※ ❧ ❧

Noah sat with her for a while but then had to return to Denton to oversee things while she stayed at the hospital for the night. She left her phone charging beneath a chair in the ICU waiting room. Once the nursing staff changed over, she and Carrieann resumed their vigil at Luke's bedside, trading off every couple of hours. He had slightly fewer tubes and wires coming out of him than before, so Josie was able to get close enough to hold his hand and speak softly to him. She talked endlessly. Not about all the horrific things she had been through since his shooting, but about all the things they would do together when he woke up, and about how maybe she would take up fishing instead of knitting, and they could have a hobby together. She was only half-joking.

She was dozing when the nurse came in around five in the morning to tell her it was Carrieann's turn to sit with Luke. As she stood to go, Luke squeezed her hand.

Josie screamed, causing Carrieann to come hurtling into the room. What followed was the kind of jumping-up-and-down, bear-hugging, chest-bumping, high-pitched-squealing celebration that normally accompanied the winning Super Bowl team. The nurse checked Luke over thoroughly, called his name into his face fifteen times and shone a small flashlight into both of his eyes, but there was no more response than that. Still, it was a start. It was enough for Josie.

She left Carrieann weeping and trembling with excitement by his side and ran into the waiting room to get her cell phone so she could call Noah. Her fingers tapped impatiently against the phone case as she waited for it to boot up. A glance at the television showed the six a.m. news. More Trinity Payne. The phone had been dead a long time. As the screen flashed on, the photo of her and Luke beneath the icons sent even more euphoria surging through her. He had squeezed her hand. He was in there. He was going to be okay.

Notifications from the last week started pouring in. Missed texts and missed calls. She saw the little number at the upper right-hand corner of the phone icon tick upward. Three, seven, twelve, seventeen, twenty-two. The missed calls stopped at fifty-seven.

Josie pressed the icon and pulled up the missed call log. It went from most recent to oldest. The most recent call had come in an hour ago. In fact, forty-nine of the calls were from the same person. A tiny photo of Chief Wayland Harris showed beside the number. Above the number was the name she had assigned in her phone's contacts: Chief (Lodge).

# CHAPTER 75

"I don't understand," Noah said. "The chief is ... well, he's dead."

Josie paced the ICU waiting room, clutching her cell phone to her ear. "Well, someone is calling me from his hunting lodge. Someone called my cell phone from his hunting lodge forty-nine times this week."

"His wife?"

"I talked to his wife. She's planning his funeral. I doubt she's had time to drive to his hunting lodge every day for the last week and call my cell phone. Why would she? She could just call the station."

"His daughters?"

"They're both away at college. They're flying into Philadelphia tomorrow."

"Did you try calling back?"

"There was no answer. I tried three times. We need to go up there."

On the other end of the line, Noah sighed. She knew he hadn't slept in days. Neither of them had. "I'm gonna have to pull people from the Coleman search," Noah said.

"No," Josie said. "We can't afford that. Especially if

Coleman is still alive somewhere. I think we should call the FBI. Ask for their help."

"I'll call them, but they're spread pretty thin from what I've gathered, with the raids and processing and all."

"Try," Josie said. "In the meantime, put Sergeant Tralies in charge. The chief's lodge is an hour north of Geisinger. How fast can you get here?"

Wayland Harris's hunting lodge was little more than a single-level two-bedroom modular home halfway up a mountain. The last two miles of road leading to its driveway was unpaved, as was the driveway. In the winter he needed an ATV to get from the road to the house, kept in a small shed at the bottom of his property for that very reason. As Josie and Noah drove, bouncing mercilessly in Noah's truck, she noticed that the padlock on the outside of the shed was still intact.

It had been a long-running joke in the police department that the chief never actually went hunting but maintained a hunting lodge so he could get away from all the estrogen in his household. When most men in the area were showing off photos of the eight-point bucks or the seven-hundred-pound black bears they'd shot, Chief Harris would return from his lodge after every hunting season empty-handed, with no stories to tell. One year, Josie remembered, he had shot a turkey. The rest of the guys joked that was just so his wife would stop urging him to sell his beloved lodge. He had called it a lodge and not a camp. Most hunters belonged to a hunting camp, which was just a house or cabin in the woods where a group of them stayed together during hunting season. But this was a lodge. His lodge, and his alone.

Josie only knew where it was because the chief had loaned the department his ATV a few years in a row—mostly to rescue dumb kids who got lost in the woods. The chief had commissioned Josie twice to go with him to return the ATV. She'd never been inside the infamous lodge though.

So that anyone at the lodge wouldn't hear their vehicle driving over the gravel, they parked at the bottom of the chief's long driveway and walked the rest of the way. Soon Noah was panting beside her. She glanced over at him, alarmed by the shade of white he had turned. He was still nursing his gunshot wound, and she was working him like crazy. "You okay?" she asked. "Want to wait in the car?"

He scoffed at her and wiped the sweat from his brow with the back of his wrist. "Are you crazy? Leave you alone? No way."

"You don't look so good."

"I'm fine."

At the top of the driveway the chief's lodge sat silent and implacable. The chief had replaced the siding since the last time Josie had seen it. She pulled her service weapon out and held it pointed toward the ground. Together they circled to the back of the house.

After two circuits of the house, Josie walked up to the front door and knocked, while Noah stayed back in the tree line, his pistol drawn, ready to fire. She holstered her own gun but left the holster unfastened. She waited several minutes, knocking periodically until finally she heard movement from inside. It sounded like more than one person—and a dog barking. She heard footsteps and what sounded like a whispered argument before the door creaked slowly open, and Misty launched herself into Josie's arms.

"Thank God. Thank God you're here," Misty cried. Josie tried to mask her shock as she attempted to disentangle herself from Misty's vise-like embrace. It was like trying to get a frightened child to let go. Josie peeled one of Misty's arms from around her neck and the woman quickly slung it back around Josie's waist. Tears streamed down her face. Her blond hair looked dull and uncombed. "Thank God," she repeated. "The chief said you would come. He said you would. But you didn't answer any of my calls. How come you didn't answer any of my calls? I would have left a voicemail but the chief made me promise not to just in case someone else got their hands on your phone and accessed the messages. He didn't want anyone knowing we were here."

Noah stepped from the tree line and approached. Misty clutched Josie harder and squealed in panic. "He promised you would come alone," she shrieked.

Josie glanced back at Noah and he froze in place. "That is Officer Fraley," Josie explained. "He's helping me. The, uh, chief said I could trust him."

Misty's body relaxed. "Okay. Okay."

Josie made one last effort to free herself, curling her hands around Misty's shoulders and holding her at arm's length. "Misty," she said. "What the hell is going on?"

A figure stepped into the doorway behind Misty. A young woman with sunken cheeks and skin so pale it had a blue, vampirish hue. A men's sweatsuit hung on her, and she too looked unkempt, her blond hair in a tangle. In her arms was a tiny dog that looked like a miniature fox. Before Josie could completely register the young woman's identity, she heard Noah murmur, "Isabelle."

# CHAPTER 76

Misty sat at the table in the Denton police department's conference room, a half-empty bottle of water in front of her. She raked her fingers through her hair over and over again, trying to tame it, her tiny dog snoring in her lap. Across from her sat Special Agent Holcomb. Josie sat all the way at the end of the table, as far from Misty as she could get without actually leaving the room. Noah stood behind Josie like a sentry. She was glad of his presence. They had had to break the news to Misty on the way back from the lodge that both Ray and the chief were dead. Josie could barely handle her own grief, let alone Misty's, which was emotional to the point of seeming insincere.

"You didn't even know the chief," Josie had snapped at her in the car.

"Boss," Noah had interjected softly. "Everyone deals with grief differently."

She had kept her mouth shut since then because she was afraid if she spoke again she would say things she would regret—even to Misty. Special Agent Holcomb readily agreed to take down Misty's statement.

Isabelle Coleman had been taken to the nearest hospital.

Josie had called her parents, reveling in the pleasure of delivering some good news at last. Holcomb would take her statement later, after she'd been examined by a doctor and reunited with her family, although she had told Josie enough to confirm what they already knew. The Gosnells had kidnapped her after seeing her at her mailbox and held her in the bunker. When she first arrived there she had been imprisoned with June Spencer. The Gosnells had been arguing so fiercely about whether or not to keep Isabelle that Sherri had unwittingly left the girls with a flashlight for two whole days. It had been Isabelle's idea to give June her tongue piercing after she heard the Gosnells talking about selling June. It was her only way to send a message in the event that June somehow escaped. Once they took June and started administering the drugs, her memories took on the same flash-cut quality as Ginger Blackwell's memories. She had escaped after Sherri was no longer there to administer the drugs on a regular basis, and had wandered through the woods for some time before coming across Misty.

"Take me through it, Miss Derossi," Holcomb said to Misty, his tone so gentle Josie wanted to slap him across the face. But then she realized that there was no reason for him not to be gentle with Misty. She had found Isabelle and kept her safe.

"Well, I was driving down Moss Valley Road," she said, referring to one of the rural roads that ran past the Gosnell property between the strip club and Denton's central area. "It was early in the morning. I was leaving work, you know, the night shift."

"What do you do for a living, Miss Derossi?" asked Holcomb.

Misty stroked her dog's head. "I'm a dancer at Foxy Tails."

One of Holcomb's eyebrows lifted. "Foxy Tails?"

"It's a strip club," Josie said pointedly, unable to stop herself.

Misty glared at her.

Holcomb watched the two of them stare icily at each other for a long moment before posing another question. "What time of the morning were you on the road, Miss Derossi?"

Slowly, Misty turned her attention back to Holcomb. "It was probably around five. I don't usually work that late, but we had a lot of private parties that night. Anyway, I was going slow 'cause of the deer, you know? They're always running out. I almost hit her. She ran out just like a deer. Stark naked."

"Who?"

"Isabelle. At first I didn't know who she was. She scared the shit out of me. I braked just in time not to hit her, and got out. She was screaming and just, you know, totally freaked out. She wouldn't let me touch her. I was going to call 911, but my battery was dead."

"What did you do?" Holcomb asked.

"I had a jacket in the car so I gave her that. I stood by the side of the road and talked to her. She said she was Isabelle Coleman and someone had taken her but she wasn't sure who. She kept talking about someone putting a needle in her arm so she wouldn't remember. She was really freaked out. Like, hysterical."

"Did she get in the car with you?"

"Well, yeah, eventually. I said I would take her to the police or the hospital. She said she just wanted to go home. I said a lot of people were looking for her but she should really go to a hospital before she went home. To get checked out, you know?"

"But you didn't make it to a hospital," Holcomb pointed out.

Misty glanced over at Josie and Noah briefly, and then back at Holcomb. Her tiny dog sighed in its sleep. "She got in the car, and I started driving. All of a sudden she started saying she could smell one of them."

"One of who?"

Misty held her dog tighter to her body. "One of the men," she said. "She said she thought there were a lot of men who, you know, did stuff to her. She said where she was she couldn't really see because they kept her in the dark, and even when they took her out of the dark, the light dazzled her eyes so much she didn't get a good look at any of them. But she could smell them. She said she . . . She said she smelled one of them in my car."

"Ray said he was never there," Josie said. Or had he lied about that as well? They hadn't found him on any of Gosnell's videos.

Wide-eyed, Misty turned to Josie. "Not Ray," she said. "Dusty."

Before Josie could respond, Holcomb said, "Officer Branson?"

Misty turned back to him. "Yeah. He had been in my car that morning. He came by my work, and we went out to the car."

Holcomb looked perplexed. "For what?"

"It was for sex, wasn't it?" Josie interjected. "You were sleeping with Dusty too? Ray thought you were in a relationship, Misty."

Misty was all wide-eyed innocence. "We *were* in a relationship. We were going to move in together." Her eyes welled up with tears. "We were going to get married."

And yet, Ray wouldn't sign the divorce papers to end things once and for all between him and Josie. Had he had reservations about things with Misty? Or had he just been reluctant to let go of a relationship that had lasted almost all of his life? Josie slapped a palm on the table, making everyone jump. Misty's little chi-wiener dog popped its sleepy head up to see what the commotion was. "Then why were you fucking Dusty in your car?"

Noah said, "Boss."

"It wasn't something we planned," Misty said. "Ray and I were already together. One night Dusty and I got drunk together and things just kind of happened. We were going to stop once Ray and I got married."

"Did Ray know?" Josie asked accusingly. Somewhere in the recesses of her mind she wondered why she even cared. But she couldn't stop herself.

"I don't know," Misty said. "I didn't tell him. I don't think Dusty did. Look, the stuff that happened with Dusty didn't really mean anything. I loved Ray. It was just that Dusty was under a lot of stress. He said he needed it."

Josie said, "Oh my God."

Noah put a hand on her shoulder. "Boss."

Holcomb said, "Okay, okay. That's not really germane to the issue at hand. Officer Branson had been in your car, and Miss Coleman said she could smell him . . . or, to be more accurate, Miss Coleman advised that she could smell the scent of one of her rapists. You believed it was Officer Branson because he had most recently been in your car?"

"Yes," Misty said.

"So what did you do at that point?"

She looked down at her dog. Its eyes were trained on her face, alert and tuned to her emotions. "Ray had told me that he thought Nick Gosnell was . . . taking women and pimping them out and that a lot of guys on the force knew."

"What?" Josie said. "When did he tell you that?"

"The day before that. He had just told me. He was really rattled over it. He thought maybe Gosnell had Isabelle, but he didn't know what to do, 'cause he said everyone was in on it.

He said guys had been killed over the whole thing. He was worried about what would happen to me if he blew the whistle or whatever. He never specifically said that Dusty knew, just that a lot of guys knew. So when Isabelle said she smelled Dusty, I knew. I knew he was involved. I realized I couldn't just take her to the police. So I took her home. To my house."

"Why didn't you call Ray?" Josie asked.

"I did. I called and asked him if Dusty was involved in the Gosnell thing, and he lied and said he wasn't. So I thought, why would he lie? Why would he protect Dusty?"

"Because they've been best friends since kindergarten," Josie said.

"Ladies," Holcomb interjected. He asked Misty, "Did you tell Ray Quinn that you had Coleman?"

"No. I didn't know what to do. So I called the chief."

Noah said, "But how did you know the chief wasn't involved too?"

Misty shifted uncomfortably in her chair. The dog whined. "Well, when Ray's friends found out that Ray and I were, you know, in a relationship, all of a sudden they all started showing up at the club. It was weird, like they wanted to check me out or something. It got to the point where it was a little creepy with some of them. Anyway, the chief never came to the club. Ever. But I met him a couple of times. I had brought Ray some coffee and food to the station during the Coleman search."

"Oh, but not Dusty?" Josie asked.

"Boss, please."

"Chief Quinn," Holcomb said.

Misty shot her a dirty look and went on as if she hadn't spoken. "I called and asked for him directly. They must have thought I was his wife 'cause they didn't even ask who I was. I told him what was going on. He came right over. He said he had an idea that something strange was going on in his town, but he didn't know what. He said he wasn't sure how far things went, and until he sorted it all out he wanted me and Isabelle to hide. So he took us to his lodge. He said if he didn't come back for us in two days, I should call Josie and only Josie. From the landline, not from my cell phone."

"Did he say why?"

"He said she was the only person in this godforsaken town he could still trust."

# CHAPTER 77

On the day of Ray's funeral, Josie woke at five in the morning. She tried on a half dozen variations of funeral attire before finally settling on a simple sleeveless black dress with a pencil skirt. Around her neck was the diamond pendant that Ray had given her before they went away to college. He had saved up for months to buy it for her. It was his parting promise to her that they would return to one another. She spent an hour pinning her hair back and then letting it flow down her back and then pinning it back again before finally deciding to leave it down. Ray had always liked it that way. She stood before the full-length mirror in her bathroom and thought how silly it was to be dressing up for the funeral of a man who had betrayed her, cheated on her, and then been complicit in the abduction of Isabelle Coleman.

Her Ray.

She slid into a pair of black heels. He had always loved her in heels. She thought about pinning her hair back up as a concession to the conflicting emotions she was having about him. But no, she decided. Today she wasn't laying to rest the man who had wronged her. She was laying to rest the sweet boy who had saved her from her childhood nightmare, who had let her push every boundary he had, who had loved her in spite of the bad things that had happened to her. Today she was laying to rest the man she had married—decent, honest, loyal Ray. She might never reconcile the boy and the husband she loved with the man Ray had become in the last year or so of his life. But she would have to say goodbye to him. She had no choice.

A knock sounded from her front door. She took her time getting downstairs, expecting Trinity but instead finding Noah on her doorstep. He wore his sling over an impressive black suit. His brown hair was expertly tousled. Only his face looked pained. Her heart leaped into her throat. "What is it?" she asked, thinking of Lisette, of Luke.

*Please, oh God, please. I can't lose another person.*

"Josie," he said. "Can I come in?"

"Just tell me."

"Alton Gosnell died in his sleep last night."

She sagged against the doorway. Noah stepped forward and took her elbow with his left hand, guiding her inside and nudging the door closed behind them with his foot. He directed her toward her living room but froze when he saw it was empty.

She smiled sheepishly. "I don't have any furniture."

He looked behind them, put a hand on her lower back and steered her in the opposite direction, toward the kitchen. She let him pull out a kitchen chair for her and pour her a glass of water. She, at least, had glassware. He sat down across from her. "You okay?"

She took a sip of water. "That son of a bitch," she said.

"I'm sorry," Noah said. "Not that he's dead, but that we didn't have a chance to put him away. The director of nursing called this morning. She said his infection had been improving. A bed had opened up at Denton Memorial. They were going to move him today. She said he was finally well enough to be moved. He wasn't in the best health to begin with, but she thought he had turned a corner, might have a few years left."

"My grandmother said he would never make it to prison. But still, I hoped..." she trailed off. A moment passed. She met his eyes. "Noah, would you mind driving me to Rockview?"

He stood and offered his good arm. "Of course," he said. "You and Lisette can ride with me to the service."

༄

Lisette waited for them in the lobby, dressed in a smart gray skirt suit, a wide-brimmed black hat elegantly covering her gray curls. When she saw them enter, she sprang up, clutching the handles of her walker and making a beeline for the double doors. "Let's go," she told Josie and Noah, pushing past them into the parking lot. Josie and Noah looked at one another, shrugged and followed her out. Josie sat in the back with Lisette as Noah drove them to the funeral home.

"Gram," she said. "You know about Mr. Gosnell, don't you? Did they tell you?"

Lisette met Josie's eyes. "Of course, dear."

"I'm really sorry, Gram. I wanted him to pay for his crimes."

Lisette reached a hand across the seat and patted Josie's knee. Then she smiled at Josie, her eyes twinkling with something that looked very close to satisfaction. It was the same look Josie had seen in her eyes the day that she finally and permanently wrested custody from Josie's mother. She was triumphant. "Oh, Josie dear, he did pay. Don't you give him another thought. Things have been set straight."

Josie's brow furrowed. "You mean you're not upset?"

Lisette turned to look out the window. "No, dear. For the first time since my Ramona went missing, I finally feel a bit of...peace."

"I'm going to find her," Josie said.

"I know."

Noah pulled into a parking spot at the funeral home and helped Lisette out. Josie followed behind them. Ray's mother had planned the service. She had wanted something quick and simple, and neither she nor Josie could afford a large affair. Josie had wanted to get there early so that she could spend a few minutes with him in private. She left Noah and Lisette chatting with Mrs. Quinn while she approached his open casket at the front of the room. The funeral home had done a good job making him look handsome in his police uniform, his blond hair neatly combed, eyes closed in what looked like a peaceful sleep. But somehow he just didn't look like the man she had loved. She touched his cold hands. This was not her Ray. It was just the shell that had held all the parts—good and bad, wonderful and ugly—that had made him hers for so many years of her life.

Still, she could not stop the tears from rolling down her face. "Damn you," she muttered to him. "Damn you for leaving me."

She felt strangely numb and adrift the rest of the day. The hours passed in a blur. She stood in the greeting line beside Ray's mother. She was too immobilized by grief to even protest when Mrs. Quinn allowed Misty to stand on the other side of her and hug Ray's mourners as though she had had any place of importance in his life. As though she had mattered that much to him. He never signed the divorce papers, Josie kept thinking. It was small solace.

She hugged every mourner, said the requisite words, half-listened as a pastor she had never met before gave Bible readings. No one gave a eulogy. Neither Josie nor Mrs. Quinn were in any shape to give one, and Ray's best friend, Dusty, was in jail. After the service, a small group of mourners followed his casket to the cemetery. Josie and Lisette clutched one another and wept as they lowered Ray into the ground. Noah stood sentry behind them. He waited until they were ready to leave, which wasn't until the graveyard workers finally asked them to go so they could finish their work.

# CHAPTER 78

The next day, Josie sat next to Luke's hospital bed, holding his warm, meaty palm in hers. They had moved him to a step-down unit, given him a private room, and taken away most of the equipment needed to keep him alive. Now he only had to wear the standard monitoring devices that checked his heart rate, blood pressure and oxygen saturation. All his numbers were stable. Carrieann said he had woken up the day before, briefly, while Josie was at Ray's funeral. He had asked for Josie. Carrieann hadn't told him anything, just that Josie would return soon. Then he had fallen back into a deep sleep. Now Josie waited. She could wait as long as she had to. Isabelle Coleman had been found and reunited with her family. The FBI was handling the Gosnell mess, which would likely take months. Ray had been laid to rest. She would have to attend Wayland Harris's funeral in a few days, which was going to be a spectacular affair befitting her beloved chief. But other than that, she was free to sit with Luke and wait for him to come around. Noah could handle things at the department for a few days.

Josie was watching Luke's chest rise and fall, her mind

back on the conversation she had had with Lisette on the way to Ray's funeral. Aside from her obvious grief over Ray's death, Lisette was right. She did seem more at peace. Lighter. Josie would even venture to say happier. She kept thinking about the sparkle in Lisette's eyes. The flash of triumph.

*He'll never make it to prison,* Lisette had said with confidence. *He's too sick.*

*I mean, we caught her outside of his room a couple of times, just standing there, staring at him. I don't think it's healthy. Last night, one of the night shift nurses found her inside his room, standing over his bed.*

*Oh, Josie dear, he did pay. Don't you give him another thought. Things have been set straight.*

"Hey." Luke's voice cut through her thoughts. His hand squeezed hers gently. She looked over to see him smiling wanly at her.

She stood and leaned over him, holding his hand against her chest with both of hers. "Luke," she breathed. "You're awake. How do you feel?"

He blinked a few times. "Fuzzy," he said. "What the hell happened?"

"You don't remember?"

"No, I remember leaving work, walking to my truck, that's all. Carrieann said someone shot me."

Josie nodded. "I'm so sorry."

He opened his mouth to speak but the effort of the few words he'd already said seemed to wear him out. "It's okay," Josie told him. "Just rest. I'm not going anywhere. There will be plenty of time to fill you in later. We got the shooter. Everything is going to be okay."

He closed his eyes. "I know it will be," he said. "You're here now."

She relinquished his hand and sat back down, studying his face, surprised at how much better the sound of his voice made her feel. He would make a full recovery. They would get married, start a new chapter in both their lives.

She might even let him put a door on her bedroom closet.

# EPILOGUE

Shortly after Luke was discharged from the hospital, Dirk Spencer's condition took a turn for the better and, eventually, he was released to home where his sister, Lara, joined him, caring for him as he recovered from his injuries. Josie checked in on them every couple of weeks. June had been committed to a psychiatric institute for inpatient treatment and evaluation while she awaited trial for the murder of Sherri Gosnell. The new interim District Attorney was hopeful that a plea bargain could be made so that June could get the psychiatric treatment she so desperately needed. Six months after Josie rescued her from Denton's holding area, she had finally started saying words again.

Isabelle Coleman's recovery moved much more quickly. The girl took on her return to normal life with an enthusiasm that, to Josie, sometimes smacked of desperation. She even decided she would attend college that fall as planned. But Josie knew that everyone dealt with trauma differently. Isabelle's parents assured Josie that the girl would receive regular counseling, even when she went away to college.

Two months after the Gosnell case broke wide open, the woman who had accused Josie of excessive force when Josie was still a detective died of a drug overdose. The Mayor allowed Josie to continue as interim chief. At Special Agent Holcomb's suggestion, the DA reviewed her statement about Nick Gosnell's death, together with his autopsy report. After talks with the Mayor, the DA's office decided not to press charges. Morale in Denton was at an all-time low, and Josie was being hailed as a hero for exposing Gosnell's horrific crimes and putting a stop to them. The families of the victims being unearthed on the mountain were effusive in the press with their praise of Josie. Because of her, they said, they could finally lay their long-lost relatives to rest. It was decided that prosecuting Josie for the murder of the most hated man in Denton history after she had been held captive by him for two days—during which she had witnessed her husband's death and nearly been raped—was public relations suicide. For this, Josie was grateful, but she was not sorry for killing Nick Gosnell.

Eight months and thirteen days after his death, little Ramona's body was unearthed by an FBI team. Alton had buried her only steps from the Gosnells' back door, which was why it had taken so long to find her. DNA taken from her remains confirmed that she was Lisette's daughter. Josie spared no expense to give her the funeral she deserved. It seemed to give Lisette some peace to choose a coffin and headstone, to choose flowers and plan the service. The attendance was larger than Josie thought it would be, and this seemed to please Lisette as well. Finally, after more than sixty years, she could give voice to her howling grief and claim the daughter who had been denied to her both in life and in death. Many of Lisette's friends from Rockview were there, as well as some members of the staff she had grown close to over the years. The Mayor, medical examiner and the new DA attended, as did Noah and a few other members of Denton PD. Luke stood steadfastly beside Josie as she watched the aunt she would never know being lowered into a grave that had been decades coming.

He slung her over his shoulder like she weighed nothing. The girl hung as though lifeless down his back, her small hands swaying as the man moved. He carried her outside. Each step sent a lightning bolt of pain through her body. Blinking rapidly, she willed her eyes to adjust to the light. Finally, the ground came into focus: grass, leaves, and twigs. She couldn't tell where he was taking her. She tried to lift her head to look around but she was too weak.

Luke had recovered, albeit slowly. He wasn't ready to go back to work, but he filled his days fishing and texting Josie endlessly. They had lunch together every day, and the nights were spent relearning each other's broken bodies. He hadn't been able to make love again until recently. He was scarred, and dealt with a great deal of residual pain, but he was alive. Luke's shooter was still in jail awaiting his trial. The DA was confident about getting a conviction. Denise Poole had tried getting in touch with Luke several times, but he had put her off, reluctantly admitting to Josie that Denise had always had stalker-like tendencies. He had promised her a painting they bought while they were engaged if she gave Josie the information on the Blackwell file. He genuinely felt badly that she had gotten caught up in the Gosnell mess but he insisted on keeping her at arm's length—which was just fine with Josie.

The boy's feet came into view. He wore white sneakers turned brown by dirt as he trudged behind his father. His eyes stayed on the ground. The girl knew it was useless, but she tried to choke out a "help me" that only came out sounding like a wet cough. The man jostled her and made a hushing sound. Tears leaked from the corners of her eyes.

As the pastor said his final words, each of them stepped forward to place a single red rose on Ramona's grave. Lisette went first, abandoning her walker in favor of Luke's arm. He guided her to the coffin, and everyone seemed to hold their breath as Lisette reverently placed the first rose. Then she placed her fingers to her lips, transferring a kiss to her long-lost daughter. Josie couldn't stop the tears from pouring out of her. Not just for the aunt she would never know, but for all the loss they had experienced. Josie's father. Ray. The chief. Josie's naive belief that her city was a great place to live.

Noah offered his arm. Together, they followed Lisette and Luke, each placing a rose and then walking off, away from the graveside. Lisette leaned against Luke and watched the mourners disperse.

After what seemed like an eternity, they stopped. To the girl it looked like some kind of clearing. From the corner of her eye she saw a set of steps. Were they near a house? Was he taking her to get help? Was he taking her home? She dared not hope. Gently, the man knelt and laid her on her back. They were behind a house. It wasn't her house though. It must be theirs. She thought she saw a movement of the curtains in one window. Then it was gone. Her eyes found the boy. He stared at her curiously. Then the man leaned closer to her, and when he smiled, she knew she would never go home again.

Josie retrieved Lisette's walker, but she refused it. Luke covered her palm with his and smiled down at her. They had hit it off far better than Josie hoped.

"You know," Luke told her, "your granddaughter has dining room furniture now, and I make a mean creamy chicken lasagna. Will you come back to the house with us for the evening?"

Lisette had chosen to stay at Rockview, in spite of Josie's insistence that she find another facility. "I didn't do anything wrong," Lisette had said. "Why should I leave my home? Why should I have to live further away from you?" Josie had to admit that she was happy to keep her grandmother close, now more than ever.

They reached Josie's Escape and Luke helped Lisette into the passenger's side. She smiled at him. "I'd love to join you," she said.

Ramona didn't look at the man again, or the boy. She would not give them that. Blue sky turning purple with dusk stretched out overhead, filling her heart with a strange kind of peace. She had longed for the beauty of the open sky when she was locked away. Her breath caught as a large, yellow monarch butterfly flitted across her line of sight. She smiled, and thought of her sister, and she didn't feel afraid anymore.

# A LETTER FROM LISA REGAN

I want to say a huge thank-you for choosing to read *Vanishing Girls*. If you enjoyed it, and want to keep up to date with all my latest releases, just sign up at the following link. Your email address will never be shared, and you can unsubscribe at any time.

www.bookouture.com/lisa-regan

With such a huge selection of fantastic books out there to choose from, I genuinely appreciate your taking the time to read the first installment of the Josie Quinn series. The town of Denton and the County of Alcott are fictional places but based very loosely on several different locations in rural Pennsylvania that I've lived in and explored over the years. I hope you'll keep reading about Josie and her adventures in Denton!

As you'll see in my acknowledgments, I am so grateful to all of you readers for taking the time to read my work. I love hearing about your reading experience. You can get in touch with me through any of the social media outlets below, including my website and Goodreads page. Also, if you are up for it, I'd really appreciate it if you'd leave a review and perhaps recommend *Vanishing Girls* to another reader. Reviews and word-of-mouth recommendations go a long way to helping readers discover one of my books for the first time. As always, thank you so much for your support! It means the world to me! I can't wait to hear from you and I hope to see you next time!

Thanks,
Lisa Regan

# ACKNOWLEDGMENTS

First and foremost, I must thank my passionate readers. Thank you for joining me on this wonderful journey. I deeply appreciate every message, tweet, email, and Facebook post. Thank you for spreading the word. I hope you love Josie Quinn as much as I do and will stick around for more of her adventures.

As always, thank you to my husband, Fred, and lovely, inspiring daughter, Morgan, for giving up so much time with me so I could work on this book. Thank you to my parents: William Regan, Donna House, Rusty House, Joyce Regan, and Julie House, who are constantly encouraging this dream of mine. Thank you to the following friends who cheered me on through the first draft of this novel and the many editing rounds, without whom I would surely have given up: Melissia McKittrick, Nancy S. Thompson, Michael J. Infinito Jr., Carrie A. Butler, Dana Mason, and Katie Mettner. Thank you to the following loved ones for constantly going above and beyond to spread the word about my books no matter how much time goes by between titles: Helen Conlen, Marilyn House, Ava McKittrick, Dennis and Jean Regan, Torese Hummel, Laura Aiello, Tracy Dauphin, and Dennis Conlen.

Thank you so very much to Sgt. Jason Jay for answering

so many of my police work questions in such great detail. I can never thank you enough. Thank you to Amy Z. Quinn for answering my journalism questions so thoroughly.

Thank you to Jessie Botterill for asking me what else I had up my sleeve; for your willingness to take a chance on me; for your passion and commitment to this book and this series; for your amazing editing work; and for your candor and your overall brilliance. I feel so blessed to be working with you. Thank you to the entire team at Bookouture, including Oliver Rhodes, Kim Nash, and Noelle Holten! It is humbling to be a part of such an amazing publishing family. Finally, thank you to Alex Logan, Kirsiah McNamara, and the entire team at Grand Central Publishing for making my dreams come true!

# ABOUT THE AUTHOR

Lisa Regan is the *USA Today* and *Wall Street Journal* best-selling author of the Detective Josie Quinn series as well as several other crime fiction titles. She has a bachelor's degree in English and a master of education degree from Bloomsburg University. She is a member of Sisters in Crime, International Thriller Writers, and Mystery Writers of America. She lives in Philadelphia with her husband, daughter, and a Boston terrier named Mr. Phillip.

For more information you can visit:
LisaRegan.com
Facebook.com/LisaReganCrimeAuthor
Twitter @LisaLRegan